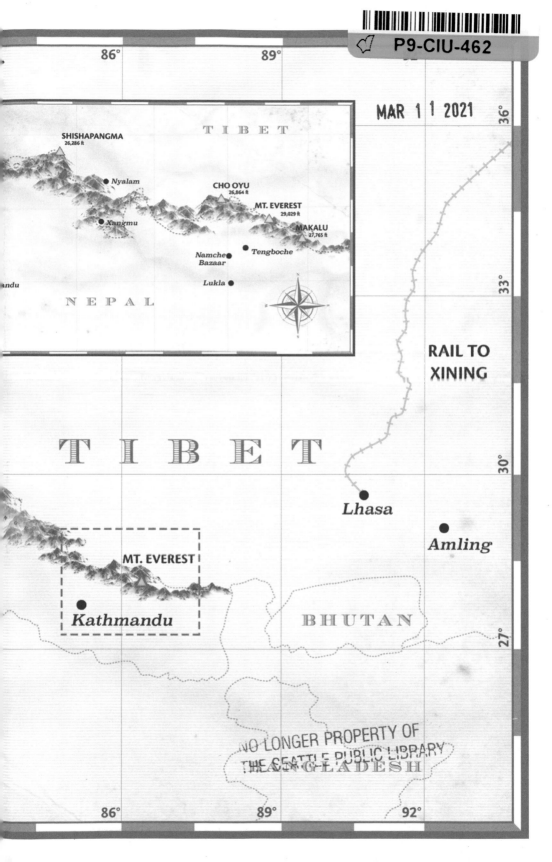

86° 89°

36°

33°

T I B E T

SHISHAPANGMA
26,286 ft

● Nyalam

CHO OYU
26,864 ft

MT. EVEREST
29,029 ft

MAKALU
27,765 ft

● Xangmu

andu

Namche ●
Bazaar

● Tengboche

● Lukla

N E P A L

N

RAIL TO
XINING

T I B E T

30°

● Lhasa

● Amling

MT. EVEREST

27°

Kathmandu

B H U T A N

BANGLADESH

86° 89° 92°

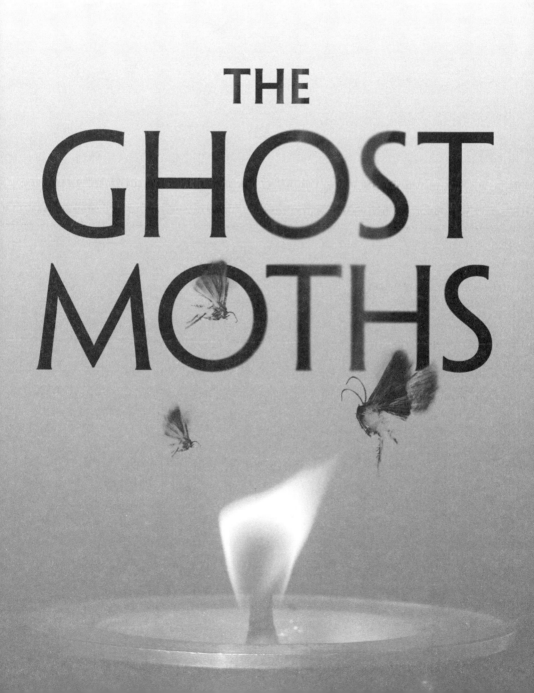

THE
GHOST
MOTHS

THE
GHOST
MOTHS

A Novel

HARRY FARTHING

**BLACK
STONE**
PUBLISHING

Copyright © 2021 by Harry Farthing
Published in 2021 by Blackstone Publishing
Cover and book design by Alenka Vdovič Linaschke
Maps and illustrations by Amy Craig

This is a work of fiction. Names, characters, businesses, places,
events, locales, and incidents are either products of the author's
imagination or used in a fictitious manner. Conversations attributed
to actual public figures contained herein are fictitious and were
created solely for the purpose of this novel.

Printed in the United States of America

First edition: 2021
ISBN 978-1-5384-6923-1
Fiction / Thrillers / Suspense

1 3 5 7 9 10 8 6 4 2

CIP data for this book is available
from the Library of Congress

Blackstone Publishing
31 Mistletoe Rd.
Ashland, OR 97520

www.BlackstonePublishing.com

Hepialus armoricanus Oberthür lives on the edges of the harsh cold night in a harsh cold land: Tibet. An ancient creature, the ghost moth silently seeks little more than survival. To do so, it must endure, escape, and evade to ultimately cast its offspring far and wide in a biological diaspora that seeks only to better the long odds of continuity on those high, frigid plains and mountainsides. However, the defenseless caterpillar that immediately struggles into the ground for its own protection can be betrayed by that same soil. For within the very earth awaits *Ophiocordyceps sinensis*—an insidious fungus that seeks to claim the larva's fleshy body and simple soul as its own.

It is apocryphal that in Putonghua, or Mandarin Chinese as that language is also known, the symbols for *crisis* and *opportunity* are the same; an oft-used, oversimplistic rallying cry of the panic-stricken in moments of calamity already beyond their control. Many far beyond the borders of that harsh cold land see the crisis of the parasitized ghost moth as an opportunity. The by-product, *yartsa gunbu,* a mummified powdery husk, is for some a needed medicine, for others a stimulant or performance-enhancing drug, a source of hard currency, a coveted status symbol, a useful "gift" that oils wheels in the salons of Shanghai and Beijing. Just one more valuable commodity from the "Western Treasure House" as Tibet has always been known in those same salons.

But, make no mistake, for the ghost moth it is simply a slow, lingering death.

The ghost moth and the fungus are old foes.

They battle on.

DRAMATIS PERSONAE

Alan "Big Al" Reid English climber on guide Neil Quinn's commercial expedition to climb the mountain of Shishapangma

Anthony Green, the Honorable New ambassador-in-waiting to Nepal for Her Majesty's Government, replacing the longstanding incumbent, Sir Jack Graham

Balkumar Venerable Kathmandu newsagent

Christopher Anderson Pioneering American climber who pushed the use of the "alpine style" in the Himalayas in the 1970s and '80s and also the partner of Henrietta Richards

Elizabeth Waterman American freelance journalist

Gedhun Choekyi Nyima The rightful eleventh Panchen Lama as chosen by the Dalai Lama in May 1995 when aged six, but missing within Chinese territory ever since

Gelu Sherpa Senior climbing Sherpa (sirdar) to the 2014 Snowdonia Ascents commercial expedition to the mountain of Shishapangma

Geshe Lhalu Scholarly monk at the monastery of Amling in the 1950s

Geshe Shep Senior monk and Chinese Communist Party member who advises the Chinese State on religious matters within the current Tibetan Autonomous Region (TAR)

Gyaltsen Norbu The official eleventh Panchen Lama appointed by the Chinese State following the disappearance of Gedhun Choekyi Nyima

Haiyang Senior general in the People's Liberation Army

Hao Ping Elderly Chinese trader in the Tibetan village of Amling in the 1950s

Henrietta Richards, OBE Retired senior staff member of the British embassy who has lived in Kathmandu for over forty years becoming the preeminent historian and record keeper of Himalayan climbing

Huang Hsu Accomplished and aggressive mountaineer from Taiwan seeking to become the first female climber to summit all fourteen eight-thousand-meter peaks in the Himalayas

Hsiao Teng Business manager, sponsor, and the lover of Taiwanese mountaineer "Lady" Huang Hsu

Inaka "Fuji" Sakata Japanese climber who went missing while climbing the mountain of Annapurna in 1985, the last summit in his quest to solo climb all fourteen eight-thousand-meter peaks in the Himalayas

Jack Graham, Sir, KCVO CMG Longstanding friend of Henrietta Richards and soon-to-retire ambassador for Her Majesty's Government to Nepal

Jin Yui Governor of the TAR

Jitendra Thanel Senior detective in the Kathmandu Metropolitan Police

Kami Sherpa Climbing Sherpa and manager of the Sunrise Café owned by Temba Chering and located in the Thamel tourist district of Kathmandu

Mao Tse-tung Founder and supreme leader of the People's Republic of China and Chairman of the Communist Party of China who died in 1976

Neil Quinn Professional mountain guide from England who has officially summited Mount Everest twelve times and unofficially once

Nima Sherpa Junior climbing Sherpa on the 2014 Snowdonia Ascents commercial expedition to the mountain of Shishapangma

Pashi Bol Sole proprietor of the famous Pashi's Barbershop in the Thamel tourist district of Kathmandu and longstanding friend of Henrietta Richards

Paul van der Mark Dutch professor of Chinese and Tibetan studies at Nijmegen University who also guides high-end tours of China and the TAR for wealthy Europeans

Pema Chering A doctor and surgeon, oldest son of Tibetan exile and successful Kathmandu businessman Temba Chering

Pema Chöje Tibetan who grew up in the village of Amling in the 1950s

Pertemba Chering Flies H125 rescue helicopters out of Lukla airport in the Khumbu Everest region, youngest son of Tibetan exile and successful Kathmandu businessman Temba Chering

Rambhadur Gurkha sergeant seconded to the British embassy in Kathmandu as head of security and logistics

Sangeev Gupta Indian born clerical assistant and secretary to Henrietta Richards

Tenjin Sherpa Senior climbing Sherpa on the 2014 Snowdonia Ascents commercial expedition to the mountain of Shishapangma

Tenzin Gyatso The fourteenth and current Dalai Lama who resides in exile in the suburb of Mcleod Ganj, situated above the hill town of Dharamsala in the Indian state of Himachal Pradesh

Temba Chering Tibetan who grew up in the village of Amling in the 1950s with Pema Chöje and, in subsequent exile, worked as a porter and "sherpa" in the mountains but would become a successful businessman in Kathmandu

Thubten Norgyu Tibetan laborer within Community Work Group 57, once the village of Amling in the region of Gyaca

Tommy Rowe One of many noms de guerre adopted by a former US Marine and CIA agent who specialized in training indigenous tribes to fight against Communism during the Cold War

Tore Rasmussen Norwegian client climber on the 2014 Snowdonia Ascents commercial expedition to the mountain of Shishapangma in Tibet led by mountain guide Neil Quinn

Wang Maozhen Chairman of the Chinese People's Political Consultative Conference with specific responsibility for religious affairs within the TAR

Wangdu Palsang Second-generation Tibetan refugee based in Dharamsala who works for the Central Tibetan Administration (the Tibetan Government in Exile)

Xi, Captain Officer in charge of the People's Liberation Army that came to Amling in 1950

Yama, also known as Lieutenant Yen-Tsun Lai Officer in the Chinese Ministry of State Security Police, Xizang division, active throughout the TAR and enforcer for Governor Jin Yui

Zhang, Captain Kathmandu chief of station for the Chinese Ministry of State Security

Zhang Li Designated Chinese Travel Agency assistant to Professor Paul van der Mark

Zhao, Lieutenant Officer in the People's Liberation Army stationed in Amling in the 1950s

Zou Xiaopeng Communist Party secretary for the TAR

A glossary of terms is included at the end of the book.

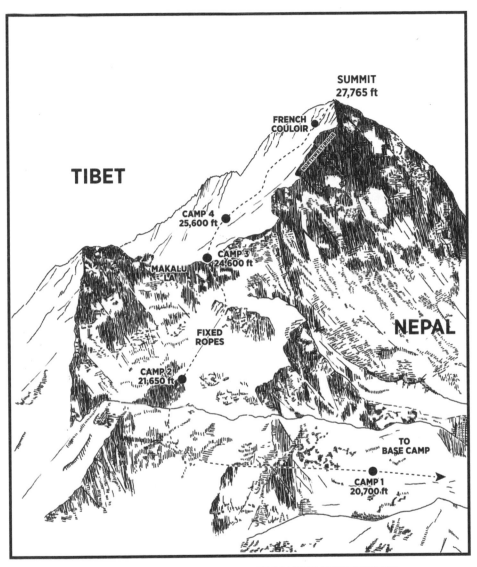

SUMMIT
27,765 ft

FRENCH
COULOIR

NORTHWEST RIDGE

TIBET

CAMP 4
25,600 ft

CAMP 3
24,600 ft

MAKALU
LA

NEPAL

FIXED
ROPES

CAMP 2
21,650 ft

TO
BASE CAMP

CAMP 1
20,700 ft

THE MOUNTAIN OF MAKALU FROM THE NORTHWEST

PROLOGUE

THE MOUNTAIN OF MAKALU

1981

A huge gust slammed Christopher Anderson hard against the French Couloir. The snow crust fractured, chunks sliding down the icy chute to oblivion far below. The American climber pulled down hard on his axe and dug in his spiked crampons to stop himself from doing the same.

Beneath a fall of freezing spindrift, Anderson pushed in close to the mountain's white mantle. His tinted goggles blanked as he leaned his face into the ice and—pinned to the mountain—shivered the hold. The empty gray of the ski mask began to flicker like a screen coming alive with grainy images.

Faces.

People. Friends. Enemies. Some true. Some not.

Places.

Countries. Mountains. Jungles. Some real. Some not.

This is nothing new.

Anderson had pushed himself beyond twenty-five-thousand feet enough times to recognize the mental kaleidoscope of an oxygen-starved brain, the cascade of unsought images, as happens in those final seconds before sleep, before death perhaps. He drew in a long, deep breath, as much to drag his brain back into his skull as to fill his chest.

Colder than its nitrogen, the thin air threatened to shatter his teeth as his lungs strained to absorb every chill molecule. He answered the pleural scream for more, permitting himself another nine breaths and counting each one. His head cleared, a little.

Anderson lifted his face back up, shook the snow from his body, and looked around. To his right, that dark cliff that they had identified in their black-and-white reconnaissance photographs jutted from the white snow like a brutal compound fracture. While the rock lacked the red ink of the pictures' route markings, he could imagine the bleeding, the rivers of red arterial blood cascading down the stone gullies, running, falling, dripping . . .

You need to move!

Wearily the American tugged the steeply angled head of his Terrordactyl free from the ice only to heft the stubby pick in again, three feet to the right. More snow shattered and collapsed as it stabbed into the hard ice beyond. Below, a spiked boot reached similarly sideways and kicked into that same frozen spine as hard as the tired leg muscles and bruised toes permitted. The other slowly followed.

Pull. Stab. Kick. Kick. Hold.

And again.

Pull. Stab. Kick. Kick. Hold.

And again.

For this is my mantra . . .

Foot by foot, Anderson crabbed across the treacherous snow face until, finally, he could hook his axe onto an edge of solid rock and haul himself up onto it, muscles screaming. The grimace of effort split his congealed upper lip and real red blood oozed out, the only warm thing in that forsaken and frozen place.

Wind pummeled the American as he took momentary sanctuary in the solidity of his new perch. He rewarded himself with ten more shuddering breaths before he continued to claw his way up the jagged rock in bullying, hard climbing that tasted of blood and bile.

Anderson lost himself in the relentless stop-start progress, until he reached the shelter of the gully riven into the rock that they had both identified in those same photographs. In the lee of the rough granite cliff, he spiked his toe points into cracks, locked his legs, and unhooked a piton from his waist harness. Probing its flat blade into the tightest fissure before him, he hammered it home. A gloved, wood-stiff hand hooked a carabiner into the piton's protruding, beaten eye, then pulled down on it as hard as possible.

The anchor didn't move a micron, bombproof solid; "bomber" as those two English brothers used to say before the mountains blew them both away. Uncoiling a purple 11/16 sewn sling, he quickly tethered himself to the piton and, trusting the nylon umbilical, leaned back to sling his backpack from his shoulders and hang that also from the same anchor.

Now free to work, he began to dig the axe's pick deep into another, bigger crack that horizontally split the rock, scraping it free of snow and ice until he could push an arm far inside to be sure it was good for his purpose. It was, so he bent down to pull from his backpack a football-sized bundle tightly wrapped in olive green gabardine and bound with bright red cord.

He rotated the package carefully with both hands, thumbs gently pushing on the surface to feel the form within as the wind picked up around him once more to pummel and pound, ice crystals drilling against his jacket. Satisfied he was holding the bundle correctly, Anderson defiantly lifted it up high into the angry air, pointing it toward the distant northern horizon, toward Tibet.

For a long, cold minute he just held it there. "See this, you fuckers? Because it sees you and everything you do," he shouted into the north wind, then lowering the green package, he twisted it around and firmly pushed it into the mountainside. The fit was perfect.

When Anderson's empty hands reappeared, he lifted his axe again. The sharp pick scraped and gouged a design into the stone, one that mirrored the outline of the smallest of the many embroidered patches stitched to his climbing jacket.

Finished, Anderson pulled back a glove cuff to look at his battered Benrus. Peering into the watch's scratched crystal as if looking into a frozen lake, he murmured to himself, "It's okay. There's still time."

The American climber turned his face upward to see the remainder of the route they had chosen together to be his variation to the summit of Makalu. His eyes stepped into the sky seeking holds, suggesting moves.

He only caught a glimpse of the tumbling shadow before the image of a woman's face flashed in front of it; the woman he loved.

Another.

An aspen lined valley; the place where he had grown up.

Another.

A Tibetan face, that of a child; he didn't recognize it.

Faces.

Places.

Some known.

Some not.

Before sleep.

Before death.

The falling rock killed Christopher Anderson instantly.

PART I

THE KAPALA

Very soon in this land deceptive acts may occur from without and within. If, in such an event, we fail to defend our land, the holy lamas including "the triumphant father and son" [the Dalai Lama and the Panchen Lama] will be eliminated without a trace of their names remaining; the properties of the reincarnate lamas and of the monasteries along with their endowments for religious services will be seized. Moreover, our political system originated by the three Dharma Kings will be reduced to empty name; my officials, deprived of their patrimony and property, will be subjugated, as slaves for the enemies; and my people subjected to fear and miseries, unable to endure day or night. Such an era will certainly come.

Prophecy regarding the "Reds,"
written by the Thirteenth
Dalai Lama, Thubten Gyatso,
shortly before his death in 1933

1

YARTSA GUNBU

AMLING, GYACA, TIBET
Spring in the Year of the Iron Tiger (1950)

Hao Ping's doors were magnificent, the only thing the village of Amling possessed to rival the ancient monastery that watched over it. It was said that their immense black beams came from the cloud forests of Pemako, the hidden kingdom of poisoners far to the southeast. Their wood was so thick and heavy, others recalled, that it broke the backs of many yaks carrying it over the Su-La, thereby costing the Chinaman an even greater fortune. The villagers firmly believed those great doors were big enough to hold back all the hells, be they hot or cold. But despite such strength and power, qualities the villagers so admired, a simple wooden sign that sometimes hung to their side always received far greater attention.

དབྱར་རྩ་དགུན་འབུ་

The fading red symbols meant different things to the different people of Amling. To the literate monks who lived in the three-sided monastery that crowned a steep conical hill that rose above the small town, the script read simply, *yartsa gunbu.*

It was a riddle for a name best explained by their ancient scholar,

7

Geshe Lhalu. Whenever his young novices asked about it, the old monk would patiently pull himself away from his lifetime's work—his study of the glorious goddess Palden Lhamo, to whom the monastery was dedicated—and extract a piece of dry fungus from his medicine cabinet. Pinching the crinkled stick of ochre between his stained fingertips, his hand would gently lift like a black crane rising on the summer air as he spoke of the summer grass, winter worm.

"A powerful medicine," he would say, "found especially on the grassy hills below the holy lake of our monastery's spirit, our protectress, Palden Lhamo. It is one of her many gifts to us, beneficial for ailments of the kidney and the lungs, the heart and the liver."

The students would be hypnotized by the spiraling crooked fingers raising up what seemed to be a dead caterpillar impaled on a burned matchstick. They always had more questions that Geshe Lhalu would answer by telling the story of a small and drab, yet hardy and determined, insect that flew as briefly as summer lasted in that high place. His wrinkled arthritic hand fluttered before their eyes as their teacher told the story of the ghost moth's continual battle for survival in that harsh cold land. Then it mimed the coiling action of the moths' newly hatched caterpillars worming their way into the earth to escape their many predators; the shrike, the owl, the fox, the weasel, and, fiercest of all, the coming winter. But even there, in that cold darkness, seemingly so hidden, so remote, Geshe Lhalu cautioned, the caterpillar was not safe.

For in that very soil, a powdery bane lay waiting to attach itself to the wriggling worm. An infection that would slowly consume its moist life until, finally sensing the arrival of a new spring above, the parasite split open the ill-fated caterpillar's mummified head to send up a black shoot alongside the new blades of grass to spore on the coming summer air.

"And thus the cycle starts all over again . . . Summer grass, winter worm. As always, in every end, a new beginning . . ." While his suede-headed novices digested this tale of a cruel samsara, Geshe Lhalu's free hand would silently rise again into a clenched fist like the head-splitting stroma. With a cheeky, toothy smile he would then chuckle and say that Chinese wives had found another most important use for *yartsa gunbu* that had made Hao Ping rich. That said, the old monk would suddenly flick his crooked index finger up in an instant erection that set the young monks giggling and Dolma, Lhalu's ever-faithful, ever-present sister monk, blushing.

"Chinamen travel far for the caterpillar fungus of Amling! We need little. They would take it all if they could!"

For the two hundred or so people that inhabited the squat community below the monastery, time and experience rather than literacy had converted the sign's dagger-like symbols into its own story, wider in interpretation than Geshe Lhalu's perhaps, but no less accurate. To them, the board's springtime appearance indicated that Hao Ping, that tiny Chinaman who had lived amongst them for as long as anyone could remember, had put away his opium pipe—his own preferred manner of sitting out the winter—and was ready to do business. The high passes would soon be open to permit the trade caravans to arrive.

Originally the sign, when it was new, said to them in Hao's spiky bird-like writing, "Bring me all the yartsa gunbu you can find. I will trade for it." But now, so many years later, that battered plank also silently asked for fox fur, yak tail, musk, wool, deer horn, quartz, even those tiny flecks of gold the villagers sometimes found in the wide river. Hao Ping, like seasoned middlemen the world over, had diversified, and those great doors had been built for good reason: to protect the huge courtyard that received the caravans, the silk-lined salon where business was transacted and celebrated, and those dark storerooms that, every year, became crammed with precious goods for barter: cigarettes, fabrics, cottons, silver, jewels, coral beads, tools, pots, pans, and most important, tea. Amling needed few staples. Barley, the villagers grew in the walled fields beyond the river. Butter, they churned from the milk of their yak that roamed the hillsides. Salt, they found large pink crystals of in a cave a week to the south. However, tea—strong, black tea—had to come from Hao Ping. It arrived at his doors in dense five-pound blocks, embossed with symbols the villagers couldn't read, to be chiseled and shaved into amounts they understood to the very last grain. Winter in that place lingered long and the tea supplies dwindled, so the painted plank's reappearance was always a relief. The children of Amling particularly welcomed its arrival. For them, that sign was just one more to accompany the heavy rattle of snowmelt in the river, the green furring of seedlings in the mud of the paddocks, and the honking of newly arrived geese from beyond the mountains that announced winter was over for another year. Their excitement was equally noisy and joyous, even if it also meant long days ahead on the sides of the cold, shadowy flanks of the higher hills, watching sheep and yak and searching on numb hands and knees for those tiny black sticks that poked up through the snow-burned grass. At least, successfully digging that dirty dead worm from the ground offered praise and reward, instead of the heavy hand of punishment that was never more than a few feet away during the cramped confines of winter.

When not on the hill, the kids would wait outside the old Chinaman's house, wrestling, shooting one another with wooden arrows, racing on imaginary ponies, or teasing the village idiot, Mad Namgi, until he would fly into a rage, to their delight, becoming a screaming whirlwind of dust in the center of the street. All the while they would remain attentive to the comings and goings of their fathers and the traders, listening for the slap of hands and shouts that signaled a deal had been done, awaiting the shower of candies and small toys, fabric animals and rag dolls that would be flung out soon after to encourage the "searchers" further. Whenever a new caravan arrived, the children would study it eagerly to see if those strangely costumed traveling players were with it. They lived for the town's annual performance of the *Warrior Song of King Gesar*. It was the event of their summer, and that old wooden sign also announced it was on its way, sooner or later.

Hao Ping's sign may indeed have been small and simple, old and worn, but it said so many things to so many people. However, that year, its appearance said one more thing that no one could be expected to understand. Life for the monks, the villagers, the children, even old Hao Ping himself, was about to change forever and not even his mighty doors were going to be able to hold that back.

2

A DISCOVERY

The tea chest was dust bare.

"You can go," a gruff voice consented.

Eight-year-old Pema Chöje didn't need telling twice. In an instant the boy's arms were forced into his sheepskin chuba, fast fingers quickly cinching the heavy jacket's cord belt and pushing inside his sheaved knife and some cloth-wrapped tsampa cakes from his mother. He darted out of the door before anyone could change their mind, hearing only half of the demands that tried to follow him into the street.

It didn't matter.

Pema knew the rules because he had broken them so often.

"Stay with the others. Watch the weather. If the cloud goes dark from the south, come down immediately. Beware the river. The water is high from the melting snows. Do not walk on the paddocks. The barley seedlings are shooting. Do not throw stones at the idiot or the dogs or the Rinpoche's novices—particularly your brother. Do not go beyond the slopes to the holy lake. Return with at least twenty pieces or else . . ."

Outside, his three friends, Temba, Dorje, and Lobsang, stopped their dusty push-and-shove to immediately race him down the street, their imaginary steeds galloping as fast as the invisible hooves could go. The four young knights of King Gesar waved and cheered as the quartet passed old Hao Ping, standing in his open doorway sizing up the new day over-head. The skies were open, the mountainsides clear, the air crisp and still: the first traders would be arriving soon. He raised his long clay pipe in return, his smile at the boys' exuberance hitching up the long wisp of white hair that hung from his chin.

At the end of the single thoroughfare, the gang kicked left in an impossibly tight turn and galloped on, keeping just beyond the reach of the mastiffs that guarded the town's perimeters. The furious dogs jumped and roared at their passing, wrenching their iron chains so hard they threatened to separate the links. The boys howled back at them only to abandon the cacophony of barking and snarling they had incited by jumping the stepping-stones that studded the wide river.

On the far bank, they cantered the raised earth walkway that ran between the barley paddocks to reach the foot of the steep hillside that walled the eastern side of their valley. Only there did the four of them slow to an intuitive, even pace that permitted air enough to banter but without the need to stop and rest; not even the knights of Gesar could race uphill in Amling.

With every step the boys' known world shrank beneath them. The village became a cluster of grubby white boxes scabbed with flat brown roofs. The wide road that ran down its middle tightened into an old scar. The river, so broad and furious when they crossed it, stretched white and thin like Hao Ping's beard. The paddocks interlocked into a single tortoise-shell of green and brown. Even that barren stand-alone hill that bore the monastery dwindled to little more than a distant mound of barley flour topped with a single white molar.

The boys joked and laughed, telling stories as tall as the valley sides until, beyond its ridge, they stepped onto the wide alpine pasture that ended in the forbidding ring of jagged hills that surrounded the Holy Lake of Palden Lhamo. Immediately they spread out and began the hunt. Huddled close to the ground, backs turned against the chill wind that always whipped that place, they searched and searched for tiny black stalks amidst the stunted new shoots of spring grass.

It took nearly an hour before Pema's shout told the others he had found a piece. The first of the year always merited special attention, so the boys quickly gathered around their friend as he took out his knife to prize the brittle worm from the earth. They watched with bated breath as the long blade slid down into the barely defrosted ground aside the small stalk. Gently, Pema levered the knife, first from side to side, then in a circular motion to make a hole big enough to insert a finger. With a fingernail he began to carefully scratch at the dirt until he could feel the side of the dead worm.

"Be careful. Don't break it," his best friend, Temba, whispered as if fearful that even the sound of his voice might cause the brittle worm to disintegrate.

Pema gave the gentlest of tugs, but the stalk didn't move.

Instantly releasing so that the piece didn't snap, he slid his index finger back in until it stopped at something hard, cold to the touch. "A stone . . . trapping the tail," the boy said, returning his knife blade to the hole and pushing straight down in an attempt to dislodge the rock.

The sharp tip held for a moment then slid off the surface to stab deeper into the earth. The boy cursed like a man and instead squeezed his bare hand back into the hole to claw at the earth again.

His fingertips began to trace an oval hole in the rock through which the worm emerged. Digging out still more dirt, he felt another crater form. Pema pushed his face to the cold ground to better see the obstruction.

From the bottom of the hole two eye sockets stared back at him. Shocked, the boy quickly pulled his face from the earth's black gaze.

"What is it?" Lobsang asked.

"A skull."

"Yak? Fox?" Temba asked.

"No. Man."

Together all the boys began to furiously dig until, with both hands, Pema finally pulled his find free.

The human skull came out in one piece, a brown muddy ball, the only white, two complete rows of long-rooted teeth held within jaws tightly clamped together with rusty screws.

Pushing the earth away and freeing the forgotten shoot of yartsa,

Pema saw that the entire surface had been cut and engraved. Symbols, figures, and signs covered every piece of exposed bone. On the forehead was carved an inverted triangle.

The boys looked at the skull in wonder and awe until Temba finally broke the silence.

"Pema has found the head of King Gesar!"

The boys began to shout and cheer as Pema slowly and theatrically offered the skull up to the blue sky with both hands. At that exact moment, a loud thump like thunder sounded, not from beyond the boy's offering to the heavens but from below, down in the valley.

There was another, then three more.

A plume of dust and smoke began to rise.

Temba, Dorje, and Lobsang immediately raced to the ridge to see what was happening below.

Pema, deserted, pushed the skull down into the front of his chuba, gathered up his knife and his single piece of yartsa, and chased after them, the heavy skull pounding against his chest as he ran from its shallow grave.

3

REDS

The gang of four encountered the first villagers hiding behind the drystone walls that bounded the barley paddocks. Mostly women and small children, they were huddled tightly against the rocks, the smallest almost squirming their way into the cracks as they cowered and shook. One of them was Temba Chering's aunt. She was on her knees, rocking backward and forward, chanting the same mantra carved into many of the stones around her.

When the handsome woman saw the boys, she immediately straightened herself into a defiant anger. A group of soldiers, she said, had appeared at the northern end of the village. Without word or warning, they had set up a single green cannon and fired five shells, one after the other, into the side of the monastery's hill. The explosions had shaken the old gompa so violently they had all feared it might crumble and fall.

Temba asked his aunt who the soldiers were.

She spat back her simple answer, "Reds." Everyone in Amling had heard of the "Reds," those soldiers who fought for control of the faraway land of China. The boys, just as boys do everywhere, also knew that it was a violent and bloody war, and that the Reds were the victors. They immediately wanted to see such famed warriors for themselves.

Despite the warnings of the villagers around them and the insistence of

Temba's aunt that they stay, the four ran on. At the river the boys passed Mad Namgi, sitting on a rock, stripped naked, tearing at his long, matted hair, and howling at the spiral of vultures overhead, certain that something below was dying. For once, the boys ignored him to jump the stepping-stones as a dull groan from the heavens began to accompany the wails of the madman.

The new sound grew, separating into loud blasts that filled the valley and echoed like brass waves breaking on the distant hillsides. Pema recognized the long horns of the monastery being blown from the high tower, calling for the dharma, the way of the Buddha, to defeat the ignorance of those who would fire cannons at them, to reinforce the spirit of Palden Lhamo, the goddess that protected them and those walls of stone that protected her — a Jericho in reverse.

The boys pressed on to reach the small crowd of men that had assembled opposite Hao Ping's great doors. Before them, standing at attention in three ranks, were thirty heavily laden khaki soldiers, without insignia beyond a single red star on the fur front of their caps and red collar tabs. Despite machine guns and bayoneted rifles, full bandoliers of ammunition and stuffed packs of equipment, the Reds did not resemble mighty warriors. The men within the bulky quilted jackets and trousers were small and sallow, dusty and dirty. Many struggled just to breathe, panting although at a standstill. The heavy eyelids of others slipped shut without control, betraying the exhaustion of the journey that had led them there.

The soldiers' captain, wiry thin, was no bigger than Hao Ping, with whom he was talking in an animated fashion. He thrust a rolled document at the old Chinaman then pushed him forward to address the small crowd.

Hao Ping reached inside his round collared jacket for a pair of tiny spectacles, letting the document unroll from his hand as he did so. All the spectators clearly saw the crimson Chinese characters at the top and the dense black orders that cascaded below but only Hao Ping could understand them. He began to read the proclamation, translating each phrase aloud as he went.

"The Advance Guard Twelve of the Eighteenth Corps of the People's Liberation Army of the People's Republic of China greets you, the people!

"On behalf of the great helmsman, Chairman Mao Tse-tung, and the victorious Central People's Government, we bring you long-awaited freedom.

"We arrive, at last, to drive out the Kuomintang's nationalist bandit regime . . .

"To end the barbarous feudalism of your own lords and priests . . .

"To destroy all landlords and merchants, those running dogs of capitalism, that rob you daily!"

Hao Ping stopped for a moment and swallowed, taking in the personal significance of what he was reading only as he said it. A prod in the back from the captain's swagger stick forced him to continue.

"Captain Xi and Advance Guard Twelve apologize ten thousand times for such a clamorous arrival, but only thus can you understand the awesome power of democratic reform that has arrived at your doors. Together we, the people, will construct with you, the people, the glorious society for which you have been yearning . . ."

The speech went on and on.

The crowd listened, trying to make sense of what they were hearing, understanding the words but not the context. Only Hao Ping got the message, the already small Chinaman visibly dwindling with every word he uttered. The boys, expecting more action, grew bored, fidgeting and looking around.

Pema noticed that many of the monks from the monastery had joined the crowd. Even the Rinpoche, the monastery's abbot, was there now and listening intently to every word.

Pema's older brother suddenly pushed in alongside him. Without even turning to look, the young monk's arm reached across to pat his sibling's swollen chest.

"What have you got in there, brother? Some yartsa I can take to Geshe Lhalu?" he asked under his breath, nudging him a little and gesturing to the monastery's great scholar, who was also standing amongst the crowd.

"Nothing," Pema whispered in reply, suddenly remembering the skull he was bearing, momentarily forgotten in all the pandemonium and performance. Surreptitiously he tried to push his brother's prying hand away.

"Your jacket seems very full for nothing," his brother hissed.

"Leave me alone."

Gritting his teeth, desperately trying not to make a disturbance, Pema twisted away but his brother grabbed at the thick sheepskin of his coat to hold him still. Pema tried again to wrench himself free, but his older brother didn't let go. Locked together they twisted and fell forward into the street.

Hao Ping, concentrating on his reading, jumped with fright at the unexpected disturbance.

The tired soldiers' eyes snapped open, the bayoneted barrels of the front rank instantly dropping to point at the boys who froze in the dirt.

A command issued by the captain ordered two men from the rear rank to approach the pair. They did so warily, looking down at them through the sights of their rifles until their razor-sharp bayonet tips were an inch from each boy's face.

A slight oscillation in the blades, almost close enough to sever their noses, ordered the boys up and onto their feet. A widening of the movement amplified the instruction further to raising their hands in the air as the captain issued another high-pitched command.

Two more of the troop approached without their rifles. Each began to pat a boy down. The soldier checking Pema soon felt the bulk of the skull. In a flash he un-holstered a pistol and pushed the barrel hard against the boy's forehead.

The steel tube seemed to suck all the air out of Pema's chest cavity, freeing his pounding heart to beat wildly against the old skull.

The soldier, his captain, and Hao Ping exchanged terse, urgent sentences.

"Young Pema Chöje," Hao Ping finally asked, "what have you got in there?"

"Nothing," the boy replied. "It's mine. I found it."

"So it is something. What?"

The soldier, growing impatient with an exchange he didn't understand, tentatively reached for the front of Pema's jacket with his free hand, screwing up his broad face as if fearing the boy might explode at any moment.

The hand gently reached inside.

First it pulled out Pema's knife. With a loud exclamation of "Ha!" it was thrown to the ground.

The fingers returned to feel inside the jacket again. Pema felt them run lightly over the curved cranium then instantly withdraw to the shout of a single word that sounded like "Zhadan!"

All the soldiers immediately pulled back as Pema was ordered to lie back on the ground again.

Other soldiers were commanded to approach. One unclipped his bayonet from the end of his rifle and knelt to slice through the rope belt that held Pema's sheepskin coat together. That soldier then quickly withdrew as another, keeping his distance, pushed his bayoneted rifle barrel forward. The long blade delicately poked apart the two sides of the sheepskin jacket to reveal the skull rising and falling on Pema's heaving chest.

A murmur ran through the crowd.

One of the watching monks began to chant, guttural and low.

It was Geshe Lhalu.

The soldier slowly inserted the point of his bayonet into one of the skull's eye sockets and lifted it. Holding the skull at rifle's length the infantryman carefully walked to offer it to his captain. But the officer wouldn't take it. He stood back, ordering the soldier bearing the skull and Hao Ping into the merchant's house. The great wooden doors opened then closed behind them.

The remaining soldiers gestured that everyone should go, which they did, shocked, bewildered, and uncertain. When Pema got home, he tried to explain himself, but nothing could stop the thrashing that came after.

4

RAHULA

AMLING, GYACA, TIBET
Summer in the Year of the Iron Tiger (1950)

Amling returned to its routine of living the summer to prepare for the winter quicker than it took Pema's bruises to fade. The Chinese soldiers stayed, but, to everyone's surprise, they were polite and courteous, respectful of monks and women alike. Hao Ping spoke often of their long march and everyone agreed they seemed to need a good rest.

Captain Xi paid for his men's food and, when they got better used to living in that high country, he released them to help the villagers with their farming and chores. On occasion, they even gave out presents of clothing and, best of all, ta yang; silver dollars. The old merchant reassured everyone that it would always be so, that all Chinese were kind parents whose goodness would continue to rain down on Amling. However, others in the village whispered that the true reason for their invaders' benevolence was the magic skull that Pema had found. They had all seen the sky god, Rahula, the year before. The comet, a wrathful deity, had brought with it fierce hailstorms, earthquakes, and, some said, the Chinese army itself. They heard from the nomads and the traders that such troubles continued elsewhere. Their village was the only one peaceful and plentiful because the skull, or *kapala*, as they called it, had put a spell on Captain Xi and his soldiers.

If Pema ever mentioned "his" find, he was told that he should forget about it, that it must stay working its magic on that captain billeted in

Hao Ping's house. If he persisted, word soon arrived to his father to beat him for the good of the town.

The only adult the boy could talk to about the skull without risk of punishment was Geshe Lhalu. Since the discovery, the old monk would send Pema's brother to summon him up the hill to the monastery. Alone, without even Dolma in the shadows, Geshe Lhalu would then ask the young boy to describe every detail of the skull and how he had found it. Although the kapala had only been briefly in his possession and unseen since it had vanished into Hao Ping's house, Pema found that he was able to describe it precisely because the skull haunted his dreams, each night-time rediscovery accurate in every detail. The only difference was that as he pushed the earth from the skull's carved face, the skull's jawbone would pivot on its rusty iron screws to tell him that a storm of pain and suffering was coming, so much worse than anything Rahula could conjure, that only kapala stood between them all and the end of days.

Whenever Pema recounted this to Geshe Lhalu, the old monk would just stare at him in silence then turn to the many texts that stacked his tables, as if desperately seeking answers to questions the boy hadn't asked. On the wall of his room, a small painting of Palden Lhamo, the fierce red-haired goddess the old monk had dedicated his life to, would silently watch him work.

That summer a traveling player came with the last caravan. The man was tall and somberly dressed compared to the minstrels who had come before. Alone, he carried no lute, no drum, just a long staff of wood. His lean, strong face bore no paint. His only colors were the red wool that bound back his long black hair and the gold and turquoise of the heavy earring that hung from his left ear.

The man spoke each night for a week. He would stand wearing his long cloak, holding his wooden staff, before a fire in the center of Hao Ping's crowded courtyard, the sky above him a dome of stars, sparks from the flames rising up into that same firmament. So noisy were their crackling and spitting, everyone had to strain to hear precisely what the man was saying, for though his words were strong, he did not make his voice overly loud.

"Bow down before me, for I am Kormuzda's son! Bow down before me for I am the servant of Buddha!"

To Pema and his friends, who had listened intently to the epic of King Gesar every year, the speaker seemed a little unfamiliar with the verses. However, told his quiet and purposeful way, the epic seemed to have a greater realism, a greater drama, as if it was the very king himself determinedly urging his people on from the flames of the fire.

"Bow down before me, you princes and tribesmen and beggars, for I will be the light of your darkness, the food for your hunger and the scourge of your evils. I wield the sword of righteousness in one hand! Let my foes beware its edges! I bear the balm of peace in the other! Let my friends savor its sweetness! The prince of warriors is come to lead you to battle!"

Pema noticed that the entire village and most of the monks from the monastery were there, crowded in tight, spellbound by the talking shadow and that wooden staff that seemed to thrust the iron words at them as if newly forged in the fire behind. Only the Chinese soldiers stayed out of earshot, huddled in their own groups as they drank and played mahjong and cards.

With the recounting of each of the great king's adventures, the man continually reminded his audience that they must be like Gesar: proud, courageous, honor bound to protect the land of their birth, the dharma, and their true king, the Dalai Lama, still just a boy. The staff pointed directly at Pema. "Just like you."

꩜

The day after the final show, the player came to Pema's house in the morning to speak with his father at length. After, Pema's father summoned him and said to take the man to the place where he had found the skull, a place forbidden to him since the discovery. Together, they took the long walk to the high pasture, following the path that led up the hill, the man questioning Pema continually about himself before changing the subject.

"Have you taken this path many times before?" he asked.

"Yes, it's our way to reach the high pastures."

"Have you ever followed it all the way to the holy lake?"

"No, that is forbidden."

"Well, today we will. Do you know that this path is known as the 'Way of Knowledge'?"

"No," Pema replied. "Why?"

"It is because the most senior lamas of our land, the Panchen Lama and the Dalai Lama, must sometimes pass this way. The spirit of Palden Lhamo resides in your town's monastery and in the holy lake. They come to seek her advice. The goddess is sworn to protect the lineage of the Dalai Lama, to ensure our faith's future. In the waters of her lake much can be seen. In the texts of the monastery much can be read."

The man continued to speak as they passed the windswept place where the skull had been found. To Pema's surprise it was now marked with a ring of stones, many holding down silk khata scarfs and strings of brightly colored prayer flags that fluttered and snapped on the breeze.

"Is the kapala really a magic treasure?" Pema asked.

"Yes."

"Shouldn't we try to get it back?"

"No, not yet," he cautioned. "There is still much to learn and much to happen. In the meantime, you must endure and have faith. There are dark days ahead."

With that said they carried on until they had left the high pastures behind and the trail tightened to thread its way through the jagged rocks that rose up before them. Climbing ever higher and higher, they finally reached a high ridge and both looked down onto the waters below. From their vantage point, Pema clearly recognized the shape of the skull in the lake's outline but saw only waves racing across the windswept waters like fleeing white horses. The man with him, silent and staring, seemed to be seeing much more.

5

UGLY MANTRAS

AMLING, GYACA, TIBET
The Year of the Fire Monkey (1956)

In time the words from those bony jaws that gnawed endlessly at Pema Chöje's sleep began to ring true. The silver coins vanished, followed by those first weary, yet oddly decent, soldiers. The troops that marched in to replace them were different; a younger, angrier cadre fanatical from battle in another place they called Choson.

For the first few years, Captain Xi remained in their charge but he began to drink the local rakshi and smoke Hao Ping's opium. Retiring into conflicting waves of oblivion, he was rarely seen. Another took control, Lieutenant Zhao, a fanatical wire of a man from Yenan who screamed until he was hoarse then installed a loudspeaker system next to Hao Ping's great doors to further murder the silence of the hills.

From that moment, day and night, the ugly gray horns screeched propaganda and squealed with feedback.

"Hail to the liberation of the Tibetans! The Seventeen Point Agreement has solved all the problems of the Tibetan people. Thank your great helmsman, Chairman Mao Tse-tung!"

"Imperialist foreigners with their long noses, round eyes, and light skins have been cast from your precious soil! See them flee before the glorious People's Liberation Army!"

"Tibet is to China as the child is to the mother. The Dalai Lama is to the Chairman as the child is to the father."

Papered decrees multiplied beneath the speakers. Hao Ping's white-washed walls became a peeling maché of red-and-black script punctuated with the stenciled head and shoulders of Mao as if he was personally supervising every complex new order.

LAND REFORM!
THE NATIONAL CAMPAIGN TO SUPPRESS COUNTER REVOLUTIONARIES!
THE CAMPAIGN OF THE THREE ANTIS!
THE FIRST FIVE-YEAR PLAN OF THE CHINESE COMMUNIST PARTY!
THE CAMPAIGN OF THE FIVE ANTIS!
THE GREAT LEAP FORWARD!

It was relentless and, to the villagers of Amling, unintelligible and, when explained, totally nonsensical.

The land was redistributed to everyone, and yet no one.

The lowest people were designated "model citizens" and placed in charge of everything, and yet nothing.

The men who once led the town, including Pema's father, were sent to build roads that led somewhere, and yet nowhere.

It was left to the boys of Amling to look after their families as best they could. A task made each day more difficult by Zhao's constant requisition of crops and animals that those new roads shipped elsewhere, no barter or payment, no tea or ta yang, in return.

The people lost belief in the magic of the kapala and began to think only of survival: denying how bad things were getting, passing each day as best able, hoping things would improve. But they only got worse when Zhao pasted up another crimson-head document that mandated the villagers must only grow wheat from that moment on.

HAIL TO THE PEOPLE'S CROP!

The next harvest failed as it was always going to in that high place where wheat couldn't grow.

The people began to starve, painful hunger making them eat the leaves on their few trees, the bitter stunted grass on the hillsides, even chew the leather in their belts and bridles. Any yartsa found now was used to try and keep the weakest alive despite the fact that the caterpillar fungus had also been "nationalized" and possession was a crime punishable by a quicker death than starvation.

Whole families began to leave without notice, usually at night. Temba's went south to the great mountain of Chomolungma, Dorje's to a place called Kalimpong in Sikkim, Lobsang's to Lhasa alongside some of the younger monks at the monastery, including Pema's brother. Pema missed Temba Chering the most, but feeling bound still to Amling, to the kapala, to Geshe Lhalu, he stayed.

Other refugees, in even worse condition, began to arrive from the north, from the regions of Golok, Amdo, and Kham. Walking cadavers, they arrived on their last legs, little to their names but whispered news of the destruction of monasteries, the burning of their texts, the theft of their treasures, the rape of nuns, the execution of monks, of nomads, of villagers alike.

Zhao's soldiers mercilessly beat them until they moved on, but many died where they lay, too weak to even move from the blows. A pit was dug on the edge of town for the corpses. The stinking hole of death soon became ringed with piles of worn shoes, thrown away by the soldiers before they tipped in the bodies to prevent the hungry ghosts of the dead from following them back into the town. Overhead carrion birds circled on the noxious vapors and grew fat on the pickings below.

Hao Ping became Zhao's much abused messenger boy until the old Chinaman, bankrupt and brokenhearted, committed suicide by eating poisonous match heads. His body also went into the pit and, soon after, his great doors were dismantled to unleash a new hell on the defenseless starving town. Their priceless wood was cut and hewn once more to make an immense stage in Hao Ping's courtyard, backdropped with the biggest portrait of Mao yet. All the villagers were ordered to attend what Zhao said was going to be a "ceremony" to mark the completion of "the Chairman's Balcony."

That night, what remained of Amling assembled to watch in silent horror as Mad Namgi was pronounced the abbot of the monastery on the hill. The rightful Rinpoche stood alongside him wearing a dunce's cap, a painted sign hung from his neck that proclaimed:

ENEMY OF THE PEOPLE!

Cadre soldiers crowded the abbot, stabbing at his face with rigid fingers, spitting on him, demanding he declare himself guilty of unspecified crimes until, silent to the end, the old man passed out onto those great black beams. His unconscious body was kicked and beaten viciously then tipped off the stage to fall heavily before the weeping villagers. He never recovered.

From that terrible night, Zhao declared open war on religion and the Chairman's Balcony was rarely empty. Night and day the soldiers pulled up monks, nuns, novices, to be reeducated in the "struggle sessions." Everyone in Amling was forced to watch the thamzing, to also denounce the trembling wreck on the stage. If they didn't do so with sufficient enthusiasm, they were hauled up also and beaten until they did.

Systematic and fanatical, Zhao pasted up a schedule of those to be struggled next.

No one was safe.

"Come in, Pema," Geshe Lhalu said, his gentle smile rendered toothier by malnutrition. The monk's room was even darker than usual and shadows pooled in the old monk's deepened eye sockets as he beckoned Pema in.

Pema bent his head to step inside—he was so much taller now—and it felt as if it was being dragged lower by the weight of his heart, for he knew that Geshe Lhalu and his sister monk, Dolma, were designated to be struggled the next day on the Chairman's Balcony. He feared deeply what

Lieutenant Zhao would unleash on a man and a woman together. Those stories of terrible and profane humiliations told by the refugees from the north had now become Amling's reality as Zhao acted them out daily on his stage of horrors.

Within the room Pema embraced the old monk, his friend and teacher, as if it was for the last time, but Geshe Lhalu seemed unconcerned, as purposeful and balanced as always. He simply touched his forehead to Pema's, then pulled away to present, without words, another who appeared from the dark boundary of the room. It was the man who, all those years before, had recited the epic of Gesar. He was also thinner, but in a lean, honed way. Two long scars now striped the left side of his face. At the man's belt hung a sword.

"You," Pema said.

The man nodded as Geshe Lhalu asked, "Pema, how are your dreams of the skull?"

"They continue."

"As they would. You did not find it by chance," the man said. "Our end is now at hand. In you and the kapala we leave our future, just as did the High Lama that first prepared it. Is that not so, Geshe Lhalu?"

"It is so," he said, pulling away a silk khata scarf to reveal, on his study table surrounded by stacked texts, the skull, whole, clean to the bone, the screws holding the jawbone shiny and new.

"But how can this be?" Pema asked in shock.

"The day before he left us, Hao Ping visited me. He was a good man, a friend to this town to the end. At my request he had kept the kapala safe in the very heart of our enemy."

Geshe Lhalu's hand traced the triangle on the forehead of the kapala as he spoke next.

"In these sad years, I have studied much and conversed greatly with the spirit of the great protectress who resides within these old walls, always asking how what you found might save us. I now understand that this was presumptuous. There is no saving us. We are the destruction necessary to sow the seeds of destiny. This kapala returned the day of the invasion to be saved for the future that it belongs to. Pema Chöje, you, as the finder, must take it far from here and hide it again until even the last free lama struggles to see the way. That is its time."

"But how?"

"Like a ghost moth, you must fly far from this soil to escape the fungus that consumes us all. Like a ghost moth, you must take the seed of our survival and hide it anew. Only alone and unseen like a ghost moth will you be able to do this. For the past to determine the future, it must survive the present."

"But how will I get away? The time for leaving passed long ago. It is almost impossible to even come to the monastery now."

"This is how it is going to be," the visitor replied.

Brutally Geshe Lhalu was pushed and pulled onto the stage by the screaming cadre, but the old monk offered no resistance. He did not even raise his hands to ward off the punches and slaps that rained down on him. Dolma followed, cowed and terrified. The cadre tore at her robes and punched her into a half-naked crouch.

On the fringe of the silent crowd below, Pema looked on in sadness and anger, wishing that this time the skull within his chuba was indeed a bomb that could destroy the invaders.

More punches and kicks bullied the old monk to the front of the Chairman's Balcony. There soldiers grabbed each of his arms, pulling and twisting them back hard to bend Geshe Lahlu's upper body forward into a painful bow to the horrified audience. Another cadre reached from behind to hook his fingers onto the top of the monk's eye sockets and pull his face back up into a rigid stare, his neck below stretched into an impossible contortion for such an aged man.

Soon Dolma was stretched equally into that same "jet-plane" posture alongside her old friend.

Lieutenant Zhao stepped forward to pace in front of them and scream at the assembled villagers.

"POISON! POISON! POISON!"

Other soldiers on the stage took up their officer's chant, shouting at the crowd to do the same but, this time, the people below remained huddled and silent.

Zhao stopped. Incensed at the lack of reaction, he seized a bayonet from the harness of one of his soldiers. Resting the long blade across Geshe Lahlu's exposed Adam's apple he began to open his mouth to order the crowd to cheer or else . . .

A single shot flashed from somewhere high on the surrounding roof.

The bullet struck the lieutenant in the forehead with the precision of a nomad hunter.

Instantly dead, Zhao fell from his stage as other bullets began to pick off the soldiers to a growing cacophony of horns.

The courtyard began to flood with monks as armed men threw off cloaks and separated themselves from the villagers to directly attack the soldiers. In their midst, directing the story just as he had all those years before, was the traveling man, now dressed as a warrior, sword flashing.

Pema darted from the chaos and began to run, once more a knight of Gesar galloping his imaginary pony as fast as it could go. The ghost of Hao Ping watched as Pema took that route into the hills those invisible hooves knew so well.

Within a week, the boy was a hundred leagues away from a place that no longer existed. The village and the monastery of Amling erased by bombers that for a week circled the sky thicker than the vultures. Alone and unseen, Pema Chöje pressed on relentlessly until he passed into the great mountains to the south, knowing only the name of the biggest, Chomolungma, and the one person he might find there: his fellow knight, Temba Chering.

PART II

GROWING PAINS

Away with us he's going,
The solemn-eyed:
He'll hear no more the lowing
Of the calves on the warm hillside
Or the kettle on the hob
Sing peace into his breast,
Or see the brown mice bob
Round and round the oatmeal chest.
For he comes, the human child,
To the waters and the wild
With a faery, hand in hand,
For the world's more full of weeping than he
    can understand.

—W. B. Yeats
"The Stolen Child"

6

TWO PICTURES

COMMUNITY WORK TERRITORY 57, GYACA COUNTY, TIBETAN AUTONOMOUS REGION OF THE PEOPLE'S REPUBLIC OF CHINA

August 11, 2014

Even with the single light bulb burning, darkness ruled Thubten Norgyu's low-ceilinged living room, day or night. That evening however, the light remained off. Instead, alone in the silence of shadows, the Tibetan laborer lit a single butter lamp. Half in prayer, half on purpose, he placed the clay dish on his only table and slightly opened the door of the iron stove that squatted in the center of the room. The lamp's amber flame flickered and the stove's red embers glowed in a valiant struggle against the night, silently admonishing him for overcaution, for fear even.

But it wasn't like that. Norgyu knew full well the low-wattage bulb that jutted from the rough plaster wall to the rear of the room never produced anything more than the weakest of illuminations. What he was really doing was hiding the only things that feeble filament could reveal: the telltales that led to that night's coming pain.

If the bulb was switched on, a picture could be seen in the lower-left quadrant of the faint light, a small painting found in the ruin atop the hill overlooking the rows of barrack-like two-room dwellings that made up the work territory's community. To its right could also be seen a stained

33

rectangle where another framed picture had blocked the soot and dust until it had become too deadly for display.

In any light, the image that remained had always been the most fearsome of the two. Within the cracked and faded paint, a blue-skinned, red-haired goddess sat astride a mule; a rampant white beast saddled with a human skin and bridled with serpents, that leapt a river of blood and viscera before a great wall of flames. Beneath a crown of five skulls—those five human poisons of anger, desire, ignorance, jealousy, and pride—the deity's ogrish visage was wild and contorted, a triangle of three eyes bulging in simultaneous vision of past, present, and future. Her fanged jaws roared, thirsting for the skullcap of blood in her left hand as the right raised a staff to wield the power of the thunderbolt against all her people's enemies.

Yet that was the picture that hung still?

To the atheism of the typical communist cadre, such smears of colored glue were a fiction, a spiritual nonsense without reality, an item possibly to be taken and sold as an antique novelty, but nothing to be feared. No, it was that other blank space in the lamplight that had held the image they deemed suspicious and wicked.

For where now remained only a stained outline, a framed black-and-white photograph of someone real had once hung, a living being, respected, beloved, and free; qualities far more worrying to Chinese pragmatism.

So it was that Thubten Norgyu's black-and-white image of a benignly smiling and very youthful fourteenth Dalai Lama had become a one-way ticket to questions, to custody, to disappearance.

For some years the monochrome icon had lain hidden within a secret compartment at the bottom of a wooden tea chest, only to appear furtively during times of private festival or prayer. However, as even just suspicious marks on walls produced wormlike questions from Community Supervisor Pie Lee during cultural conformity inspections, the blank rectangle left behind on the wall had been constantly covered by their children's drawings.

First, the drawings came from their eldest son, pictures of imaginary boats, cars, and airplanes—usually confused in their never-seen combinations of waves, wheels, and wings. Then it was their second son's pictures of people, stick figures going about their daily lives with equally simple yaks and sheep and dogs. That night, if the light had been left on, it would have shown the photograph's bare stain revealed once more, along with a tattered corner of pinned brown paper, all that remained of the last picture to have been stuck there: the second drawing of their youngest child, Yangchen.

The five-year-old's first picture had been surprise enough; a drawing of a monastery on a hilltop that would have been an achievement even for an accomplished ten-year-old, every wall, every door, every window perfect in proportion, perspective, and place.

When Thubten Norgyu first saw it, his heart had almost stopped. Immediately, he demanded of Lhamu, his wife, to know from where she had got the photograph Yangchen had copied; a photograph he himself had not seen for over twenty years and then only once. She had looked back at him as if he was mad. "What photograph? Have you gone crazy?"

Thubten had taken down the drawing and pushed it in front of his small child to ask what it was.

The reply had been immediate, unconcerned and casual.

"My house."

"Say that again."

"My house on the hill above your house."

But there was no house on the hill, no monastery for that matter; just ruins and picked-over rubble—the small painting of Palden Lhamo had been found there long ago. All that remained now was shattered masonry, a few unscavenged wood beams, the odd tatter of weather-bleached material that together, some sixty years before, had been the town's ancient gompa before the days the bombers came.

Thubten Norgyu had slept poorly that night, racked with questions. In the morning he said of the matter only, "no more drawing," but returned home from the fields that evening to find a new one on display. This time, a scrap of brown packing paper was covered with a triangle of black scribbles veined with red pencil lines. The picture resembled some immense erupting volcano.

When Norgyu had angrily torn that paper from the wall to ask what it was, the answer again had been immediate and direct.

"Mother Kali. She has my treasure."

Another sleepless night passed in many more questions. So did the days that followed until Thubten Norgyu did what others whispered you must do if you became convinced that the soul of your child was special, and if your belief was strong and your love of the Dalai Lama was true. With a piece of chalk he drew the faint outline of a moth to the side of his front door.

By evening, the mark was gone, rubbed away so perfectly the image itself could have flown.

A week had become a month, then two, until Thubten Norgyu had left the house to see that the mark of the moth had returned. A tiny hole gouged into the plaster below contained a tightly rolled tube of paper as thin as a white straw.

Thubten Norgyu had followed the instructions to the symbol, despite the fact he would have preferred to organize his own execution.

The quiet knocking came at the time and to the number stated.

"Come in," Norgyu whispered as he quickly opened his front door.

A hooded figure stepped in on a gust of cold wind that instantly overpowered the butter lamp's flame.

The shadow crouched before the glow of the open stove, face completely hidden.

"Tell me everything," the man said in a strangely accented Tibetan as he warmed himself.

Thubten Norgyu passed over Yangchen's drawings and explained.

While the farmer spoke, the two pictures, particularly the second, were studied in the red glow of the stove's embers before being folded and inserted into the man's robe. The hand holding them reemerged clutching a tightly tied bundle of dried plants.

The end was pushed into the stove, the tinder flaring yellow, momentarily illuminating a haggard and aged Asian face until the flame was quickly snuffed against the metal side. The visitor stood and walked the smoking bundle around the room, inserting it into every corner, and then circling it before the small painting. The smoke seemed to thicken before the flame-haired goddess. The man's free hand reached into it to make a complex sign; sweeping, twisting and circling to cut the swirling tendrils of smoke like a knife and set its musky wood scents—agar, juniper, and cedar—free.

Turning to Thubten Norgyu, the man said, "It is time."

The Tibetan laborer moved to the bedroom door and tapped on it.

His small child appeared first, followed by Lhamu. At the sight of the stranger, the mother's lip trembled then hardened. Resolutely she knelt before her offspring. "I am your mother. Remember me," she said as she tied a khata scarf around the infant's tiny neck, tucking the cream silk into the new thick cotton tunic in which she was dressed.

Lhamu stood to pass to the stranger Yangchen's small pack of belongings. Among the few possessions inside was the family's photo of the Dalai Lama. The man seemed to weigh the pack in a hand that, even in the shadows, Thubten Norgyu could see was missing the ends of two fingers. Passing the smoking incense bundle to Norgyu, the man opened the pack and reached inside.

The framed picture was taken out.

"You will need this for what lies ahead of you," the man said as he exchanged it for the bundle of half burned tinder that he cast into the stove. In the light of another yellow flare of fire he crouched in front of the child to stare deep into the small face.

"I see you."

His hand pushed into the child's wild mane of unusually long and thick curly hair.

"Do not be afraid, fire child," the man said as the other hand unsheathed a long knife.

The narrow rectangular blade raised above the tiny head, suddenly panicking the two parents. But before they could say or do anything the blade fell, a quick downward stroke that just sliced away a bunch of the long curls that spat and crackled when they were thrown into the stove.

The cutting continued until all the hair had been removed and the head shaved to the skin with that same razor-sharp blade. Throughout it all, the small child never flinched, never spoke.

"Hat?" the man said to Lhamu whose tears began to drip to the floor as she fetched a woolen cap and passed it back. The man pulled it down over the child's now naked head.

The mother moved forward to hand her child a tattered and ancient cloth toy. The stranger's broken hand reached toward the small stuffed animal but seemed to relent as the child clutched it tight.

"So I go now?" the child asked the stranger.

"Yes. You are special and you must fly far from here."

"Like a bird?"

"No, like a moth, quiet, hidden, in the dark," the stranger said as he lifted the child.

"Are you a moth?" the child asked.

"Yes, I am a ghost moth."

No sooner had the words left the man's mouth than he began to cough so violently that he doubled toward the floor until the paroxysms finally settled. Seemingly recovered, he raised up the child, hooked his cloak over the small body, and walked out into the cold Tibetan night.

Left alone with his sobbing wife, Thubten Norgyu looked at his picture of the Dalai Lama for comfort as Lhamu knelt to pick up a lock of her child's hair that had missed the stove. Her tears dripped onto a stone floor that she saw was speckled with blood from the stranger's coughing, the spots glistening in the light from the curls of hair still burning in the iron hearth.

7

VERDOMDE YINGYING

XINING TO LHASA RAILWAY, AMDO COUNTY, TIBETAN AUTONOMOUS REGION OF THE PEOPLE'S REPUBLIC OF CHINA
September 11, 2014

Sound!

Light!

Nighttime in train T27 was officially over.

Paul van der Mark awoke with a jolt.

The fluorescent fanfare bleached away a final nightmare quickly replacing it with a rhythmic pounding in his head and liver.

"Shit!"

The sixty-two-year-old professor of Chinese and Tibetan studies at Nijmegen University growled in a simultaneous curse of his bad dreams, the train's brutal alarm call, and the cheap baijiu he had drunk too much of the night before.

That "hard class" carriage he had made his way to once he had safely tucked his own tour party into their "soft sleeper" berths had been crowded with black-suited PRC administrators, homesick Han transplants, Hui traveling salesmen, even a few Tibetans, all set on drinking, talking, and gambling away the small hours of what—for them—was the boring imprisonment of the twenty-four-hour train journey from Golmud to Lhasa. Van der Mark had thrown his cards to keep them playing and led the cries of "Gan bei!" to keep them downing the hooch, to keep them talking.

Lying there, the professor momentarily tried to recall anything useful he had learned from the increasingly drunken chatter but that instantly became impossible as every loudspeaker on the train began to blare the Chinese national anthem.

起来！起来！起来！

ARISE! ARISE! ARISE!

The piercing commands of the people's choir and marching band were impossible to resist, so Van der Mark unfolded himself from his bunk to drop his big feet into his black slippers and pull his down jacket over his cotton pajamas. Stepping out of the sleeping compartment into the tight side corridor, he pushed his face close to the double-glazed window to take in the new day as a final crescendo left the train's speaker system buzzing. In the momentary silence that followed, the professor touched his throbbing forehead against the glass, seeking relief in its chill and the rhythmic mantra of the racing train. Almost immediately, the train's public information system burst back into life. The pre-recorded female voice spoke first in a pitchy Putonghua and then a sickly English, thereby doubly irritating the hungover professor who was fluent in both.

"Dear passenger friends, good morning! To your night of sweet repose now comes the most happiest of endings!"

The Dutchman groaned to himself as other awakened passengers began to squeeze themselves free of the carriage's tight sleeping compartments.

The train's "soft class" tourists were mostly nouveau riche Chinese from Beijing or Shanghai. Van der Mark's party was the only big Western tour group amongst them; twelve good-natured Dutch and Belgian retirees nearing the end of a luxury three week "Dragon Tour" of China led by the learned, if slightly grumpy—*Depressed?* they wondered—professor and his delightful STA assistant, Miss Zhang Li.

"Gentle pilgrims, see with wonder most joyful the Tibetan Autonomous Region of the People's Republic of China, land of legend revealing its ancient mysteries before your wide eyes!"

Eyes peered as instructed through the dirt-streaked glass, anticipating vast turquoise lakes, rolling grasslands studded with yaks and nomad tents, distant walls of immense white mountains touching limpid blue skies, all those things so seductively offered by website or brochure. Instead they saw only a wall of gray cloud dragging on a broken wasteland like a lead curtain.

"Look there! Perhaps it is a chiru—our most precious Tibetan antelope!" the prerecorded script ordered, as oblivious to reality as an automatic traffic light. "Fun facts for travelers! It is said the chiru with the long horns was the sideways mistake of the unicorn. Did you know that Yingying, one of the five mascots of the glorious 2008 Beijing Olympics, was a chiru? Enjoy the eyes' feast bestowed by nature! Hello, good boy Yingying!"

Bloody Yingying was nowhere to be seen.

Instead an abandoned farm emerged from the fog, roofless and jagged. The broken, once-white building sped by like a rotten molar on a conveyor belt to final extraction. The rapidly receding end wall was crowded with Chinese characters that surrounded a stenciled image of the head of Mao Tse-tung, the eyes chipped out, the teeth as black-stained as they had once been in real life, the trademark army cap denuded of its single red star.

Krijg de klere, Van der Mark thought as the Chairman disappeared east, *would that it could be so easy . . .*

A hailstorm replaced the paramount leader.

Ice pellets raked the carriages with a machine-gun rattle and bounced wildly on the wide highway that began to run parallel with the tracks, the undulating power lines above seemingly stitching the low cloud with black thread. That morning, China National Highway 109 was as vacant as the view. Its rough drivers knew their dangerous trade as well as the professor knew his. "The Road to Heaven" was always potentially literal, but particularly so on bad weather days, mandating that drivers stay in whatever bar, billiard-hall, or brothel they had marooned themselves in the night before.

The professor envied the brute truckers' day off. With conditions like this he was going to have to supply his disappointed party with endless stories and explanations to keep them entertained until the train pulled into Lhasa. The thought made him hungry for a solitary breakfast, for some time alone to dissipate his hangover and gather his thoughts before their onslaught of earnest interest started.

Pulling his jacket tight around his pajamas to avoid having to return to his bunk and risk getting caught in endless conversation with any of his tour party, the Dutchman quickly turned down the corridor to make his way to the dining car. As he walked away he considered what he had gleaned so far from that trip, recalling again what that old man in Xining had told him, had shown him, wondering if his contacts in Lhasa had been able to find out anything about it.

Over his first bowl of tea in the dining car, which the professor was relieved to see was still mostly empty of other travelers, he replayed the encounter.

The roadside noodle bar had been steamy and sour smelling, little more than a Perspex-enclosed counter despite being grandly called the Golden Dragon, as if the grubby white surfaces stained yellow by years of cooking grease were somehow intentional. At least the dive's cocoon of moist warmth offered a temporary respite from chilly Xining's choking traffic fumes and the constant bleating of Van der Mark's dull charges, mercifully at that moment being led by his commission-hungry assistant around a state souvenir shop.

The old man had entered to sit next to the professor despite other free seats. He had said nothing, looking resolutely ahead as he seated himself, even if there was an air of silent expectancy in his subsequent wait to order that the professor had interpreted as a desire for a free bowl of noodles from a rich gweilo. The Dutchman had obliged, finishing his own noodles to the sounds of the old man noisily sucking and slurping the white tapeworms from the edge of his bowl, constantly stoking them forward into his mouth with twinned chopsticks as if they might escape.

Van der Mark had no scheduled contact in Xining—the next was Golmud—but something in the old man's manner prompted his instinct to take a risk. From a hidden fold inside the back cover of his leather-bound notebook the professor slipped out a small photograph that he kept hidden under the flat of his hand. Only when the old man had finished eating did the professor tap his index finger on the scratched vinyl surface to summon attention to his hand.

Seeing the old man's rheumy eyes fix on it, the Dutchman slightly spread his fingers to reveal the head and shoulders image.

A young boy peered out between the living bars.

The old man looked down for an instant, then stared straight ahead again. His eyes watered as he began to speak in a mumbled Mandarin to the mirrored back wall of the noodle counter.

"They told me to teach him calligraphy. Despite being young, he had a natural talent, a great intelligence. I can still see how his ink brush swept and stroked the page as if guided by an older, greater hand than my own. Whenever I complimented him on it, he replied that one day he was also going to be a teacher like me."

Van der Mark's heart had lurched. He was finally hearing tell of the boy he had searched for across the length and breadth of China for more than twenty years.

"I enjoyed my lessons with him but one day we had some visitors," the old man continued. "Party officials and a large monk from Lhasa. They instructed me to write something on a page in order that they might watch the child copy it and assess his progress."

"What did you write?" the Dutch professor said to the man in the mirror as he opened his notebook at the last blank page and laid on it his uncapped pen.

"This."

Still looking forward, the man's hand took up the pen and lightly danced its black fiber tip on the page.

Three symbols soon latticed the top of the cream paper.

毛主席

"Chairman Mao?" the professor asked.

"Yes. That's what they wanted him to write."

"What did he do?"

"The boy did nothing. He didn't even breathe. He just stared at the symbols for what seemed like an age. I watched as a big drop of ink grew on the end of his brush, shiny, black, and round, until it fell and blotted the page.

"The boy just looked at the mark then dipped the brush back into the ink. Holding it over the page again, he let another drop grow and fall."

The old man's hand urgently began to illustrate his words by drawing two circles below the Chinese symbols that he quickly filled in, blackening them with strokes of ink.

"I watched the boy begin to paint around the two marks until one of the visitors shouted 'enough!' and stopped my lesson. They took him and the page away."

"When was this?"

"The year of the earth tiger."

The man finished his own drawing and shut the notebook before sliding it back to the professor.

"How old was he then?"

"Maybe seven, maybe eight. It was a long time ago. I never saw him again."

The old man hesitated before continuing.

"It is whispered that you are the gweilo that searches for him still. But, alive or dead, you should know that he is gone. You should also be careful, as those whispers are becoming too loud if they are reaching deaf ears such as mine."

The old man's crooked index finger pushed between the professor's digits and dragged the small photo away under the flat of his hand.

"Permit me the memory," he said as he got up and left with the small photograph.

Alone at the counter, the professor had waited until he was sure no one was watching him before he reopened his notebook.

Beneath Mao's name, two black pits stared back at him. They were the eyeholes in a sweeping drawing of a skull that was totally covered in lines and symbols as if the very bone had been tattooed. On the forehead was an inverted triangle. Another triangular line surrounded the whole image as if it was contained within a pyramid.

The professor had contemplated the image for some minutes, then left the noodle bar to resume his tour. The next day he had passed through Golmud and shown the drawing to his contact there. The Tibetan had no answer to what it meant, but photographed the page and said that perhaps his contacts in Lhasa might know.

Needing more tea to ponder what they might tell him when he got to Lhasa, the professor looked up for a waiter only to realize he was now alone in the carriage. He had been so lost in his thoughts that he had not noticed the few others in the dining-car leave.

The public address system shouted once more, making him jump. It was a new voice this time, less automated but louder and even more abrupt.

"Dining carriage closed for cleaning!
Dining carriage closed for cleaning!"

The announcement had barely finished when the tinted glass sliding door that led back to "soft class" opened and four black-suited Chinese entered. The professor recognized them from the night before; particularly the one bearing the tall tea thermos Van der Mark required. The man had a featureless face, a blank canvas that had creased to cruelty when he had described himself as traveling to Lhasa to take up a senior position within "the CPC Sewage Treatment Division."

Before the doors could close behind them, the Dutchman caught a glimpse of other men standing beyond. In their midst was his STA assistant, Zhang Li, and she was talking fast. Her anxious, urgent manner instantly told the professor everything he needed to know, so he ignored the cellphone he had very deliberately set on the dining table to prepare a text message on a second he pulled from his jacket pocket and kept hidden in his lap as he looked out of the window.

Snow had replaced the hail; thick, heavy flakes curving to the rocky ground like the strokes of a white scythe. *Early, even for here,* the professor thought as the man with the teapot sat opposite the Dutchman.

"Professor van der Mark, let me exchange you some tea for your cellphone."

The professor gestured to the one on the table and said, "Please, be my guest," as he hit Send with his thumb on the other and then Off.

"I'm not interested in your decoy, Professor. The alternate cellphone ploy may work on stupid peasant-soldiers but not me. Give me the other one."

The professor raised the second phone to place it on the table.

The man looked at it then refilled Van der Mark's empty bowl.

"So I can assume that you are not part of the CPC Sewage Treatment Division?" the Dutchman asked.

"Actually, I do dispose of sewage," the man replied, his eyes so dark brown they seemed black. "You should know that any message you think you have just sent will not be received. All cellular traffic has been blocked for the remainder of this journey. Everything in both of your cellphones, the official and the secret one, will have been analyzed and traced before this train arrives in Lhasa."

The Chinese man passed the professor's phones across to one of the other men who had set up a black laptop on the next table. The man nodded urgently to immediately attach the second phone to the larger device by cable. The obvious look of fear in his eyes identified the superior to the professor.

"So I finally get to meet the infamous Yama," Van der Mark said. "I knew that sooner or later it would be you."

"Yama." The nearly lipless mouth laughed with no smile. "The name of the Tibetan 'Lord of Death.' Ridiculous. My name is Lieutenant Yen-Tsun Lai. But then again, if calling me Yama helps them better understand my role in their traitorous lives, then so be it."

He paused for a moment.

"As you knew our meeting was inevitable, Professor van der Mark, then you will also not be surprised that I am mandated to have zero tolerance for an ethnic separatist operating within our territories, whatever his standing or nationality."

The professor countered with an empty hand. "I have a tour party on this train. As it doesn't stop until Lhasa, I hope you will let me complete my duties."

"You have been very clever, Professor van der Mark. Offering your services as a prestigious guide has been an excellent cover to permit you to roam our territories and spy on us. This train will indeed shortly be making an unscheduled stop. Follow me please."

Yama reached for the professor's leather-bound notebook and stood from the table. Without alternative the tall Dutchman rose also. Passing through the final sliding door of the carriage that Yama opened with a swipe of his own smartphone, they walked through into a final freight car that had been fully prepared for what the professor realized was going to happen next. Baijiu laced bile flooded his dry mouth like acid.

"Your jacket and slippers?" Yama asked.

Van der Mark handed him his thick down jacket and took off his thin slippers. Suddenly vulnerable in just his pajamas, a man on each side took the professor by the shoulders and arms.

"It is necessary that I ask some questions first. We can start with your notebook."

Yama flicked through its pages before settling on the last.

He looked at it and then turned it toward the Dutchman.

The inked skull within the triangle leered at the professor.

"What is this?"

Van der Mark looked at the drawing and said, "Of that I also only have questions."

"We'll see."

An hour later train T27 suddenly slowed as if a dead man's handle had been released.

With a long screech of metal on metal the carriages juddered to a reluctant halt that ended in a final lurch of inertia that upended people and possessions throughout the length of the train. Unseen at the rear, a single sealed door hissed and released outward on hydraulic hinges. The icy cold burst in as Professor Paul van der Mark was pushed out into the snowstorm in just his bloodstained pajamas.

The train soon resumed its journey through the elements, the public information system seemingly reinvigorated by the momentary stop.

**"And now, happy travelers,
welcome to Shangri-La!"**

8

LIVING BUDDHA DATABASE

TIBET AUTONOMOUS REGIONAL OFFICE, NO. 1 KANG'ANGDONGLU, LHASA, TIBETAN AUTONOMOUS REGION OF THE PEOPLE'S REPUBLIC OF CHINA
September 17, 2014

The two most senior officials of the Tibetan Autonomous Region of the People's Republic of China were seated at each end of the long table that dominated the executive boardroom at the top of the Party's headquarters at No. 1 Kang'angdonglu in Lhasa.

Zou Xiaopeng, the Communist Party secretary for the territory, and Jin Yui, the governor, were both ambitious men with little love for the land they ruled and even less for each other. Zou was an out-and-out Party man, hard-working, intelligent, patient, dogmatic; while Jin was his own man, venal, connected, cunning, ruthless, corrupt. Both were following one of the two well-trodden roads, that familiar yin and yang of Chinese power politics, to reach that lacquered table. Between them, on each side, were the chairman of the Chinese People's Political Consultative Conference, Wang Maozhen, and a corpulent Tibetan monk called Geshe Shep.

With his characteristic lack of emotion, Chairman Wang, another Party man in the mold of Zou, was explaining to the assembled "Dragon Committee" how the priority project of the Religious and Ethnic Affairs section under his charge was nearing completion. Casting from a laptop to a large plasma screen on the wall, he was demonstrating his new database of "Living Buddhas," as he called them.

"We have one thousand, three hundred, and twenty-one approved entries," Wang reported. "All those we deem significant within this regional religious grouping. We now know everything about them." His cursor danced energetically from photograph to photograph and section to section to highlight recorded personal details: places of residence, positions within the hierarchy of Tibetan Buddhism, and known loyalties and affiliations to the Party. "Such knowledge permits complete control," he concluded.

"Good. But what happens when your 'Living Buddhas' are no longer living?" Governor Jin said, smiling at his own wit as Zou gave him a look of barely concealed loathing. "Do you also have complete control of their rebirth?"

Wang responded like the automaton he was to clinically explain that in case of vacancy of a registered position due to death, full details of the search process to find the replacement—he did not say "reincarnation"—would also be included and procedurally monitored. He added that all monks in the database involved in such a search process would be automatically placed under enhanced surveillance and supervision to ensure they followed approved procedure. "Nothing will now be left to either local superstition or chance."

"Well done!" Party Secretary Zou congratulated his political understudy. "As we all know, this work is of paramount importance for the number one ethnic priority of this region: the selection, when necessary, of the next Dalai Lama. Only then will we finally rule this territory and people."

"That splittist monk's escape was the Chairman's greatest mistake," Jin interjected, desirous to irritate the staunch party man and loyalist to the memory of Mao with whom he had disagreed over policy toward the Dalai Lama for years.

"That was a long time ago. Things are far different now. Few escape today, as you well know," Zou snapped back, instantly rising to his rival's bait. "Beijing has granted huge investment for us to close the traditional exit routes into Nepal, Bhutan, and India. We have increased patrols, motion sensors, and UAV drones that have turned the Himalayas into a second Great Wall. In addition, heavy financial and penal sanctions on remaining family members as well as bounty payments to neighboring border authorities for the return of apprehended transients have had great effect."

"Yet still some get away," Jin needled.

The monk, appearing to wake from a postprandial slumber, spoke. "Yes, I heard recently that a possible soul child had gone missing in Community Work Territory 57. Did not Community Supervisor Pie Lee make a report?"

"I think you misunderstand the point, Geshe Shep," Wang said dismissively to the corpulent monk. "Our database is now the only authority. If a vacancy is not on the list, then it does not exist. In that case we questioned the parents at length. I suspect the infant was actually kidnapped or sold by the parents because of a particular 'difference' in that it had red hair. I hear that people pay highly for such oddities."

Geshe chewed on Wang's hubris as if it was one of his five meals a day, but chose to say nothing more that might jeopardize them.

It was Zou Xiaopeng who spoke again. "Perhaps that is so, but we must also be diligent. This is a delicate moment for us all. Need I remind any of you that our territory is the key to the next five-year plan? The president has mandated the production of new power technologies as a priority to combat our nation's pollution and to render the oil dominion of others obsolete. The extraction of lithium, graphite, and heavy earths from the Tibetan Autonomous Region has to increase dramatically as does utilization of our abundant natural water resources for additional energy. No one can be allowed to stand in the way and nothing, I repeat nothing, can be left to chance."

"But, Party Secretary, you know well that while the Dalai Lama lives that is impossible," Jin interjected, turning the screw of their ongoing disagreement over how best to deal with that matter.

"Patience has never been your strong point, Governor." Zou scowled. "How old is he now, Geshe Shep?"

"Seventy-nine, I believe. Tenzin Gyatso has already outlived every other dalai lama, with the exception of the first."

"That devil cannot live forever and when the time comes we will choose a suitable replacement from within our territories using this very database. No stone is being left unturned to prepare for this moment. Our much-loved Panchen Lama is now of age and ready to lead the process. All the registered living buddhas in this very database will fall into line if they value their freedom. Is that not correct, Geshe Shep?"

The large monk grunted his agreement as Jin pressed a button on the table and said, "Please show in the lieutenant."

Lieutenant Yen-Tsun Lai entered to stand before the screen displaying the database.

Jin looked at his protégé and wished he could let him loose on Zou—that would be something to watch—but said, "Lieutenant, welcome. I thought the Dragon Committee, particularly Party Secretary Zou, should hear your news given the subject matter of our meeting today."

Yama licked the dry edge of his mouth.

"I report to the Dragon Committee that a key splittist cell in Lhasa has been broken up following apprehension of the Dutch professor, Paul van der Mark, a foreign spy whose identity had eluded us for years. Fortunately, the person that he had searched for many years had also eluded him."

"And who was that?" Jin asked, already well aware of the answer but looking at Zou to see him receive it.

"The boy the Dalai Lama chose against our wishes to be Panchen Lama."

"Did he get close?"

Yama's hooded eyes blinked once. "No."

Geshe Shep stirred. "Was the Dutchman the ghost moth?"

"No," the lieutenant said. "I am sure of that."

"Why do you ask, Geshe Shep?" Governor Jin asked.

"The subject came up in respect to the missing child in Community Work Territory 57 that I mentioned."

"What or who is this?" Wang demanded.

"No one knows," the monk continued. "Many Tibetans think that the ghost moth is a tulpa, a spirit; others think it is another living Buddha, a saint even. The name has long been linked with people and precious relics from our monasteries and communities disappearing."

"Superstitious nonsense, Geshe. It is just a myth, another code word for an all-too-human resistance," Jin warned. "The lieutenant catches everyone in the end, and when he does you can be sure there will be no reincarnation. No one would risk such a fate twice."

"Our inquiries of the Lhasa group have left us with many leads to follow and details of a new route through the mountains that is being used to cross into Nepal. We are monitoring them all," the lieutenant added. "If he exists, I can assure you that the ghost moth will soon be found and destroyed."

"Good, then you should proceed," Zou ordered. "This is a crucial time. Nothing can be left that might jeopardize the future of this process."

"Before I do, I would like Geshe Shep to tell me about this." Yama passed the monk a leather notebook opened to the final inked page.

The monk looked at it, noting the brown smear of dried blood on the paper. "Did this come from the Dutch professor?"

"Yes. Do you know what it signifies?"

"Yes. I saw this likeness once before." The monk stopped, tasting once again his bitterest shame.

"Speak, fat man," Jin ordered.

Geshe Shep glanced nervously at Yama and immediately began to sing for his multiple suppers for the next thirty minutes. Before he had finished earning the first, Jin had beckoned Yama to his side and quietly ordered him to visit Community Work Territory 57.

PART III

PATHS THAT CROSS

The mountains, the forest, and the sea,
render men savage; they develop the
fierce, but yet do not destroy the human.

—Victor Hugo

9

ACHES AND PAINS

MCLEOD GANJ, DHARAMSALA, HIMACHAL PRADESH, NORTHERN INDIA
October 7, 2014

The old monk's mood matched the darkness: fatigued, achy, constipated; all too human at his habitual 3 a.m. rising. Time, solitude, and silence would be the required remedy before another busy day of appointments.

With all three at his disposal, he knelt to the polished wood parquet. As had become usual, his legs were reluctant to bend, his body equally stiff to follow them down to the floor. The monk let out an involuntary sigh from the effort, answered by a watery knee's cry, as if it had been stabbed by the touch of the hard wood floor, despite the thin velvet-covered pad. A new pain in his left wrist introduced itself in piercing sympathy when he pushed his hand against the floor to relieve the knee.

Getting old . . .

Years amass a corporeal toll, however spiritual their passing. Lines deepen, wrinkles multiply, folds hang, blotches bloom, muscles shrink, bones weaken, organs slow, gray hair, no hair; silent messengers of age that congregate to collectively shout their presence even in those who countenance calm.

The monk stiffly submitted his body fully to the floor, flat to this earth, in prostration before Buddha, of Buddha, in Buddha.

Settle . . .

Difficult!

Release . . .

Reluctant!

His brain was stubborn, willful from too many travels, too many people, too many complications . . .

But aren't these just alternative explanations for one more symptom?

He was tired.

Age had changed sleep from sound to fleeting, from friend to enemy, from peace to war. Night was now a black amphitheater of wakefulness. Seconds felt like minutes and the minutes like hours; hours and hours for the smallest thought to expand infinitely like a drop of oleic acid on water until it filled the void with an equal enormity.

He was weaker too.

Aches and pains multiplied and grew. Colds and fevers attacked and lingered. The natural remedy of youth was long gone.

Yes, all the signs are there.

Except those he sought.

After all, age demands an end; an end that needs to be understood to permit a new beginning.

When?

How?

Who?

Where?

But there was still nothing from the inside, and yet more silence from the night outside.

It was enough to try the patience of a saint.

10

THE BROCKEN SPECTER

MOUNTAIN OF SHISHAPANGMA, NYALAM COUNTY, TIBETAN AUTONOMOUS REGION OF THE PEOPLE'S REPUBLIC OF CHINA
October 7, 2014

Dawn at twenty-four-thousand feet in the Himalayas was a slow, mostly silent affair. That day it was no different. Mountain guide Neil Quinn could hear only the occasional sounds of his high-altitude penance—the climbing hardware rattling like Marley's chains, spiked crampons scraping against rock, the occasional buzz of radio static—over the constant backbeat of heavy breathing, heart pounding, every bone, muscle, and sinew protesting.

It had been going on for hours. The remaining members of the 2014 Snowdonia Ascents Shishapangma expedition—three Sherpa, two client climbers, and Quinn, the expedition leader—had left their Camp Two tents a few minutes after 1 a.m. to climb through the night toward the summit. The commercial climbing operators may describe the highest Himalayan peak located entirely in Tibet as "a sleeping snow giant," or "one of the easier eight-thousanders," even as an "ideal stepping-stone for Everest," but going for its top was still brutal. For hours of freezing darkness, the six climbers had been a summit team in little more than name only, each lost within the individual roundel of snow and rock that fell under the beam of their headlamps as they worked their way up the steep northwest ridge.

The gradual realization that the softer, grayer light of dawn was finally fraying the edge of his pool of lamplight made the Englishman stop for a moment and take stock of how his charges were faring. At first, it was all he could do to lean over his ice axe, drag in some deep breaths, and repeatedly curl his fingers and toes in order to bring back some semblance of life. "Shit, it's cold!" Quinn muttered to no one as he forced his head up from the ice-encrusted front of his down suit to look around.

In the east, a red line sliced the horizon as if night's throat had been cut. Crimson, orange, and yellow welled up into the dark above. The sight promised continued good weather, even though Quinn knew it wasn't going to get much warmer. Shishapangma was always a cold mountain and they, the last team on the hill, were climbing it late in the autumn season. The region's hard fall into winter was just weeks away.

Watch them for frostbite, Quinn reminded himself as he turned his eyes up the ever-steepening ridge to seek Gelu, the expedition's sirdar, and his cousin Tenjin. He soon picked out the two Sherpas' climb suits bright and high in the golden light that was now crowning the mountain. They were already fixing rope up the snowy channel that marked the entrance to the "central" summit, exactly as they had agreed. It was always super windy up there and no one wanted anyone flying away.

Quinn wondered what the two Sherpas were seeing. The summit just above them at the top of the couloir was actually false, some forty-five feet or so lower than the true apex of the mountain, which lay at the end of another crest, a fifteen-hundred-foot fin of snow that was heavily corniced and prone to avalanche. More often than not, climbers arrived exhausted at the central summit, took in the life-threatening tightrope walk that offered so few meters more of altitude, and declared the job done. A hair over the mythical eight-thousand-meter mark, it pretty much satisfied everyone except Henrietta Richards, the self-appointed record-keeper of Himalayan climbing.

Even up there, it was easy for Quinn to imagine the equally frosty post-climb interviews at Henrietta's book-lined apartment in Kathmandu that verified every Himalayan summit claim. He could hear that upper-class English accent, undiminished by forty years of living in Nepal—the faintest trace of humor perceptible only to those who had met her often—as it asked the unsuspecting "central summiteer" of Shishapangma, "But I assume you do understand what a 'false summit' is?" If they didn't when they stepped into that fabled living room, they certainly did by the time they left.

Quinn smiled to himself at the thought. He and Henrietta had become friends since "that awful Sarron business" as she referred to it. She knew everything there was to know about the mountains that he loved and in return he enjoyed feeding that knowledge with reports of his own experiences up there. Turning his mind back to that day's summit for them, false or otherwise, Quinn told himself he'd call it with Gelu Sherpa when he got up there, false summit or not.

With a look back down the steep ridge, Quinn quickly saw Tore Rasmussen not far below, relentlessly plodding upward. Despite having no previous Himalayan experience, the blond Norwegian bricklayer was a natural mountaineer; a by-product of his lean yet muscular build and resting heart rate of forty. From the first day of the expedition, Quinn had the feeling Rasmussen would summit, even if the dour loner was difficult to please—or like for that matter. The coarse man might go on to top every other eight-thousand-meter peak, or just as easily shrug his shoulders and say, "Horrible! Never again!" as if the "disgusting food" and "bloody cold" he had complained about continually were all Quinn's fault.

Still farther behind, Quinn saw Alan Reid and Nima Sherpa. "Big Al," as he'd introduced himself, seemed to be hardly moving despite the fact he was the only one of them using bottled oxygen. The heavy, ex-Army Cockney with the "Everest Dream" had talked a good game—in fact he never stopped talking—but he had always been going to struggle; the reason Quinn had assigned the fit young Sherpa to keep a close eye on him.

Quinn had weighed telling Reid to sit out the summit attempt, but with two other team members already calling it quits, Bill Owen, the owner of Snowdonia Ascents, had asked Quinn to give Reid a chance using O's. "Let's try and keep the dream alive a little longer, eh, Neil? You never know." But Quinn did know. He had led many Himalayan climbs, summited Everest one way or another thirteen times, seen and experienced pretty much everything the "death zone" had to offer and then some. Even with supplemental oxygen, Big Al was unlikely to make it. This "stepping-stone" was just too high. In the half-dark that lingered lower down the mountain

Quinn watched confirmation of the fact as Reid's bulky figure crumpled into the snow like a marionette with severed strings. Soon after, Quinn's radio crackled to life.

He tugged it from his icy breast pocket, holding it close to his face to hear, "Mr. Neil? Nima Sherpa here. Mr. Neil?"

"Go ahead, Nima. Over."

"Member Al going down . . . I think time now. Necessary."

"Does he accept? Over."

"Yes, Mr. Neil." There was a pause. "He say, he fucking well had enough."

I bet he has, Quinn thought only to reply, "Okay, Nima. Keep me advised on your descent. Over."

"Yes, Mr. Neil."

"Good. Over."

Quinn put the radio away and looked beyond the knife-edge of the ridge onto a bed of dense cloud, a soft sea of gray that masked the steep gorges below that fell into Nepal in treacherous cascades of broken rock and ice.

A smudge stained the haze.

The shadow darkened as if sucking up all the remaining ashes of the night.

A faceless head grew.

Long limbs extended.

Unasked, Quinn's hypoxia quick-fired fantastic explanations for the strange black suited figure rising up before him.

Ghost.

Bat.

Vampire.

An iridescent halo began to shine around the towering shadow's head.

Angel?

At 25,000 feet, understanding arrives like the dawn, slowly and silently. Quinn deliberately raised his right arm and moved it from side to side. The shadow waved back as if sluggishly beckoning him forward into the abyss.

"It's a Brocken specter," an internal voice with a refined German accent—another ghost—told Quinn. "Your own reflection cast by the rising sun onto cloud below."

It was the first time Quinn had seen the phenomenon in all his years of climbing.

He stared at it, thinking, *Now you really have seen it all,* until, with almost a start, he realized he should try to get some video of it. Flicking off a mitten to hang on its lanyard, he dug deep inside his down suit to pull out his new iPhone. He risked baring his hand farther by taking off his fleece liner glove to clumsily switch it on.

Faintly surprised to see it even worked up there, Quinn took some video of the specter until it vanished, evaporating as quickly and quietly as it had appeared.

Rasmussen arrived alongside Quinn to replace the strange figure. The Norwegian looked equally ghostly. His down jacket, his fleece hat, his ski mask, all were rimed with ice. Only his mouth was uncovered, the yellowed teeth exposed in a tight grimace of exertion that stretched his lips into thin blue rubber bands.

"Did you see it, Tore?" Quinn asked as he tucked away his phone.

"What?" came the gruff reply that set the two icicles hanging from the ends of Rasmussen's blond mustache trembling.

"The Brocken specter."

"No. I didn't, and you didn't say it would be this cold, Neil Quinn. Really crappy stuff, you know?"

Quinn's enthusiasm for what he had witnessed couldn't be punctured. "It was amazing, first time in all my years of climbing. And here? Incredible."

The icy Norwegian leaned over his long ice axe, looking down at the snow and dragging in deep, shuddering breaths. Finally he turned his frozen face back up at Quinn.

"Don't be so damn pleased with yourself, Englishman. Where I come from a Brocken specter is an omen . . . an omen of death."

Without waiting for a reply, Rasmussen resumed his miserable journey up the mountain.

11

BEWARE THE LAUGH

MANDALA HOTEL, DHARAMSALA, HIMACHAL PRADESH, NORTHERN INDIA
October 7, 2014

Journalist Beth Waterman had been told that Dharamsala in Northern India took its beat from a single heart. When its owner took it elsewhere, the place inevitably slowed, its residents suffering the absence like a loyal dog: sad-eyed and insecure until the master's return. The Dalai Lama needed to be there in his residence, his unique combination of parental love, protection, and discipline present in the scruffy hilltop town to grant its quiet sense of purpose for the many exiles that now called it "home." For the visitors to "Little Lhasa"—the robed pilgrims of many faiths, the fresh-faced backpackers, the neo-hippies of all ages, the single ladies of a certain one— His Holiness's presence produced more tangible levels of anticipation and euphoria, the promise of epiphany filling every bus and taxi that arrived and electrifying the hotels and cafés.

Beth didn't need her appointment to interview the Dalai Lama to know he was indeed there that day. While the thirty-six-year-old writer from New York struggled down a plate of syrupy mango slices paired with the bitterest cup of instant coffee she could remember—and she had had a few in her career—she could feel his presence all around her. However, neither the obvious excitement—a buzz of conversation that hovered over the full dining room like a swarm of invisible fruit flies—nor the nauseating coffee could lift the leaden blanket of her thirty-hour journey to that breakfast table.

Poking a last fluorescent slice around the slippery plate, she told herself that it was no bad thing. She hadn't come all that way to eat, pray, and love but to complete a tightly timed three-thousand-word commission from *Rolling Stone* that came with a golden ticket to interview the man himself. Detachment and lucidity were going to be necessary if she was to avoid getting sucked into the cosmic lovefest building up around her.

Some impressively cynical colleagues had warned her that it wouldn't be easy, that the Dalai Lama was a surprisingly difficult study, charming, clever, enigmatic, and funny, very funny. "Beware the laugh," they had all said. "It takes up your valuable time . . . It disarms your tough questions . . . It converts you from inquisitor to disciple . . . It masks a true sadness and pain that you cannot begin to imagine."

Beth looked at her notepad set next to one of the many books about the Dalai Lama she had read in her rushed preparation for the surprise project. The smiling face on the cover beamed back at her as she scanned an introductory paragraph she had written on the plane.

WHAT NEXT FOR THE DALAI LAMA?

Approaching eighty years old, His Holiness the Dalai Lama Tenzin Gyatso is a living icon, as recognizable as Barack Obama, as revered as Nelson Mandela, as compassionate as Mother Teresa, as cool as Miles Davis. But as he ages and China grows ever stronger, financially and militarily, what comes next for him, his people, and the land of his birth?

"Jesus," she said to herself, jet lag momentarily vanquishing the bad coffee.

"No, madam. Dalai Lama!" the waiter triumphantly replied, looking at her book as he automatically refilled her cup.

Beth nodded, trying to raise a smile equal to that on her book. It wasn't as easy as it looked. The cover reminded her of the words of the sad-faced man who had bagged the book in his tiny "Tibetan things" store in the East Village.

"I think that it is all over for us once His Holiness is gone," the shopkeeper had said. "He is old. They say he is often ill now. He cannot live forever. No one knows what will happen then. We are worried."

Beth returned to her notes, scrolling down her researched bullet points as if cramming for a looming test.

- *Sacred Buddhist scriptures first crossed the Himalayas into Tibet from India in the fifth century. Their amplification beyond the mountains increased in the seventh century with the support of the thirty-third Tibetan king, Songtsen Gampo (known as the first Dharma King), whose two queens, one Chinese, one Nepali, were both Buddhist.*

- *Buddhism was adopted as the state religion by the thirty-eighth Tibetan king, Trisong Detsen (the second Dharma King), in the eighth century. Tibet's geographic isolation and existing Bön, Mi Chös, and Hindu traditions endowed these Buddhist teachings with existing tantric and shamanic elements and a pantheon of ancient supernatural beings.*

- *A sequence of schools of Tibetan Buddhism have risen to dominance through key teachers, the discovery of holy texts, and periods of specific political patronage: the Nyingmapa or "Red Hats" in the eighth century, the Kagyupa or "Black Hats" and the Sakayapa also "Red Hats" in the eleventh century, and the Gelugpa or "Yellow Hats" in the sixteenth century.*

- *Each sect reveres and respects the "lama" as priest, teacher, guide, and guardian, primarily within monastic hierarchies. The "Ganden Tripa" is the most senior monk of the Gelugpa, the "Sakya Trizin" that of the Sakayapa, and the "Karmapa Lama" of the Kargyupa. In some cases, but not all, such senior figures are reincarnates—the rebirth of a holy soul into a new body.*

- *Within the Gelugpa school, dominant for the past four hundred years, another senior reincarnate lama has traditionally held greatest sway over Tibet itself: the Dalai Lama. The Dalai Lama is an emanation of the Bodhisattva of Compassion, Avalokiteshvara, or Chenrezig, the patron saint of Tibet, and seen as both the spiritual and secular head of the country since the days of the Khans. The name "dalai" signifies ocean, a historic metaphor for boundless knowledge.*

- *Tenzin Gyatso is the current and fourteenth Dalai Lama. He was born one of sixteen children in the village of Takster in the region of Amdo, now part of Qinghai province, the People's Republic of China, on July 6, 1935. Identified as the reincarnation of the thirteenth Dalai Lama, he was enthroned in Lhasa, capital of Tibet, on February 22, 1940, aged five. He was subsequently given his full political powers, de facto rulership of the historic territories of Tibet, on November 17, 1950, in response to the Chinese invasion from the east.*

- *The Dalai Lama escaped to India in 1959 during the Tibetan uprising that began 1956. Since then, more than 200,000 Tibetans have followed him over the Himalayas in a worldwide diaspora that is led by a Tibetan government in exile—now known as the Central Tibetan Administration and situated in Dharamsala, India. The Dalai Lama has since traveled the world advocating for autonomy for his former country with a consistent message of compassion and non-violence despite the fact that for nearly seventy years the Tibetan territories have been subject to one of the worst human rights records in the world.*

- *Tenzin Gyatso was awarded the Nobel Peace Prize in 1989, becoming a symbol of the "new hope '90s" that followed the fall of the Berlin Wall. Rock musicians, Hollywood film stars, and media celebrities adopted his cause, lionizing his peaceful struggles on both stage and screen. However, post-9/11, world focus shifted elsewhere and the growing economic might of China has been increasingly directed at governments and multinational corporations in a way that has sought isolation of the Dalai Lama, whom they vilify as a "dangerous separatist." More often than not, world leaders now avoid him even if their own peoples continue to admire him.*

- *In 2011, citing his advancing age, the Dalai Lama stepped down from his political leadership role of the Central Tibetan Administration conferring it to an elected prime minister. He has however continued his spiritual leadership to the Tibetan Buddhists, constantly reiterating his message of peace and non-violence.* <u>*As he ages, talk of the Dalai Lama's*</u> <u>*succession grows . . .*</u>

The last line was heavily underlined.

Beth had decided the focus of her story lay there.

She glanced at her watch. It was less than an hour before that morning's "open audience" with the Dalai Lama at the Namgyal Gompa, the monastery within the main Tsuglagkhang complex. After, she was to be shown the other key spiritual centers of the town by a member of his office before the interview itself at His Holiness's private residence the next morning.

It was time.

⋇

Beyond the hotel lobby, the receptionist's annotated street map was immediately rendered redundant. Amidst conflicting wafts of joss and body odor, spices and drains, and the constant bombardment of offers of food, trinkets, and bright silk cushions from darting street vendors, Beth just joined the flow of humanity already heading up the road. The walkers around her already seemed enraptured, remarking lyrically on every detail of the place: the fluttering strings of prayer flags—their bright hues of blue, white, red, green, and yellow—the golden temple roofs reflecting the morning sun; the tails of smoke from wood fires and incense bundles that rose up between the deodar pines and junipers; the white clouds that floated free over the distant snow summits, roaming that lost land beyond them that dominated every facet of life in Dharamsala.

Beth listened in on a chatter of travels and religions, spouses and lovers, hopes and dreams continually peppered with references to Mahatma Gandhi and Martin Luther King, Richard Gere and Julia Roberts, Bob Dylan and Bruce Springsteen. It felt more like the walk up to a big rock concert than a religious audience.

As if perfectly timed to counter this impression, a short, shaven-headed monk in bulky crimson robes began to walk alongside Beth, who took in the

68

long dark eyelashes and the soft bare skin of the monk's faintly rosy cheeks to understand it was actually a young woman. The nun turned her face, and with a serene smile, reached into a leather satchel to hand Beth a postcard. Unlike the noisy street vendors or the beggars, no word or request for money followed. The nun simply stopped in her tracks, instantly swallowed by the human tide that carried Beth on up the hill.

Beth's feeling that she was going to a sold-out show was only confirmed by the rough squeeze through the tight security cordon at the entrance to the Tsuglagkhang complex. Sniffer-dogs, metal detectors, bag inspectors, and burly Sikh policemen armed with submachine guns guarded the entrance to check everyone and everything before it was permitted to pass. The sight of the weapons was somewhat shocking in the context, but Beth told herself not to be naive.

Signing in at a VIP reception desk, she was immediately introduced to Wangdu Palsang, an athletic Tibetan in his late twenties who was dressed in a white polo shirt and pressed jeans. Assigned to be Beth's guide and photographer for the day, Wangdu showed her where they should meet after the audience, then left Beth to rejoin the crowd filing into a large open courtyard telling her, "I am going to photograph your attendance so it would be good if you could sit in the middle, somewhere near the front if possible."

There were no chairs inside the open courtyard Beth entered. Without instruction, the growing audience either sat cross-legged on the floor in neat rows, or stood to the rear in lines of ascending height as if attending their first school assembly. She squeezed her way forward and sat down on the bare concrete, understanding immediately why multicolored cushions had been one of the street vendors' many offerings. She hoped it wasn't going to be a long wait.

To pass the time, Beth looked again at the postcard given to her by the nun. The color picture on one side was a portrait of an Asian boy seated in a brown vinyl-covered armchair. Photoflash reflected in both its shiny surface and the illuminated, faintly surprised expression on the face of the subject. The little lad was very young, five or six perhaps, with the oval, open features of the Tibetan plateau—of the nun who had given Beth the postcard. The child's eyes were jet black, as if red-eye had been replaced with wet ink. The ears were pushed out and forward like little wings. Two front teeth protruded beneath the upper curl of a mouth that—despite the straight-bottomed seriousness of the picture—looked as if it could easily chuckle. The nose was pert, clean, and unwrinkled.

Beth turned the postcard over.

A single line of bold print read:

HIS HOLINESS, THE ELEVENTH PANCHEN LAMA, GEDHUN CHOEKYI NYIMA

Beth recalled something from her research and opened her notebook to look it up, but a murmur of recognition pulled her attention back to the event. Slipping the postcard inside instead, she watched as the Dalai Lama walked onto the small stage.

His raised hand of silent greeting unleashed an audible wave of joy that rolled back over the ranks of the assembled faces and left a loud applause in its wake. A blond woman next to Beth—a German or Scandinavian perhaps—began to gently cry. Another, already in the lotus position, brought her hands together in a yogic Namaste then began to rapidly mouth a silent mantra. A man's hand reached for Beth's. Surprised at the touch, Beth turned to look at a blond surfer type with tied-back dreadlocks and tugged her hand away with a shrug, irritated by the opportunism.

The Dalai Lama stood before them all as the applause rose into a loud cheering. Attendants and security silently lined the wall behind him, including Wangdu, already training his camera on Beth amongst other people in the crowd. It crossed her mind that he was scanning the audience with the long lens as much as he was photographing it.

Gesturing for a quiet that was reluctantly conceded, His Holiness began to address his audience. The animated bare right arm that projected from those familiar gold and magenta robes seemed to offer each thought by hand. If he smiled or joked, the audience instantly rippled with laughter and more applause. If he looked serious, they silently mirrored his gravity. If he looked quizzical, they internally answered the unspoken question.

Yes, we can do better . . .

The Dalai Lama spoke eloquently, evenly, without note or pause for the next thirty minutes. To Beth, it was actually a somewhat confusing message of peace and goodness, but one that was somehow being collectively understood to the last syllable.

". . . Sensory level of experience has some satisfaction but no effect on the problem in mental level. So the mental level—faith also in some extent very helpful—but mainly love, compassion—not at sensory level of love, not that way, but use intelligence, through training, through awareness, through investigation then gradually develop firm conviction . . ."

Beth Waterman, despite her long and arduous journey to that place, her abandoned Catholicism, her hateful ex-husband now living with the "soulmate" he met at his gym, her honed professional cynicism, now found herself beginning to float on every word. She had to forcibly tug her backside back down onto the hard concrete, wishing she'd bought one of those damn cushions.

12

THE TOP

SHISHAPANGMA CENTRAL SUMMIT, NYALAM COUNTY, TIBETAN AUTONOMOUS REGION OF THE PEOPLE'S REPUBLIC OF CHINA

Quinn and Rasmussen joined Gelu and Tenjin on the central summit of Shishapangma at 10 a.m., the four of them crowding a precarious stamped-out snow platform little bigger than a pool table. The driving wind quickly bullied them into a huddle as lengths of old rope and tattered prayer flags whipped the snow as if to punish it for shouldering the intruders.

Hunched down side by side, Quinn and Gelu looked across at the main summit those few meters higher. The Sherpa's experienced hand rose and fell on the gusts, wordlessly indicating what both could see: the white plume of snow crystals blasting the vaporous sky; the harelip in the heavily corniced ridge; the northern snow slope below so slabbed and full, ready to avalanche at a touch; the wind-scoured black rock that fell almost vertically to the south like a cheese-grater. With a nod, Quinn quickly called the climb. None of them were trying to break any records. The central summit was summit enough for that trip.

He broke out the radio to breathlessly announce their success to Nima and the rest of the team at the Base Camp, then for the brief twenty minutes that stabbing wind allowed, they all took in the fact that they had made it to the top of the highest mountain within Tibet.

It was still a fine day with clear, long views in every direction that

Rasmussen photographed from every angle—until he thrust his expensive Canon at Quinn and demanded the obligatory summit photo as a statement rather than a question.

"The top," he grunted.

It crossed Quinn's mind to lob the damn man's camera into Nepal but, ever the professional, he obliged, questioning who the hell the antisocial Norwegian was even going to show the photos to.

His mother?

Chiding himself for pettiness rather than savoring the twenty-six-thousand-foot vantage point they had worked so hard to reach, Quinn did as he was asked, rewarding himself with a moment to appreciate his surroundings.

To the north, long striated glaciers curved out from the mountain like unraveling question marks that tapered into brown badlands, rugged and seemingly infinite. To the west, the lower peaks of the Langtang—that jagged frontier to the tight valleys of Nepal—punctured the low-lying cloud. To the east through more tattered cloud, he saw the summits of Everest, its sister peak, Lhotse, and farther on still, Makalu. The trio rose up like the fins of prowling sharks.

Quinn's gaze lingered on Everest's north ridge as a brief but violent shudder shook his body. He told himself it was from the cold, but from the corner of his eye he caught Gelu watching him intently. Gelu was one of the rope-fixing Sherpa who had found Quinn already on the summit of Everest that day in 2011 when they thought they had opened the route to the top.

He returned the Sherpa's look with a simple tilt of the head that said nothing of that desperate morning on top of the world, but instead offered a silent, "Time's up. Let's go down."

Gelu agreed with a similar nod of reply and a single word of Sherpali to Tenjin.

Quinn, thinking again about the black figure of the Brocken specter and Rasmussens' even darker comment about it, made sure he had his ice axe—there are some mistakes you don't make twice—and set off down after the others.

13

SIGNS AND QUESTIONS

RETING ROAD, DHARAMSALA, HIMACHAL PRADESH, NORTHERN INDIA

Wangdu Palsang was setting a strong pace around the hilltop town, expertly pointing out buildings and buddhas in his faintly American accent; a product, he explained, of three years studying political science at the University of Washington. Jet-lagged and struggling a little with the altitude, Beth kept up as best she could, but finally had to ask her benign guide if she could stop for a rest. They did so in front of a large green billboard. Catching her breath, Beth was surprised to see the image from the nun's postcard staring down at her.

She retrieved the card from her notebook to compare. The two pictures were identical, but this time the young face was set above a big black question mark. Below that, in recently repainted gold capital letters, the sign read:

TIBET'S STOLEN CHILD—The 11th PANCHEN LAMA GEDHUN CHOEKYI NYIMA
THE WORLD'S YOUNGEST POLITICAL PRISONER

Beth read the English portion of the multilingual text that lined the board, the paint older, cracked, and fading.

- *HE WAS BORN IN APRIL 1989.*
- *MAY 14, 1995, HIS HOLINESS THE DALAI LAMA OFFICIALLY PROCLAIMED HIM AS THE REINCARNATION OF THE 10TH PANCHEN LAMA.*
- *MAY 17, 1995, HE & HIS PARENTS DISAPPEARED FROM THEIR HOME AFTER BEING TAKEN INTO CHINESE CUSTODY.*
- *MAY 28, 1996, CHINA ADMITTED TO HAVE THE CUSTODY OF THE YOUNG BOY AND HIS PARENTS.*
- *HE IS DEPRIVED OF HIS RELIGIOUS EDUCATION & TRADITIONAL UPBRINGING ESSENTIAL AT THIS AGE.*
- *HIS SAFETY AND FUTURE REMAIN A MAJOR CONCERN.*
- *HE IS CONSIDERED THE WORLD'S YOUNGEST POLITICAL PRISONER.*
- *THIS YEAR GEDHUN CHOEKYI NYIMA CELEBRATED HIS 25TH BIRTHDAY.*

The "25" had been recently repainted in a bright red.

Beth immediately took the easy leap to the fact that the unsuspecting boy in the photograph was no longer the world's *youngest* political prisoner. That sign had been repainted many times. Seeing her interest, Wangdu suggested to Beth that he take her photograph standing next to the sign. While he did so, she noticed another man from across the street do the same but quickly move on when he saw her looking. She alerted Wangdu, to which he casually replied, "Local pervert or Chinese spy, Mrs. Waterman, not to worry!"

Shaking off the explanation as a little odd either way, Beth turned back to the sign. In the bottom right corner of the billboard's painted frame she noticed a design cut into the wood. No hastily scratched mark, it was a carving of a butterfly.

Beth asked Wangdu if the insect meant anything in Buddhist culture. Momentarily fumbling with his camera, the youthful Tibetan dropped his lens cap, saying only as he picked it up, "No, not really. Let's move on now, Mrs. Waterman, much still to see."

With her phone, Beth quickly photographed a reminder of both the text on the board and the carving, then ran the tip of her finger around the winged symbol. While she did this, another figure, unseen, tugged hard on the back of her shirt. She jumped, turning around quickly to the further shock of a face that had lost most of its nose and one eye, revealing much of the skull within, and an outstretched hand. More from the twin nasal cavities that ruptured the face than the toothless mouth below, Beth heard an unintelligible sound somewhere between a wheeze and a mumble.

"Mrff . . . mrff . . . mrff," the broken face repeated.

Horrified at the sight, she seized a few rupees from her pocket, handed them over, and then set off after Wangdu, who was already heading up the steep road.

"Did you see that beggar, Wangdu? Why is he not better cared for here?" she asked when she caught up with him.

"We care for everyone we can, Mrs. Waterman, but that man is very damaged by what was done to him in Tibet. He often roams free, however much we try to help him."

With that said, they walked on in silence for a little while until Beth broke it by asking about the lost boy in the billboard, as she showed Wangdu the postcard she had been given.

"You must understand that your world really only knows the one, the Dalai Lama, but we actually have two equally important lamas that preside over many hundreds of others," Wangdu replied.

"Go on," Beth said. So while they walked, the Tibetan told how the Dalai Lama and the Panchen Lama were the two dominant pillars—the heart and soul—of Tibet's Buddhist faith; a faith that, despite over sixty years of atheistic occupation of its land, could not be extinguished.

Chairman Mao, he explained, had tried everything in his almost unlimited power to eliminate it through persecution, destruction, and political dogma, but had failed—especially because the Dalai Lama had escaped his grasp in 1959. In counter maneuver, Mao had attempted to utilize the Panchen Lama who remained, but that also failed when he proved to be both devout and unafraid to criticize Chinese rule, submitting his famous *70,000 Character Petition* to Chinese Premier Zhou Enlai in 1962; a detailed report that identified the many failures of Chinese rule in Tibet. It quickly led to his imprisonment.

As both the existing Dalai Lama and the tenth Panchen Lama were born before the Chinese occupation, the death of the latter in 1989—some said under mysterious circumstances—was seen as an opportunity in Beijing. His death and subsequent reincarnation presented the possibility for the Chinese to coordinate the selection and enthronement of one of the most senior positions in Tibetan Buddhism, to effectively arrange a new "made in China" Panchen Lama who would toe the party line. However, underestimating the complexity of the search for the reincarnation and the ongoing loyalty to the Dalai Lama within their Tibetan territories, the Chinese authorities failed in their plan when, independently from his exile, the Dalai Lama announced that Gedhun Choekyi Nyima, the boy on the billboard, was the reincarnated eleventh Panchen Lama.

The Chinese were furious. Almost immediately the boy and his family were taken into custody. Moreover, the leader of the search committee within the Tibetan territories, Chadrel Rinpoche, himself still clandestinely supportive of the exiled Dalai Lama, was arrested and charged with treason. A new leader for a new search was appointed in order to present other politically acceptable candidates. The Golden Urn, an archaic Manchu ceremony that Wangdu described as "having slightly more historical precedent than Harry Potter's Goblet of Fire but not a lot" was dusted off from the eighteenth century and utilized in a televised ceremony in Lhasa to "select" another boy that the party had already prechosen. This time, the People's "Living Buddha," their reincarnate Panchen Lama, was Gyaltsen Norbu; also six, also from Nagchu, but conveniently with Chinese Communist Party parents despite the fact he was being deemed a reincarnate . . .

All the while, a single, simple truth of the process—*that a new Panchen Lama can only be confirmed by the existing Dalai Lama*—was being conveniently ignored. "And in that you have it all," Wangdu Palsang concluded. "Because when the time comes the Chinese will suddenly 'remember' that the reverse is actually true."

"What do you mean?" Beth asked.

"I mean that a new Dalai Lama can only be confirmed by the Panchen Lama. The Chinese will undoubtedly use their counterfeit Panchen Lama to lead any future search for the next Dalai Lama. A search that I assume will show all the faith and freedom of his own selection. A search that will produce their man for our future. In that way they will finally have control of our two most important figures."

When Beth asked Wangdu what he thought had happened to Gedhun Choekyi Nyima, he had replied gravely, "No one knows. Official requests for information are always met with either silence or, as you say where you come from, bullshit, that he's attending school and living a normal life somewhere in China. Whenever the precise location or a meeting with him is requested, it is declined with replies that it is not possible because 'his security has been threatened' or 'that he is at risk of being kidnapped by separatists'—which is pretty stupid when you think about it. *Kidnapped from his kidnappers?* I don't think so, Mrs. Waterman.

"In 2007 the UN Human Rights Council itself asked about him and the Chinese authorities stated words to the effect that, 'Gedhun Choekyi Nyima is a perfectly ordinary Tibetan boy, in a good state of health, leading a normal, happy life, and receiving a good education and upbringing in traditional Chinese culture, and that he enjoyed studying calligraphy. But after nearly twenty years there is still no sign of him. That's a long time to be invisible. Your postcard is the only picture of him that you will ever see."

"Do you think he's dead, Wangdu?" Beth said.

Wangdu paused, wrestling with the question before answering.

"It is difficult to say. Possibly, but the Chinese are complicated. Despite being Communist for over seventy years, they have thought like Confucius for more than a thousand. It creates a deep conflict in them. Whilst some of them might say all religion is nonsense so, dead or alive, the boy makes no difference, others would argue that if perhaps Gedhun Choekyi Nyima really is the true Panchen Lama then it is best to keep him alive because if he dies then he may reincarnate elsewhere beyond their control . . . Their 'middle way' approach always wars with a ruthless pragmatism. The dominance of one or the other attitude varies depending on who is calling the political shots."

Beth and Wangdu walked on together until they stopped before another banner tied to the same fence that held the billboard. The long vinyl panel roped to the railings featured row after row of similar portrait photographs to those of the STOLEN CHILD billboard. However this time the faces of the men and women displayed were older, adults this time, even if some were anonymous, featuring only a white silhouette. Beneath each face, actual or invisible, was a name, a place, and a date.

"More political prisoners?" she asked Wangdu.

"No, Mrs. Waterman."

"What then?"

"Those are our people who have burned themselves to death in the name of Tibetan freedom."

Beth thought of her coming interview with the Dalai Lama the following day. *"But most of all that smile masks a true sadness and pain you cannot begin to imagine . . ."*

14

THE WATCHER

The morning after the summit, the Snowdonia Ascents team got up slow, waiting for the sun to warm the day as much as it was ever going to, before they took down the high camp. Quinn and the three Sherpa divided the heavy gear between themselves to give their two still-fatigued clients an easier time of the descent.

Job done, they slowly spent the day filing down the steep snowfields, through the ice labyrinth of the upper glacier, and on to the rocky moraine path that led back to the Base Camp. Despite raw lungs and leaden legs, gravity pulled them all down as relentlessly as Rasmussen's complaining until finally, Big Al, laboring under the additional burden of the death of his Everest dream, told the Norwegian to shut up in no uncertain terms.

The silence after was colder than the glacier.

Quinn was happy to see the first splashes of color from the tents and prayer flags amidst the snow and rocks that announced they had finally made it back to the Base Camp. The Snowdonia Ascents team was the last summit party of the season and the camp was much emptier than when they had left four days earlier. Only the big Czech team and a guided expedition run by an outfit from New Zealand, as well as a host of Tibetan yak-herders and their families who were waiting to ferry those last teams' gear the twelve miles or so back to the roadhead remained.

Walking in, Quinn also noticed an Asian climber—he thought Korean or Japanese—who must have arrived after they had set off for the top. The solitary man stood at the edge of the camp watching as they filed in. He was a strange sight, old and dressed in dated insulated mountain clothes, once white but now gray with use and age. Quinn wondered what such a man was doing there. It was too late to make any new summit attempts, particularly alone. Winter would soon be on the mountain.

To confirm the thought, Quinn took a look back at the mountain. It was already lost within a shroud of cloud. For a moment he half-expected to see the Brocken specter staring down at him, but he felt only its chill. When Quinn turned back, he thought he saw Gelu nod his head in the direction of the Asian climber who quickly stepped down behind the huge boulders that ringed the camp. The Englishman sensed something in the moment, but it was soon lost in the relief of abandoning his pack at the entrance of the team's mess tent to receive a scalding cup of chocolate.

After the summit team had rested, the Sherpa amiably organized a small party in the mess tent. There was food, a cake, and the expedition's remaining beer and whiskey—but not much goodwill despite the Sherpa's best efforts to celebrate the climb.

Big Al and the two other team members who had sat out the summit attempt were sullen and unhappy they hadn't made it to the top, and Rasmussen—the man who had—was just a malcontent. If the Norwegian had been more excited about what he had achieved, Quinn thought it might have soothed matters. They weren't bad guys and would at least have been pleased for him, but he wasn't, and they weren't. In return Rasmussen wouldn't even show them the summit photographs he had taken. The domed tent above slowly filled to bursting with a simmering resentment until pure exhaustion deflated it and everyone drifted off to their respective tents too tired to argue.

Quinn remained alone in the mess tent using the communications equipment to file a brief report of "expedition completion" to Bill Owen.

His phone recharged from the solar battery cell, he also watched his video of the Brocken specter. Grainy and eerie, it showed surprisingly well. For a moment Quinn recalled again the ornery Norwegian's words about the sight and felt a surge of relief that he had gotten everyone, including himself, off the mountain and heading for home, however miserable they might be.

After he had replayed the short clip again, he included it in his email to Henrietta Richards in Kathmandu with his notes on the climb for her records. Video of such a mountain phenomenon was the kind of thing his friend, the famous "Historian of the Himalayas," enjoyed seeing and he hoped it would make up for his team's otherwise rather uninteresting summit performance. He looked forward to hearing her thoughts on it when he got back to Kathmandu. She always had an interesting observation or two, and, in his way, Quinn was no less a student of those ancient mountains than she was a teacher.

15

MASTER OF COMPLICATIONS

HHDL'S PRIVATE RESIDENCE, MCLEOD GANJ, DHARAMSALA, HIMACHAL PRADESH, NORTHERN INDIA

The Dalai Lama got up from his armchair in the reception room, that same bare right arm that had conducted the audience now outstretched toward Beth. His mottled right hand took hers firmly as the other closed around the grip in confirmation of welcome. His eyes creased behind slightly tinted bifocals and that familiar oval face broke into the sort of smile that made the recipient feel that by prompting it he or she just might not be completely lost.

"Hello, Mrs. Elizabeth Waterman of the *Rolling Stone*, the popular music magazine!" he said jovially. "But I am told to be ready for hard questions from a tough lady. No moss on you they say. Ahaha!" There it was immediately—the laugh, even if it seemed to be followed by a bit of a cough. "Sit. Sit. Please," he urged.

"Thank you, Your Holiness."

"I meet many rock star. Do you know Gaga?"

Here we go, Beth thought.

"No, no. I can't say that I do, Your Holiness."

"Mr. Bono then?"

"No, him neither, I'm afraid. I don't actually write about music." she countered quickly. "But many people describe you as a 'religious rock star,' others, as a 'god.' Are you either?"

"Hmm! Straight to business I see from the lady who must not be afraid that she does not know Mr. Bono." His eyebrows raised to hover for a moment above the top frame of his thick lensed glasses, their curves reflecting the almost cheeky smile below. "Mrs. Elizabeth, I not sell many record, and partake in no sex or drug either, so not much of a rock star I am thinking. No cover of the *Rolling Stone* for me. Ahaha!" The Dalai Lama paused for a moment before continuing with a more serious, almost stern look that drilled into Beth's pupils. "But not god either . . . just simple Buddhist monk who is human like you, flesh and bone. Just tired old man who needs more sleep to shake off cough and cold." He pinched his cheek in demonstration, tugging on its elasticity, then pulled down on it to remove the bag beneath an eye.

Beth nodded gently, smiled kindly, but continued determinedly. "You escaped Tibet in 1959. Ever since the Chinese have described you as, I quote, a dangerous 'splittist,' the leader of a 'separatist clique,' 'the double betrayer.' They paint a picture of you as a 'false lama' who wears Rolex watches while others starve. They even call you a 'demon' . . ."

"Yes, very tough indeed . . ." The Dalai Lama momentarily made another grave face, then, raising two index fingers above his head like Angus Young hamming the devil across a stage with AC/DC, said, "But not demon either. Ahaha!" He wiggled the fingers so as to look completely comical before another pause. "But Rolex watch? Hmmm," he mused.

Tenzin Gyatso pushed his left arm out to show that, on his wrist under a wrap of prayer beads of a dark polished wood there was indeed a Rolex watch on a steel bracelet.

"Yes. It is true. I have nothing to hide. It was a gift. Some people happy to give me time, I think. Chinese never give me Rolex even though they make many fakes. Prefer my clock to stop perhaps?"

More laughter followed his rhetorical question as Beth quickly made a connection to her own research in an effort to keep things moving forward, to get some answers rather than questions in return.

"I read that our own President Franklin Delano Roosevelt once gave you a Patek Philippe pocket watch when you were just a boy."

"Yes. Also true. I still have it. That watch is my favorite, very beautiful. A masterpiece of complications."

The Dalai Lama switched language to address his senior private secretary and the equally aged Tibetan shuffled to a side table to retrieve an old copy of *Time* with the Dalai Lama on the cover.

Quickly flicking through the magazine, the Dalai Lama settled on a page and passed it to Beth. "Not *Rolling Stone* magazine I am afraid, but look here."

The page showed an advertisement, a timeless black-and-white photograph of a handsome father looking with pride at an equally handsome son. Below was a Patek Philippe wristwatch and the by-line: *You never actually own a Patek Philippe. You merely look after it for the next generation.*

"So actually, Mrs. Elizabeth, I not really own. I merely look after for next generation." His face then became strangely quizzical and he raised a single finger as if pointing to the sound of silence. "But . . . in my case I am also my next generation so maybe I do own forever? Interesting philosophical concept, perhaps."

Beth didn't let up, sensing her own clock running.

"But will there be another generation or, if I am right in thinking, a reincarnation? You are getting old if you permit me to say it. What comes next?"

"Perhaps this room looks too much like 'Exit Lounge,' Mrs. Elizabeth? Ahaha!" The bare arm drew a circle around the neat reception room clearly attempting to draw Beth away from her questions.

"But you can't live forever—well, not in that body—so what happens then? Your freedom has been a constant thorn in the side of the Chinese. Your death would be an opportunity to finally remove it. For a long time they have been doing everything in their power to undermine and confuse the matter. I understand that your choice for the Panchen Lama vanished some twenty years ago. In his place they installed another boy who has now come of age and plays the part of the Panchen Lama in Lhasa. It is even said by some that your own reincarnation cannot be recognized without finding 'your' Panchen Lama, but I am sure that the Chinese feel that they can do so with theirs." Beth cringed inside a little, thinking she might have overstepped the mark even if the smile in front of her remained.

"Yes, strong questions indeed. The power of the female spirit is always very strong, also in Tibetan Buddhism." The Dalai Lama paused to look at her closely. "Maybe, Mrs. Elizabeth, someone like you can win Pulitzer Prize by finding the lost Panchen Lama? But be careful what you wish for, not an easy thing to do in an area of 9.6 million kilometers and 1.3 billion people, as others have found. It would be like looking for the smallest of needles in the biggest of haystacks perhaps? Ahaha!"

For the first time the laugh felt out of place and a harder face framed the brief smile.

"However please understand, Mrs. Elizabeth, that whatever happens the Chinese cannot control my future reincarnation any more than I can choose your next Pope."

Beth realized that he'd been well briefed about her as she asked, "But then what will happen? In other interviews you have said that your reincarnate might not be found in Tibet, that you might return as a woman, that perhaps the institution of the Dalai Lama has served its time and you will choose to not come back at all, that something else will replace you . . ."

"Maybe all of those things, maybe none of them, Mrs. Elizabeth. We will see what happens but, for now, I am very much still here so I think, I consult, I listen, I pray. I wander places in my mind that might be forbidden to my feet to seek guidance, to understand the path ahead . . ."

He hesitated.

For a moment, Beth thought she caught a glimpse of a well-guarded fatigue that released a physical ripple of uncertainty through his body, but both were mastered before her eyes with another smile.

"Like Roosevelt's watch, it is very complicated, Mrs. Elizabeth. One thing however of which I am certain is that an eternal faith seeks to preserve itself one way or another."

16

AVALANCHE?

ADVANCED BASE CAMP, MOUNTAIN OF SHISHAPANGMA, NYALAM COUNTY, TIBETAN AUTONOMOUS REGION OF THE PEOPLE'S REPUBLIC OF CHINA
October 9, 2014

A sullen Snowdonia Ascents team packed the next day, only for it to emerge that the Czechs and the other big group were already booked to leave so there was not the full complement of yaks available to ferry out all the team's gear to the roadhead in one go.

The already dour mood darkened further on the news. Reassured by Gelu that more yaks would be returning the following day, Quinn sent the team on ahead with all of the Sherpa, except for Nima, to assist. The walk out to the roadhead was just over twelve miles. There were some built facilities there. It would at least get them all moving toward home with their essentials and hopefully focus their minds on happier things than bitching at an empty camp.

Quinn saw them off, unable to deny that he was looking forward to an evening's peace and quiet in the deserted camp. Leaving Nima to amiably sort the bulkier expedition kit for when the yaks did return to collect it, he turned in early to his personal tent, thinking that once the trip was finished in Kathmandu, a two-week detour to Goa was the necessary reward for spending the best part of six weeks shepherding the charming Rasmussen and friends up and down the sides of Shishapangma.

✦

Neil Quinn was treading a wave-lapped beach when, with a rending groan, the golden sand erupted as if he had trodden on a land mine. Instantly blown back into the freezing pitch of a Himalayan night, the ground beneath him seemed to have liquefied, rippling and rolling as rocks rattled and crashed around his tent. Blind in the dark, Quinn's instinct screamed, *Avalanche!*

Slapping around for his headlamp, his brain ordered, *Get out! If one of those boulders hits . . .*

His hand made contact with his phone.

Squeezing it, the screen faintly illuminated the thin fabric of his domed tent bowing and flexing wildly around him, ice crystals sparkling and falling from the inside.

Trapped inside a snow globe, Quinn struggled from his thick sleeping bag, determined that it not become his feather-lined coffin. Still on hands and knees, he crawled toward the tent's zippered door, snatching at his cold-weather gear as he went.

Before he could reach his boots, the ground shuddered violently another time. The Englishman was flung forward onto his face as outside another barrage of rocks released down the steep scree slope that over-looked the west side of the camp basin.

Quinn thrust himself up again from the thick material of the sleeping bag as a metal point stabbed into the tent's nylon skin. Flashes from the falling, sparking boulders illuminated a dark silhouette beyond. The razor-sharp metal sliced the Englishman's left ear. Warm blood spurted onto his cold cheek and down his neck.

"What the fuck!" Quinn shouted, jerking himself away from the long rectangular blade continuing to slice through the tent's double skin in a single sideways arc as if it was paper.

A gaping hole opened in the side of the tent.

A hand thrust in to snatch at Quinn's head, the fingers digging into his bloody hair like a claw.

With an immense pull, it wrenched him free.

Sprawled in the dirt, Quinn found himself looking up at the face of the old Asian climber he had seen before, now holding a gleaming knife that resembled a short samurai sword.

Quinn tried to speak but the man just shouted, "GO!"

The viselike grip tugged Quinn up onto his bootless feet and into a run just as a rock smashed into the remains of the tent, crushing it.

Stumbling and tripping in just his socks, choking on the cordite stink of broken rock, Quinn raced after his rescuer. As he fled, he caught a glimpse of Nima also running for his life, his right arm clamped close to his body by his left, his face twisted in agony as he too fled.

Relentlessly, the pale figure led Quinn and Nima beyond the camp area, across the wide but shallow river that filtered from the snout of the glacier and into the dark shadows of the moraine fields beyond.

Finally, the man stopped at what resembled, in the dark, a low burial mound. Quinn, head spinning, lungs heaving, socked feet battered and freezing, dropped to his knees exhausted. The young Sherpa fell to the rubble next to him and passed out.

Their rescuer soon loomed over the both of them and pointed Quinn around the steep side of the hump. "Not stop here, Quinn," the stranger said in heavily accented English. "We must get the Sherpa boy to other side first."

Together they lifted Nima and carried him around the hump. There, Quinn saw in the shadows that the mound was naturally hollowed and edged by what remained of a low wall of stones, no doubt erected by nomads sheltering from that place's harsh wind and weather. Between the ring of rocks was stretched a tarpaulin that, even in the dark, Quinn could see was blotched and patchy, seemingly camouflaged to the rocky terrain.

The Asian man pointed Quinn under it and said, "Okay. Safe here. For now." He then reached in himself to pull out a small gas lamp that he quickly lit. As the light grew, Quinn saw there was a tent set up beneath the tarp. Together they helped the Sherpa inside and onto a sleeping bag that the man took from a high pile of equipment that blocked the far end of the tent. Despite all their pushing and pulling, Nima remained unconscious, his pulse and breathing weakening, shock consuming his broken body.

The other man returned to the pile of equipment to pull out a thick pair of socks and a medical dressing that he gave to Quinn, pointing at the Englishman's feet and head before quickly setting to work tending Nima. When Quinn had covered his cut ear and massaged his numb broken feet back to some semblance of life, he recovered himself enough to say to the shadowy figure, in part statement, part question, "You saved us?"

The man said nothing in reply.

"Who are you?"

Still the man ignored Quinn, his bare hands moving lightly and quickly to help the Sherpa. In the flickering gaslight, Quinn could see that the ring and little finger of the right hand had been amputated at the second knuckle. That sight, the man's Asian accent, the fact that the hands were also heavily tattooed, made Quinn think of the Yakuza even if, in this case, the finger-shortening was more likely from frostbite than vengeful Japanese gangsters. He wondered, however, if this man was Japanese.

Quinn saw that each knuckle was tattooed. The ink had leached with time like a letter left out in the rain, but with difficulty, he could still make out the Western letters that ran across the stunted hand.

$$I \ldots B \ldots E \ldots T.$$

When the hand closed into a fist, Quinn saw another *T* on the thumb.

$$TIBET$$

The other hand, fingers intact, was similarly marked, but with different letters.

$$EKKLM$$

Those meant nothing to Quinn.

Looking around he saw something else written on the inner skin of the tent. He squinted to pick out what it said in the shadows.

PROPERTY OF SNOWDONIA ASCENTS EXPEDITIONS

Quinn began to say, "But this tent is . . ." but the mutilated hand raised to stop him talking.

"Enough questions, Quinn-san. I must concentrate."

The man turned his attention back to Nima, taking off his dirty down jacket and using it to make a pillow for the Sherpa. Beneath he was wearing a gathered white robe, woven and pleated. Over it hung a thin red surplice of embroidered silk material, each strip to the front embellished with two wheels of gold. The collar was joined at the bottom by a looped length of thick red rope. Another was double-tied around his middle.

Quinn was completely dumbfounded by the sight of the strangely attired figure slowly chanting over the unconscious body of the Sherpa. At first, it was little more than a whisper, a repeated sound that seemed to echo in a faint rising and falling sigh from the end of the tent. The utterances then changed, sustaining and growing into prolonged vibrations, impossibly low, from somewhere deep, deep inside the man. Other sounds from the same pair of lungs began to intermittently puncture the drone.

"En . . .

"No . . .

"Gy . . .

"Oja."

Suddenly the sound stopped.

The man was consumed by a fit of coughing that seemed to momentarily tear him open, his eyes rolling back into his head to release fast-falling tears while one of the tattooed hands shook uncontrollably as it tried to cover his mouth.

Only slowly bringing his body back under a shaky control, the man reached for something at the back of the tent, digging deep into the stack of equipment before quickly returning to his mouth. He wiped away the trickle of blood that had formed at its corner with the back of the same trembling hand, then took a long drink of water from a flask.

Quinn understood that the man was taking some type of very necessary medicine as the disturbed pile of equipment that filled the end of the tent rustled—then shook, threatening to topple.

The tattooed hand returned to gently pull it over, letting the wall of kit fall as if releasing something. The man spoke quietly, then recommenced the chant; first, as a still breathless muttering but slowly becoming stronger and louder.

The sound seemed to expand the very volume of the tent, ballooning it out into the troubled night. The man's inked hands linked above the still-unconscious, trembling body of the Sherpa, beginning to twist and turn in strange couplings that ended in a slashing cut of the chill air. Quinn noticed that he himself had begun to shiver violently from the freezing night beyond the tent.

Nine times the man made such a move then he stopped, becoming perfectly silent and still.

Time passed.

Sweat began to glisten and bead on the weatherworn face.

An intense heat grew, filling the tent space.

The warmth seemed to reach inside Quinn, exorcising the cold from his frozen feet, his numb fingers, his face, his heart.

Feeling drowsy, his eyes began to involuntarily close.

He forced them back open to vaguely take in that the man was now stripped of his robe to the waist. The totally tattooed torso was almost inhumanly pale, like engraved ivory. The creatures in the designs, the snakes, the dragons, seemed alive, twisting and coiling under the wet skin. Amongst them monks, warriors, geishas, wild-haired deities with piercing, almond-shaped eyes, and screaming mouths stared at Quinn.

Quinn looked away to see another face, another set of eyes staring at him from within the pulled-apart pile of equipment at the end of the tent.

They were those of a small child sitting cross-legged, one hand resting on its right knee, the other in its lap. The infant's gaze was locked on Quinn as if scrutinizing his very soul.

The heat inside the tent was becoming suffocating.

Quinn's head began to spin.

Everything around him, everything he was seeing merged into a single spiraling vortex of shadow and light, his ears roaring with a sonic thunder.

Unsure if anything was real, Quinn tumbled face-forward into the Asian man's discarded down jacket.

Out, but not cold.

17

STEEL JADE

MANDALA HOTEL,
DHARAMSALA, HIMACHAL PRADESH, NORTHERN INDIA

The Dalai Lama's voice and laughter filled Beth's hotel room as she replayed the recording of their interview while she worked late into the night. She had enjoyed their talk and was, despite her best professional intentions, as charmed as her colleagues had warned.

Listening to their discussion again in the small hours of the morning, she let her mind freestyle around his answers to the questions, her pad filling with random words and doodles, seeding the key elements of her article. Beth focused on one of the words scratched and underlined across the page—*reincarnation*—acknowledging to herself that the word still immediately took her beyond her own reason and into unknown territory.

Do I even believe in it?

She had already confessed the same doubt to Wangdu who had worked hard to try to explain to her the subject's complex puzzle of prophecy, portent, geography, and time as it might relate to the Dalai Lama.

She considered his explanation again. It was a process, he had said, that started while the Dalai Lama was still living through his consideration of the writings of his predecessors, consultation with oracles, and, when it used to be possible, meditation and contemplation at a holy lake—the place of the protectress deity of Tibet, Palden Lhamo. There, in those restless wind-swept waters set high in the gray jagged hills of Gyaca could be seen symbols, letters, shapes, numbers, animals; all possible clues to the identity and location of a future reincarnation. But that place was off-limits to him now, a forbidden zone to anyone outside of the People's Armed Police.

The Dalai Lama would also consider his own thoughts and dreams, combining all his findings in additional new writings. Beth realized that she had heard this very same process in His Holiness's own words when she replayed her recording.

"... *for now, I am very much still here so I think, I consult, I listen, I pray. I wander places in my mind that might be forbidden to my feet to seek guidance, to understand the path ahead ..."*

After his death, a search committee would take over. To the Dalai Lama's writings, they would add details of the last words he spoke, any natural phenomena seen at the precise moment of his death such as rainbows or the shape of the clouds, the final position of his body, any distinctive marks that might appear on his corpse, even the direction taken by the smoke of the subsequent funeral pyre.

From all these indicators the search committee would determine the possible locations of suitable candidates and seek young children there that might be deemed auspicious because of distinct physical markings, precocious abilities, or affinities and passions similar to those of the deceased. Committee members would visit them all, then make a recommendation based on intense discussion with the children and tests such as the recognition of possessions of the former lama. In the case of the Dalai Lama, the final arbiter of who was the reincarnation would be the Panchen Lama and vice versa in the case of the Panchen Lama. Enthronement and education of the selected child would then follow as he aged.

Considering the case of Gedhun Choekyi Nyima, the missing boy, Beth had asked Wangdu, "And what if that subsequent education and enthronement is denied?"

His reply had been grave.

"That would prove to be extremely dangerous for the child. If he is a reincarnation, he must be trained to handle it correctly. Without such guidance, some have gone mad, others have committed suicide. Being denied their true selves is incredibly destructive to such children."

Every way she looked at it Beth saw little possibility of the boy still being alive, but then again, she thought, if Gedhun Choekyi Nyima was dead and reincarnation was real then didn't that mean . . .

The chime of an incoming message on her phone stopped Beth's train of thought.

The text was from her editor.

Unlike everything else before her that evening, this time there was no equivocation. The message was direct and simple.

> Due to scheduling conflict DL story is on indefinite hold.

> Agreed fees and incurred expenses will be paid in full.

> Frank

Beth cursed as she turned to her open laptop to search for news of the passing of any famous musicians; they had been dropping like flies recently.

Nothing new came up to justify an immediate need for column inches, so she switched to the magazine's website for possible answers.

The homepage was newly emblazoned with a fiery banner advertisement for a forthcoming action film.

STEEL JADE

A Chinese-American coproduction, the film looked overblown and asinine, yet it also figured. People had warned her this could happen, that Chinese influence might well curtail such a visible Dalai Lama feature. Instantly angered, Beth told herself that no one was going to shut her down. Defiantly she typed the name "Gedhun Choekyi Nyima" into the search engine and hit Enter.

The homepage immediately dissolved to black. A white dot appeared, growing into a golden star as the background turned blood red. The star twisted and bulged, morphing its shape into that of an equally golden cat. The cat split into two. The two became four. The divisions accelerated to line Beth's screen with ranks of grinning felines that waved their curled left paws to the beat of a Kylie Minogue song. At the end of each chorus of "I should be so lucky, lucky, lucky, lucky," the screen blanked to flash the word "CAT" at her in golden capitals.

"What the hell?" Beth shouted, the keys of her laptop no longer responding to commands. Tearing her eyes away from what she understood must be some sort of malware, she stabbed instead at the computer's power button. She held it down hard until all the shiny cats were extinguished and it was only her fingernail that continued to pulse with the pressure.

18

BLACK HELICOPTER

ADVANCED BASE CAMP, MOUNTAIN OF SHISHAPANGMA, NYALAM COUNTY,
TIBETAN AUTONOMOUS REGION OF THE PEOPLE'S REPUBLIC OF CHINA
October 10, 2014

Quinn awoke with a start. Freezing air chilled his face and watered his bleary eyes as he understood that the entrance of the tent was beginning to lighten from the new day. Raising his aching head to look around, Quinn questioned everything that had happened the night before as if piecing together the incomplete fractions of a surreal high-altitude dream.

He touched the dressing on his ear for verification that it had actually happened. The wound within was all too real, rhythmically ticking with pain. Quinn again saw that blade slicing through his tent's double-fabric skin like paper, felt the sting of the razor's edge and the viselike grip that followed to drag him free. If he had exited through the zipped door that final rock would have crushed him.

Seeking the man who had saved him, Quinn found only Nima. The young Sherpa was sitting up, seemingly lucid, his arm expertly strapped close across his chest.

"It's you, Nima," Quinn said.

"Yes, Mr. Neil."

"How are you feeling?"

"Arm hurts a lot but able to move, thanks to you, Mr. Neil," Nima replied, smiling, clearly much recovered.

"Good. But where is the other man, the one that did help you?"

"Who?"

"I think it was a Japanese man."

The Sherpa tried to shrug his shoulders but stopped short, wincing at the pain it caused. Instead he looked down at the sleeping bag and said firmly, in almost a mutter, "It is only you, Mr. Neil. You save me."

"No, there was another man who cut me from the tent then brought us here. His knife did this."

Quinn pointed to his bandaged head in evidence.

"Sorry, Mr. Neil, but I think that a rock did that. Confused you perhaps."

For a moment Quinn questioned himself but then asked, "But what about this tent?" As he said it, Quinn noticed that except for him, Nima, and the sleeping bag the Sherpa had been lying on, the tent was now empty and bare.

"I know. Our tent. You did good work, Mr. Neil."

A dull thudding in the distance interrupted their discussion.

It was the sound of a helicopter.

Leaving the tent Quinn saw that the tarpaulin that covered their hollow in the mound had been removed. He clambered up to a small opening in the ring of rocks at the top—clearly some sort of spy hole. He looked through at a sky heavy with gray clouds bruised yellow and brown by dust from the night's disturbance. Below it, the terrain of the Base Camp had substantially changed. The stacked margins of moraine that surrounded the area had collapsed. The abandoned puja altars and prayer-flag poles of that season's expeditions had toppled. Immense boulders had moved or split into pieces as if chiseled apart. New ones the size of small cars had appeared.

From the north, the black form of a military helicopter came into view, flying low beneath that same cloud. When it reached the campsite, it hovered, then landed heavily in a spinning maelstrom of tattered material and dust. Quinn had never seen such a helicopter in Tibet. Everything about the predatory beast, encrusted with antennae, domed receivers, and weapons pods, said "Search," rather than "Rescue." Unsure, he pulled his face down tight to the edge of the rocks and urged Nima, who had scrambled up to join him, to do the same.

The pair watched as a number of tactical soldiers dressed in black jumped from the machine to take directions from a single man in their midst then fan out to inspect the remains of the camp, assault rifles at the ready. Another team of two set up a small platform that released a drone to shoot up into the air like an angry wasp skimming the tops of the glacier's icy penitentes to fly farther up the valley.

One of the patrol soon stopped, looking straight in one direction like a German pointer dog and raising a hand in a clenched-fist signal that brought the others running to his side. Aiming his gun, he called out loudly.

Three Tibetans, dressed in heavy sheepskin jackets and draped with thick blankets, stood up warily. Quinn recognized them as one of the yak-herder families that had been staying at the camp. With gun barrels pointed at them, they flung their arms into the air in immediate surrender. Surrounded, their blankets were tugged away and, hands held high, they were brought at riflepoint before the commanding officer.

Quinn noticed that the leader very deliberately removed his helmet and dark glasses to show the Tibetans his face as he began to shout and point toward the mountain. Nima mumbled something under his breath at the sight but when Quinn whispered "What?" he received no reply.

The commander's questions were met with shrugs and arm waving from the Tibetans. He began to push at them, screaming all the more. Other soldiers crowded in to kick and threaten them with their guns. The three Tibetans began to plead as one was pushed to his knees.

Quinn found himself edging forward against the rock, wanting to do something, but felt Nima's good arm restrain him. "Stay down, Mr. Neil. Please. We can do nothing."

"The hell we can't."

Quinn pulled himself back below the lip of rocks. Huddled down he thrust his hand into his jacket to get his iPhone only to find it blocked by a small wad of fabric. He tugged out the soft impediment and cast it to the ground without a look, his hand instantly returning to the pocket to get the phone as fast as he could.

Once it was out and on, he rested the device on a rock, zoomed in as much as he could, and began to film the questioning of one of the Tibetans as it grew increasingly violent. Another twisted and slipped from the soldiers' guard. The figure made a break for it, trying to run away amidst the rocks and debris of the devastated camp.

Without wait or warning, there was a burst of automatic fire.

The body jerked, a flailing, stuttering rag doll, before falling to the rocky ground.

The two remaining Tibetans immediately began to cower and plead for their lives only to be slammed faces forward to the ground, gun barrels to the backs of their heads.

The commander just walked away from them all and looked up the glacier's tail of ice toward the snow peak hidden in cloud. He called over to the pair operating the drone. Receiving a shake of the head from one, he looked up the glacier again, issued an order, then pointed back to the helicopter making a whirling motion with his hand. The helicopter's long multi-bladed rotor lumbered into life.

The sonic roar of the engine grew as the drone obediently returned to be stowed aboard by its operators, and the two remaining Tibetans and the corpse were shoved and pushed into the helicopter.

The helicopter soon rose to hover noisily above the camp, the fierce downdraft blowing tattered tenting and equipment around like dead leaves until it rotated 180 degrees on an invisible axis and thundered away. Quinn continued filming as something fell heavily from the side door to thump into the tundra that lay beyond the glacier river.

Two more black silhouettes fell before the helicopter finally disappeared to the north.

PART IV

JATRA

There's a one-eyed yellow idol to the north
    of Kathmandu,
There's a little marble cross below the town;
There's a broken-hearted woman tends the
    grave of Mad Carew,
And the Yellow God forever gazes down.

—J. Milton Hayes,
"The Green Eye of the Yellow God"

19

THE MENTAL NOMAD

BUREAU DU TIBET, PARIS, FRANCE
October 15, 2014

The prostrate body slowly dissolved into its mantra, consciousness unlocking, expanding into every dimension, known and unknown, limitless. Once more, the old monk was a mental nomad wandering freely, no aged legs or lungs, no politics or borders, no concerns or fears to hold him back. Temporarily transhuman, he let his mind graze freely in places long denied his presence.

The homes: the dust of his childhood still in their corners.

The monasteries: the faith of his youthful prayers still in their air.

The towns: the blood of his people still on their streets.

Leaving them all behind, he hiked on, passing old scattered ruins and the regimented ranks of modern work compounds to climb up through high pastures that dwindled into a narrow path between jagged rocks and boulders. A high ridge lined with snapping prayer flags applauded his arrival.

The old monk took his rightful place at the Throne of Kings and looked down.

The sun broke through the heavy cloud overhead.

The skull shaped lake below shone like mercury.

Waves rippled.

Lines formed and twisted.

The hint of an image . . .

But somewhere much nearer, a police siren passed. The sound tore the night's silence in two, slamming its gateway to contemplation shut like a portcullis. The old monk's mind was immediately fettered anew within aged bone and gristle, conscious of an inescapable reality; day began when it chose, not when others might will it.

20

MOMOS AND WI-FI

XANGMU, NYALAM COUNTY, TIBETAN AUTONOMOUS REGION OF THE PEOPLE'S REPUBLIC OF CHINA

October 15, 2014

After weeks spent in the deserted, silent mountains of Tibet, Quinn always found the town of Xangmu a difficult return to civilization. Stacked on the steep side of the Sun Kosi River gorge, the town was a rough, alcoholic frontier post that offered quick-boil noodles, cheap consumer electronics, and mother-daughter prostitution teams to travelers as the only permitted solutions to the pain of desire. At its dusty feet, the Friendship Bridge crossed the turbulent river to Nepal beneath the unfriendly gaze of ominous buildings bristling with antennae and satellite dishes. Young PLA soldiers, brutish and bored, deliberately posted far from their homes, patrolled the queue of filthy trucks created by unexplained customs closures that lasted days. They itched for trouble.

Quinn itched to leave that place.

He sat in the Snowland Café—*Momos and Wi-Fi*—while Gelu and the other Sherpa worked their local contacts to establish when the border might reopen. The team had been stuck there for days since their hasty exit from Shishapangma and it was getting very old. Earlier that afternoon however, there had been word that things would finally get moving again in the morning, so Quinn had given Gelu some of the expedition's petty cash to make sure they were at the front of the queue when it did.

Gelu had been optimistic when he left. Quinn, however, still sat waiting for more news in the café, drinking endless cups of green tea served by a sulky second-generation Han Chinese girl in tight, electric-blue pants. Since she seemed more interested in her pink mobile phone than serving him, Quinn had followed her lead. He again watched the video of the Brocken specter, then, muting the volume, that of the murder at the Base Camp, reliving what happened afterward.

For a long moment the Englishman and the young Sherpa had been shocked to silence by what they had witnessed.

"Bastards," was the only word Quinn would eventually utter as he continued to hang his head in disgust and horror, staring at the small wad of material lying on the rocks at his socked feet. For a while it hadn't registered. Nothing did, until, reaching down, Quinn picked the object up, understanding it to be the lump of material he had discarded from his pocket in the rush to get at his phone.

It appeared to be a tiny stuffed animal. Old, filthy, misshapen, many times repaired, it was difficult to say for sure what it was even meant to be: a once white dog or horse maybe?

He raised the small fabric toy to Nima's face to show him.

"Your summit mascot, Mr. Neil?" the young Sherpa responded. "Sure saved you last night."

Quinn knew full well that people did take such toys and mementos up mountains as lucky charms, but he was not one of them. Looking at it, he remembered the small child who sat lotus-like within their hallucinatory rescue. He considered saying something more about it to Nima, but hesitated. Putting the little cloth animal back into his pocket, he turned his attention to the more important task of what to do next.

After a short wait to be sure it was safe to leave their hiding place, they cautiously made their way to where their tents and the remaining expedition equipment had been. At worst, Quinn needed to retrieve his boots to walk out of that place, at best, they might also be able to recover the more important of their belongings.

As they crossed the glacial runoff, Quinn expected to hear the sound of more helicopters, but the eerie silence had sustained beneath the somber sky.

When they arrived, the camp resembled a bombsite. What remained of Quinn's tent was partially beneath a massive boulder, as were most of his things—including the boots he badly needed to walk out of that godforsaken place. He dug around the detritus to retrieve what he could, relieved to at least find his documents and wallet, before moving on to what was left of the team's duffel bags that Nima had piled together the night before.

They were also badly damaged; contents being blown free by the wind. One was already completely empty. That kitbag had been sliced open, the cut as clean and precise as the one that had appeared in Quinn's tent fly. Picking up the empty vinyl skin, he saw that the bag had no identification tag on its label, just the outline of some sort of butterfly or a moth drawn in black marker on one end. Confused, Quinn tossed the material aside to rummage through what remained of the other bags in order to at least find another pair of socks and some sneakers that fit him.

Just when he had finally assembled a collection of gear that could suffice, a single boulder crashed down the hill and through the camp like a deadly bowling ball. Heeding the warning, Quinn looked back up the mountain as if it was to blame. Through a break in the cloud, he glimpsed a distant figure emerging from the snow at the bottom of the first slope like a corpse freeing itself from a grave. It shouldered what looked to be a large rucksack before setting off back up the route to the mountain to vanish once more. Quinn asked himself how cold it must have been hiding from the drone in the snow and ice, but said nothing aloud to Nima other than that it was time for them to go.

It wasn't long into their walk out that Quinn and Nima sighted the body of the first Tibetan thrown from the helicopter.

The corpse was buckled by the fall, grotesquely twisted, bloody punctures in the thick clothing identifying it as the one that had been shot. It was a young woman. Quinn could do nothing for her but record her murder with some more video and photographs. Afterward the pair continued in silence until Quinn decided to mention again the man that rescued them.

Once more Nima denied knowledge of anyone else having been there, even though Quinn could feel that the young Sherpa was unsure of himself, not a natural liar.

"I think those soldiers were looking for him. That he hid in a crevasse to escape the sensors of that drone," he said, but Nima just remained silent and walked on until—with obvious relief—he pointed out two figures in the far distance, moving toward them. Despite his arm injury, Nima quickly pushed ahead to greet Gelu and Tenjin with loud cries of relief. The two Sherpa had immediately broken out flasks of hot tea as Nima babbled in Sherpali, the three of them continually looking back up the mountain as he spoke.

The senior Sherpa then turned to Quinn. "Mr. Neil, it is good to see you alive. We are in your debt for helping Nima so."

Quinn began to say something in reply but Gelu continued regardless. "It was a small earthquake, Mr. Neil. Much mining now in Tibet, happening more and more often, very dangerous."

"It didn't feel so small from where I was. Did Nima tell you about the helicopter?"

"Yes, we saw it come over the road camp. Special I think, at the limit of the possible to fly so big in this weak air. Nima says you film what happened?"

"Yes."

Quinn broke out his phone and replayed the recording of what they had witnessed. The two older Sherpa crowded in to watch it, heavy concern etching their faces. When it was finished Gelu looked at Tenjin and said something to him that sounded like little more than a mumble. Nima nodded.

"What is that?" Quinn asked.

"Not what, Mr. Neil, but who. Yama. He was the leader of the troop. He is a very dangerous man, a Chinese that hunts Tibetans who want their freedom. You must keep that film hidden, Mr. Neil. Say nothing, show no one, or we not get home."

"Did Nima tell you about the man that saved us?" Quinn asked as Nima, hearing Quinn's question, began to speak in Sherpali once more.

Instantly Gelu turned away and started walking, saying only, "We must go. Hurry."

Nothing more was said until they finally arrived at the roadhead, where they met up with the rest of the team, all of whom were hugely relieved to see them except for the Norwegian, Rasmussen. He just threw a fit when he saw Quinn wearing his sneakers.

"Bloody bad you know."

A Chinese liaison officer surrounded by soldiers from the local garrison, all ragged and poorly equipped when compared to the elite troop from the helicopter, questioned them about what had happened. When they described the earthquake but nothing else, the Chinese liaison officer seemed relieved. Almost immediately after, all the Western climbers were bundled into one minivan, the Sherpa into another. The drivers' instructions were clear; get them away from the earthquake area as fast as possible and on their way back over the mountains to Kathmandu where their expedition had started. They should treat their remaining equipment as lost.

The team had been stuck at the border in Xangmu ever since. Quinn had done little but think about what he had witnessed on the glacier. He was at a loss to know what he should do with the video he had taken. Memory of that broken body from the helicopter stopped him from deleting it, even though he knew Gelu's warning was more than valid. The only conclusion Quinn could arrive at was that he should keep the footage to himself and show it to Henrietta Richards when he got back to Kathmandu to ask her advice.

As for his mysterious rescuer, it dawned on Quinn that perhaps he had seen the man's face before, but only in photographs. The visage he recalled was much younger and surrounded by the type of fur-edged hood used more often in polar exploration than mountaineering.

A Baidu search on his phone soon offered the image he remembered. The accompanying article was entitled: DESTINY DENIED: INAKA "FUJI"

SAKATA LOST ON ANNAPURNA. It was an obituary. Quinn read again the short but spectacular life story of the shy young adventurer from the mountainous Yamagata prefecture of Japan who, in the late 1970s and early '80s, had briefly become a climbing superstar.

Rising up alone and perfect, like the famous Japanese volcano other climbers nicknamed him after, Inaka Sakata scaled the five highest mountains in the world—Everest, K2, Kangchenjunga, Lhotse, Makalu—in rapid succession, using deeds, not words, to fight the accepted wisdom that huge teams and massive resources were needed for success on those mountains. Thinking about the achievement of climbing those five peaks alone at that time, Quinn remembered those tattooed initials on that twisting and turning left hand as it wove its strange magic above the sick Sherpa.

EKKLM

With those five summits the young Japanese had become a late entry into the "race" between two other iconoclasts of mountaineering—the Italian, Reinhold Messner, and the Pole, Jerzy Kukuczka—to be the first to climb all fourteen eight-thousand-meter peaks. A queue of Japanese sponsors—Honda, Shiseido, Toshiba, Comme des Garçons—lined up to help him win. And for a while it looked like he would. But then just before the seemingly inevitable moment of greatest glory, it was all over. In May 1985, Fuji vanished climbing a new line up the northwest face of Annapurna. Avalanched, the Sherpa later said. It would have been Sakata's fourteenth and final eight-thousand-meter mountain. The race would have been won.

With a ripple of recognition, Quinn saw that the tribute had been written by Henrietta Richards. Whatever way Quinn looked, his blocked road seemed to lead back to her, so when Gelu returned to say that he thought the border was indeed going to reopen the next morning, Quinn felt a surge of relief that they were finally going to get out of that place and back to Kathmandu.

After they had discussed the details, Quinn asked Gelu to stay for some tea. As they were drinking it, Quinn passed his phone to the Sherpa with a picture of young Fuji on the screen. Gelu looked at it with a face like granite and said nothing.

"I think this was the man that saved me at Shishapangma and that you and other Sherpa were helping him in some way, Gelu," Quinn stated directly. He pulled the small stuffed animal he had found in his pocket after his escape from the earthquake and placed it next to the phone. Quinn said nothing about it, but saw Gelu's eyes take it in, then harden as he replied, "That man died a long time ago, Mr. Neil. You were lucky, but your wound has confused you. We have all made a big climb with a difficult ending. We are tired and need to get home. I have much work to do now to make that happen."

Leaving no moment for reply, the Sherpa got up and left. Quinn's eyes fell back to the photograph of the Japanese climber as his hand squeezed the soft toy so hard it almost vanished within his fist.

21

FOOLISH HUANG

APARTMENT E, 57 SUKHRA PATH, KATHMANDU, NEPAL

Two short rings of the entry bell interrupted Henrietta Richards while she watched again Quinn's video of the Brocken specter on her laptop, remarking to herself on its exceptional clarity. Her glance from the screen to the brass carriage clock on her living room mantelpiece was unnecessary.

Six p.m.

Of course it was. Sir Jack Graham, the outgoing British ambassador to Nepal, was, without fail, as punctual as the politest of diplomatic kings. He would be down there exactly as agreed, waiting for her in the back of his aging limousine, an island of calm amidst Kathmandu's toxic hurricane of buzzing motorcycles, effete microcars, and smoke-spewing buses and trucks. Henrietta was going to miss Sir Jack. Like her, he was one of the last of the "old crowd."

Urgent and shrill, the sound of the bell caused her to shut the laptop and gave a final stir to the insults that had been curdling the cool air of the top-floor apartment that afternoon since the door-slamming departure of the Taiwanese mountaineer, Lady Huang Hsu, and her entourage of manager and sponsors, that had rattled the pictures on the walls like a minor earthquake.

The Taiwanese hadn't minced her parting sentiments even if she had struggled with their English pronunciation, her *r*'s and *l*'s constantly swapping their stories.

114

"You no crimber, Miss Lichards," she had screamed. "No summit any mountain, ever. You just old bitch with no light to doubt Lady Huang Hsu to be first woman in whole world to successfully crimb every eight-thousand-metal mountain."

The prim old lady cast her eyes around the living room for her handbag, smiling to herself at the thought that while Huang might be technically correct on her first two counts, she was very much mistaken about the third. Henrietta Richards had made a lifelong pursuit of doubting every summit ever claimed in the Himalayas. Her records of the past forty years were the benchmark for the sport, her books on the subject, the reference. Make no mistake, she most definitely had the right.

Locating her handbag, Henrietta took out her compact and lightly powdered her face. She smoothed her blouse and skirt—her uniform, she called it—to a spark of excitement at attending that evening's religious festival, the Kumari Jatra. It was one of her favorite nights of the Kathmandu year.

Down on the street, Henrietta expected the familiar sight of Sir Jack's bronze Jaguar, the increasingly battered yet still dignified ambassadorial transport that had been in service since 1986. Yet that evening a new vehicle awaited her. High-wheeled, dark-tinted, glossily robust, the brand-new SUV seemed purpose built to anonymously bully its way through the old city's congested streets like some sort of luxurious tank.

More change, Henrietta thought as a Gurkha soldier, who was known to her, escorted her to the vehicle, opening the rear passenger door as if to a four count. Within the cocoon of black leather and polished alloy, she was pleased, almost a little relieved, to see Sir Jack's craggy face. But that too was different. Instead of angling down at the stack of diplomatic papers that habitually lay on his lap whenever he waited for her, it was looking directly at her, a smile curling the pronounced crow's feet that fanned out from his eyes as he said a warm hello. The only thing on his lap was a catalogue of military models, his passion.

Henrietta inhaled caustic "new car" smell before saying, "So they've not only pensioned off our ambassador, but also his car?"

"Sell-by dates long expired for both, Henrietta," Sir Jack replied with another smile as the vehicle began to force its way out into the traffic, careful to give space only to a skinny cow nonchalantly crossing—and confusing—the flow of the busy highway. "The old Jag's gone. Off to be a prop in Bollywood, I heard, and as you know I'm being 'wound down.' Retirement beckons."

"Well at least El Alamein can finally be won," Henrietta said, referring to Sir Jack's seemingly endless construction of the great battle's diorama that he retreated into during his spare time with just as much diligence as Henrietta put into her mountain research.

"Yes," Sir Jack acknowledged looking down at his catalogue. "Just in time for it to be boxed up and sent to England where I can reassemble it all over again. Small pleasures! Anyway, how are you?"

"So-so, Jack," Henrietta replied. "None of us is as young as we once were. My own eccentricities keep me busy; summits, writing, Sherpa welfare—always playing part historian, part mother hen, full-time referee." She smiled wryly at him then said, "I was actually called an 'old bitch' this afternoon so I guess I'm still doing something right."

"Charming. Who was that?"

"A female Taiwanese climber who self-styles herself 'Lady Huang' despite a foul mouth that clearly suggests otherwise."

Sir Jack laughed.

"She has climbed thirteen of the eight-thousand-meter peaks—no mean feat actually—but became evidently fatigued by it all when I wouldn't accept her claim to have summited the fourteenth and final one for her: Makalu. When I then asked her to explain the photographs on my laptop taken by a solo Italian climber, Marco Uncini, who summited the day after her claim, a sequence of images that clearly showed the only other tracks up there—the very tracks that he had been following—stopped approximately four hundred feet below the final apex—that pretty much did it, as you can imagine."

"I can indeed. Foolish Huang. Nothing like the combination of mountains and photographs to stir up trouble, as we both know well."

"We do indeed, Jack. On that subject of mountains and pictures, I was recently sent a most amazing video of a Brocken specter by Neil Quinn, who's in Tibet. Have you ever seen one of those, Jack?"

"Yes, actually I have. On a Munro once in Scotland."

"Yes, more likely to see one there in fact, rarer here. A very eerie sight. By the way, as we are on the subject of Tibet, has there been any word on that missing Dutchman I asked you about?"

"Not a lot. Bert de Jong, deputy at their embassy, told me the Chinese authorities said he committed suicide by jumping from the Lhasa train. Depressed, they said. Anyway, what's the interest? He was a professor not a mountaineer."

"Just someone I met a few times to compare notes with on what is happening in Tibet. He said he was going to come and see me after his last trip, but he never showed up. The next thing I heard was that he was dead."

"Hmmm." Sir Jack ruminated before saying, "The one thing I am currently hearing is that there seems to have been another big crackdown in Lhasa, a lot of arrests. Bad stuff."

"That would suggest that the governor, Jin Yui, must be getting the upper hand over Zou Xiaopeng. That's not good at all. Jin's a brute."

Henrietta was lost in thought for a moment then asked, "Tell me about your replacement, the Honorable Anthony Green? The young man certainly has an impressive CV. Thank you for sending me that. First impressions?"

"Not dissimilar to the new embassy cars that arrived with him. Shiny, modern, badged as English but available to anyone with a few quid." Sir Jack emphasized his analogy with a role of the eyes and a devilish smile.

This time it was Henrietta's turn to laugh.

"Actually given his career path to date, I'd suspect he's just passing through, cutting his teeth on an ambassadorship in a minor nation before the bigger and better role elsewhere. He's already spent some time kindly explaining to me how Nepal is little more than a rickety bridge between two of the most populous, economically powerful nations in the world. I'd wager it's one he means to traverse as quickly as possible."

"In which direction?"

"North, undoubtedly. Green is young for a posting like this, only thirty-five—you've been here longer than he's been alive. He was at

Oxford University with our equally youthful chancellor of the exchequer. My contacts in Whitehall tell me he has many 'friends in high places.' As all the man talks about is trade and business, a lot of it in quite fluent Mandarin, I suspect that's what he and his friends are after."

Sir Jack paused.

"A hundred years ago, 'trade mission' used to mean something quite different. A euphemism for some fly-blown outpost manned by a well-spoken chap juggling the demands of being an English gentleman and keeping his head attached to his shoulders. Today however, I fear that is exactly what diplomatic corps have become, a bloody trade mission in the truest sense of the words. Glad to be getting out really."

"When do you leave?"

"Less than a month now. We'll be having a do at the embassy to pipe Betsy and I out, but I wanted Green to meet you today so that if he needs any help in learning about the region, he knows where to ask."

"And will he?"

"Yes, if he's as smart as he thinks he is. I've told him that he should make use of your local knowledge before you also take the boat back."

"Jack, you know I won't be taking any boat anywhere. This is my home now, for better or for worse."

"I admire the sentiment, Henrietta, but you should really think about it. Kathmandu may well be an ancient city but, more and more, it is one only suitable for the young."

Sir Jack and Henrietta chatted on like the old friends they were until the SUV, pinched by the crowds spilling into the roads that lead into Durbar Square, slowed to a crawl.

"It's already busy, Ambassador Graham, sir," the driver said as a wall of people necessitated the vehicle come to a halt.

"Don't worry, Biraj," Sir Jack replied. "I think it is fine for us to get out here. Sergeant Rambhadur, will you see Ms. Richards to the palace steps?"

With a brisk "Yessir," the Gurkha immediately got out and opened

Henrietta's door, almost having to force it back against the dense yet good-natured crowd.

Rambhadur then strode ahead through the people with Henrietta following close behind. Overhead the first streetlights were flickering into life, the daylight beyond the pagoda roofs of the surrounding temples declining into a green-tinged azure glow. Beyond a bobbing sea of baseball caps, multicolored topis, and shiny mops of black hair, the Gaddi Baithak—where the city's great and good would watch the festival—rose up. Whitewashed and colonnaded, the Royal Palace had always struck Henrietta as unlikely; a hundred-year-old chunk of Victorian neoclassicism completely out of context with the far older pagoda-style buildings of the Hanuman Dhoka that surrounded it.

It was a tight squeeze through the writhing mass of people, and Henrietta had to quicken her pace to stay close to the Gurkha. With every step it became more difficult, the crowd pressing in ever tighter until forward progress became impossible.

Henrietta found herself beginning to float on the ebb and flow of the crowd. Adrift, she lost sight of the sergeant.

A gloved hand suddenly seized her left wrist. Henrietta's nerves shocked in electric response.

Flight?

Wedged solid, she couldn't escape in any direction.

Fight?

She tried to wrench her hand free but to no effect. The grip was tight. In secondary reflex, she forced her elbow down to clamp her handbag tight against her body—if that was what this was about. She then attempted to twist her hand away again, but such was the pressure of the hold, the movement stung like a Chinese burn.

Desperate to alert Sergeant Rambhadur to her plight, she raised her eyes only to start a second time at the sight before her: a bulging blue face; a staring triangle of red-rimmed, bulging eyeballs; a diadem of five bloody skulls surrounding an explosion of wild red hair. Henrietta instantly recognized the mask staring back at her as Tibetan not Nepali, as Buddhist not Hindu. She wondered what . . .

The gaping mouth, tusked like a wild boar, spoke.

"Henrietta Richards."

"Yes," she replied.

Bowing gently, the figure released its grip to take a long string of beads and a handheld prayer wheel from within the white silk khata scarf and the worsted robe that fell beneath the mask.

The pair of artifacts were offered to her with the words, "For us all to meet on Mount Yudono you must finish what Christopher Anderson started. Neil Quinn will help you. You and he are the keys to the future."

A moment later, the dense scrum of people parted, restoring a clear path to the Gurkha sergeant. Henrietta Richards twisted her head around seeking the masked figure, but only his gifts and scant words remained.

22

ABACUS

GADDI BAITHAK PALACE, DURBAR SQUARE, KATHMANDU, NEPAL

Sir Jack was waiting for Henrietta at the entrance to the Royal Palace, newly garlanded with two bright strings of orange marigolds. "Bit of a scrum, wasn't it?" he asked, smiling. "See you also received some offerings. Shall we go in?"

Henrietta was still stunned by her encounter, struck by that name from her past as if it had been a blunt instrument. For a moment she didn't reply, she couldn't. Instead she just looked back at the crowd seeking some explanation.

"Henrietta?" Sir Jack asked with a growing concern. "Are you all right? You look like you've just seen a ghost . . ."

She scrambled for an excuse. "Sorry, Jack . . . not so good in crowds these days."

Sir Jack nodded with understanding and gently took Henrietta's arm to guide her into the palace and up to the terrace. Effortlessly switching into his well-practiced diplomatic persona, he led her through the tight islands of politicians, ambassadors, NGO representatives, and local businessmen. There was a greeting here, a handshake there until they arrived behind a tall man with parted black hair, a good foot higher than the ring of Chinese he was talking to in quick-fire Mandarin.

Anthony Green was wearing a well-tailored dark-blue pinstripe, more suited to St. James Square in London than Kathmandu. The blond assistant close at his side was dressed as if she had been transported directly from some glazed office tower as well. The Chinese to their front were also besuited, but gray, ill-fitting—except for a pair wearing the uniform of the People's Liberation Army. From the golden insignia on their pine green jackets, Henrietta knew they were generals, the shorter of the two looking at Green's assistant as if she were a plate of Peking duck.

Despite Sir Jack's gentle tap on Green's elbow to announce their arrival, the younger man continued to talk, without urgency, until he eventually said goodbye to the generals and turned. With a glance at Sir Jack, the new British ambassador carefully looked Henrietta up and down, and asked, "Cultural relics?" Henrietta, mind still elsewhere, instantly prickled, missing the interrogative despite the items she was indeed holding. Green's sharp eyes noticed her reaction with a faint smile that hovered on the disputed border between charm and superciliousness. "From what I'd heard I didn't expect you to be a Buddhist, Ms. Richards. Are those things for me?"

"No," Henrietta replied curtly.

Green continued regardless. "Sir Jack has told me that you know everything about this region: the places, the peoples, the religions. So why don't you start by telling me about this 'Ku . . . ma . . . ri . . . Ja . . . tra' we have been assembled here for?"

Trying to focus for Jack's sake even though her thoughts were still scrambled, Henrietta began to explain to Green the story of Kathmandu's Royal Kumari.

Of how a young girl was selected from amongst the city's Newari community by form, horoscope, and portent to be raised as a living goddess, a human incarnation of the Hindu divine female energy, a protector spirit for the city.

Of how that evening's jatra, or festival, was one of the rare occasions when the tiny deity was permitted to leave the seclusion of her holy rooms to be seen in public and worshipped by Hindus and Buddhists alike in that strange intersection of religions the city specialized in.

Of how—

Green's cellphone rang loudly. The man instantly took the call, pausing only to say, with a desultory hand draped across the phone's face, "Sorry. Absolutely must take this. Do carry on though. Cassie is clearly fascinated." He winked at his assistant. "She can type it all up for me later."

With a smug grin, the British ambassador-in-waiting to Nepal returned his attention to the call, saying loudly, "Yes, in a few weeks, but thoroughly immersed in local history already," before deliberately moving away from the others and lowering his voice to talk more.

Henrietta looked down at the prayer wheel in her right hand. With every rotation a Tibetan prayer wheel was said to release compassion and understanding, much as prayer flags did on every gust of wind. It seemed a suitable moment to conjure such feelings, so she gave the wheel a spin and walked away herself.

Green's assistant, seeing her leave, called after her, "But what about the Kumari?"

"Google it, my dear."

Below the terrace, Durbar Square was now full to capacity. The staggered steps of the surrounding temples were so tightly crammed with onlookers that they resembled human pyramids. The lamps of the streetlights and the spotlights angled to illuminate the ancient buildings were now shining brightly, the burning air around their bulbs alive with fluttering insects. Looking out on it all, surrounded yet alone, Henrietta's left hand squeezed on the mala, the Buddhist rosary the masked figure had given to her. She repeated to herself that first name that had accompanied its delivery.

"*Christopher Anderson.*"

Her eyes, heavy with the memories it conjured, dropped to the smooth cylindrical bead she was clutching, a tassel of red threads projecting from one end. It was the guru bead, both the beginning and the end of the loop. With her thumbnail she hooked it down into the palm of her hand, the action automatically calling the next bead up onto the top of her index finger.

This one was smaller, rougher edged. It was fashioned as a tiny human skull. Henrietta pressed the pad of her thumb onto its tiny, yellowed temple and pushed. Hard as marble but not as cold, it too obediently rode the string down into her hand.

"One," she counted.

Her thumb pushed forward again, searching for the next tiny cranium. "Two."

The beads of the mala began to click quickly through her cupped hand like an abacus.

"Three. Four. Five."

Each skull was as exquisitely crafted as the one before, the workmanship too fine for the secular needs of the Kathmandu tourist, too intricate for the discarded bones of a yak or a goat. In the Kenyan savanna, Henrietta told herself, they would have been made of ivory. In the Arctic, walrus tusk or perhaps the tooth of a luckless sperm whale, but here, she knew beads such as these were made from something else. For they were kapala, carved from human bone, each one originating from a different skeleton.

The understanding made the rosary's one hundred and eight beads immediately hang heavier on her hand with extinct life, their rotation posing unanswerable questions.

"Six."

Who were you?

"Seven."

When did you live?

"Eight."

How did you die?

"Nine."

Where?

It was an abacus of death. Yet, Henrietta also understood that those tiny, hand-carved skulls also thoroughly signified life. To the adept, each was its own mantra, a circular devotion of affirmation, of positivity, of the continuity of the very life force itself through the cycle of rebirth: the samsara.

The little skulls continued to click through her hand, uniting with that name she had not spoken aloud for years to question Henrietta about her own life, but numerically, linearly, bead by bead, with one beginning and one end, unknown but inevitable.

"Twenty-two."

Her age when she first came to Kathmandu to work at the British Embassy.

"Thirty-four."

Her age when Christopher Anderson, the only person she had ever truly loved, didn't return from the mountain of Makalu.

"Forty-five."

The number of years she had lived in that ancient city.

On and on they went, the beads plucking out her memories until a loud blast of horns shattered her reverie and instantly energized the crowd below.

The kumari was finally arriving.

A squad of policemen in blue shirts and beet-red berets immediately pushed outward from the foot of the Royal Palace. Their line forced itself against the crowd to clear an area they held open with linked arms like a human perimeter fence. Above their heads, other arms raised, not in salute but to lift cellphones in twisting, searching anticipation of filming the goddess-child's arrival.

To a new cacophony of piercing whistles, squealing oboes, clashing cymbals, and banging fireworks, an immense wagon was slowly pulled into the cleared area by a team of straining men. Before the great cart, a vanguard of masked figures, Ganesha the elephant-headed god, the eagle-beaked Garuda, others, ran, dancing, circling, leaping. Whenever one neared the crowd, people screamed in mock fear and cowered back in exaggerated panic, whistles and trumpets blowing.

Amongst the masked dancers, Henrietta searched for the blue-faced deity that had given her the beads and the prayer wheel, but it was nowhere to be seen. Her eyes turned instead to the golden pagoda on the cart, a three-tiered miniature of the same temples that surrounded the square. Within sat a small child dressed in impossibly fine red-and-gold robes.

Her large eyes were further emboldened by thick lines of kohl. Her rose-bud lips were painted blood red. The child's tiny head was swaying gently from side to side as if she was hovering on the very edge of consciousness, human or otherwise.

The wagon carrying her was slowly turned to face the terrace of the Royal Palace as burly attendants climbed aboard to ready the little princess for the coming ceremony. Curls of smoke from the incense bundles tied to the wagon caught the same breeze faintly rippling the fringes of red material hanging from the square's tiered temple roofs. The sweet, spicy scent drifted up to perfume the terrace of the Royal Palace. Henrietta inhaled deeply as she continued to click through the beads and take everything in.

"Ninety-six. Ninety-seven. Ninety-eight. Ten beads to go . . . " she told herself just as a scuffle broke out in the crowd to her right.

The disturbance buckled then broke the blue wall of policemen.

A solitary person pushed through the gap to run into the space between the chariot and the palace terrace just as one more bead dropped into Henrietta's hand.

"Ninety-nine."

The figure stopped in the center of the open area. Its head was covered, bound with a khata scarf but it seemed to have vision through the tight silk skin. The amorphous white face turned from side to side to scan the terrace above. The unseen eyes within seemed to lock onto Henrietta's as the gloved hands unrolled a tube of white material the figure was holding.

A sign was held open for all to see.

LONG LIVE THE DALAI LAMA
LONG LIVE TIBET

Henrietta sucked in her breath at the sight of the small banner, the distinctive moth symbol immediately taking flight to settle in her mind next to the name, the memory of Christopher Anderson. This further shock of recognition made her shudder.

From the surrounding crowd, the sign inspired loud shouts and screams. Some began to chant the words displayed. Fists punched the air in support. Others gripped and held back the policemen struggling to break up the demonstration. Alert to the disturbance, the men on the Kumari's wagon huddled around their small charge, blocking her vision as others below strained to push the heavy wagon away, leaving the figure to stand alone silently displaying its message. Lights flashed all around the lone demonstrator. With every burst, the figure and its white sign, seemed to glisten in reply. The air above shimmered, vaporous.

A more pungent smell began to corrupt the incense as another bead slowly clicked through Henrietta's hand. The hundredth small skull brought with it a terrible explanation for the new odor.

Gasoline.

Henrietta squeezed the bead as hard as she could, pinching her own flesh and bone until it hurt. Shaking her head in horror and disbelief, she shouted at the stationary figure, "No!" But the silken face remained fixed on her even as more policemen tried to cut through the crowd, whipping at the onlookers with long lathi sticks until they could burst through and make a grab for the protester.

Their reach met an intense flash. The nearest policemen were thrown back onto the flagstones as the stationary figure in front of everyone transformed into a blazing pillar of orange fire. The crowd began to scream in panic and shock, stampeding in every direction. Blinded by the sight, nauseated by a sweeter, sicklier odor overpowering that of the gasoline, Henrietta felt her thumb rest against not another skull but the guru bead, once more.

Eight beads missing . . .

Henrietta Richards immediately understood.

Eight beads missing.

Quickly she pushed the prayer wheel and the beads deep into her handbag, checking to see if anyone was looking. She needn't have bothered. They were too busy watching a man burn beneath a spiraling, dancing swarm of moths, ghostly against the pale smoke rising into the black night sky.

23

TIBETAN TRANCE TRACK
DHARAMSALA, HIMACHAL PRADESH, NORTHERN INDIA

Although the other hotel guests reported mournfully that the Dalai Lama had left on his travels once again—some said to Buenos Aires, others said Paris—the streets of Dharamsala were still busy that evening. After a slow dinner alone, Beth drifted through illuminated stores and cafés, more tourist than journalist since the termination of her mandate. Nothing was working for her. She had come to India optimistically believing the Dalai Lama story might take her beyond the dead ends recently plaguing her. Instead circumstance had conspired to create one more. She was returning to the States in the morning empty-handed. The thought made her angry, and she found herself trying to paraphrase the Dalai Lama himself, instructing herself to try and move beyond it. It was not as easy as he made it look.

Half by accident, half by design she found herself once more at that same billboard she had seen with Wangdu Palsang. The sight of the painted panel only increased her sadness. Its tragic story was largely forgotten in the West—if it had ever been really known. The bold appeals painted at the bottom of the sign shouted at both her conscience and her craft.

THINK ABOUT PANCHEN LAMA!
ASK ABOUT PANCHEN LAMA!
TALK ABOUT PANCHEN LAMA!
WRITE ABOUT PANCHEN LAMA!

She again touched the butterfly carved into the wood frame, this time, bracing herself in anticipation of the beggar with the hole in his face. But as Beth traced the design with her fingertips—the four wings like spearheads, the dagger-shaped body, the two stubby antennae—the only sound she heard was the rattling of insect wings beating frantically against the overhead lamps that illuminated the panel. For a second, Beth burned her retinas to look up at the fluttering moths.

The symbol is not a butterfly but a moth.

Beth took the thought with her and continued up the road. As she walked on, she imagined herself as one of those small pale moths pulling itself free from its light to fly north into that forbidden land beyond the mountains, free to roam, free to search. A certainty grew inside her.

They must have looked for that boy.

The street had grown darker and emptier before Beth realized the immolations banner that had been her next subconscious target must have been taken down for the night. She took out her phone to orientate herself, shivering at the thought that she might have gotten herself lost.

Before she could even switch it on, a figure darted from the shadows. This time, instead of the beggar's tug, there were two strong hands that pushed her hard in the small of the back. Beth fell forward, her arms spontaneously flying up into the air, the phone slipping from her grip as they did so. She crashed forward onto the hard pavement seeing stars as her head hit the curbstone. Her phone clattered into the gutter.

A hand stretched down to seize the device just as another leg kicked out in the dark. The white Nike sneaker on its end struck the wrist reaching for Beth's phone with the force of a fifty-yard-goal attempt.

The impact produced an audible snap and a low grunt of pain that Beth heard above her own shock and confusion.

Her attacker stumbled and fell, only to roll expertly back onto his feet and flee, clutching his arm. Moments later the distant clunk of a car door and a squeal of tires announced a hidden escape.

Looking up from the ground, dazed, Beth saw that it was Wangdu who had come to her aid. The Tibetan reached out a hand and helped her to her feet while asking, "Mrs. Waterman, are you okay?"

Unsteady on her feet, head spinning, shocked and shaken, Beth leaned forward, hands on her thighs, taking in some deep breaths to be able to answer. "I think so," she said as she felt the broken skin and the growing bruise on her temple.

Wangdu carefully helped her to the side of the pavement and sat her on a low wall to recover. He then retrieved her phone and handed it back to her, "I am sorry, but the screen is broken."

Beth looked at the spider-webbed glass. "Who was that, Wangdu? A mugger? Here?" she asked, still breathless.

"No, Mrs. Waterman. It was a Chinese agent. After your phone, for sure."

"But how come you were here to help me?"

"Rest for a moment, then I know a place we can go where we can talk."

Beth regathered her senses before they slowly walked down the hill, back into the busier part of the town. There, Wangdu pointed Beth into a side alley and a modern-looking bar called Eye3. Inside was bright, crowded, and loud. A headphoned DJ in a raised corner booth was playing a trance track interlaced with the guttural chants and horns of Tibetan monks. A crowd of equally noisy young partyers danced below; at their center was the guy with the dreadlocks who had taken Beth's hand during the Dalai Lama's audience. Stripped of his shirt, he was spinning like an Egyptian tanoura, lost in the groaning, pounding music.

Wangdu directed Beth around the pulsating crowd and through

another door to a quieter bar area beyond. There he sat her down and ordered the straight whiskey she requested, with a Coke for himself. Beth sipped the whiskey medicinally as the young Tibetan began to talk.

"I was following you, Mrs. Waterman," he said. "Ever since you have been here you have been under my protection. You must understand, Mrs. Waterman, that Dharamsala is much more than some Indian hill town full of refugee monks and partying travelers. It is the world center of the 'Free Tibet' community. As a result, everything the Chinese have is brought to bear on this place. Can you imagine what that means?" Beth nodded, contemplating what Wangdu was saying as he continued to explain. "We are tiny and they are immense. They hack our computers and plague them with viruses—you have heard of Lucky Cat I assume?"

Beth recalled her computer crashing when she had tried to search for information about the lost Panchen Lama but said only, "Yes."

"They plant spies. They bribe or smear our people. They deter or harass our visitors. Everywhere they seek to disrupt everything we do. We might believe in peace, but this is a war. You are a career journalist, Mrs. Waterman. They knew you had come here to interview His Holiness. From the moment you arrived they had you under their constant observation just as you have been under mine as a counter. Theft of your phone for its contents or maybe just to hinder you as a foreigner who might struggle to replace it so far from home is a standard obstruction."

"My phone is the least of it, Wangdu," Beth spontaneously confessed. "I think my article on the Dalai Lama has been canceled so as not to upset some big Chinese-backed movie."

"Most probably. More and more the world is being shuttered to us by their influence. In Tibet there is a saying; 'Your mouth becomes smaller after eating other people's food, your hands become softer when holding other people's gifts.' Chinese business is a most powerful medium. It offers much food, many gifts. So what will you do now?"

"I'm scheduled to go home tomorrow but I don't want to. One story may have been denied to me, but I sense so many others. I think that was why I was walking that road, returning to that sign of the lost Panchen Lama. Its message urges me to stay and do something." She drank some more of the whiskey, then asked, "But how, Wangdu? It is not as if I am just going to be able to waltz around China and find someone who has been lost for twenty years."

"Mrs. Waterman, it is worse than that for you now. You are an American journalist who is on Chinese records as having interviewed His Holiness. They wouldn't even permit you a tourist ticket to the Great Wall. They will watch you closely from now on wherever you are."

"But others must have tried, surely?"

"They have and some have paid the highest price."

"Did you know any of them, Wangdu?"

Wangdu seemed to consider his answer before he replied.

"Yes, there was a professor, a Holland man, who often visited us here. He was a great expert on our culture and our religion, a friend of His Holiness. It was said that he searched far and wide."

"What happened to him?"

"He went missing last month. The Chinese said he committed suicide by jumping from the Qinghai to Lhasa train, but we know that is not possible as that train is pressurized and sealed against the altitude when it crosses our high country. No passenger can just open a window or door." Wangdu shook his head and fell silent.

"What was his name?" Beth tapped her phone to life even though the screen was badly shattered.

"I can tell you the name, but you cannot search for it here. Just typing such a name in these territories will create an alert elsewhere I'm sure."

Beth slid her finger from the screen, the broken glass catching skin with a sting. She put it to her mouth sucking away the blood then tapped again on her photos. Passing the phone to Wangdu, she asked, "So what does that symbol really mean, Wangdu? Is it a moth?"

He looked at the image displayed; the moth outline cut into the painted wood frame.

"That is a ghost moth, Mrs. Waterman. It is a creature that lives on those same high planes of Tibet where we lost the Dutch professor and so many others before him. For a long time it has been a symbol for independence, survival, and evasion. It has been carved there by someone as a call to save our lost Panchen Lama."

"Why?"

"It is said that there was once a group of people who called themselves the 'ghost moths' who worked to help Tibet by saving our people and our holy relics from the Chinese destruction."

"Who were they?"

"No one knows. It was a long time ago during the worst excesses of the Cultural Revolution. Some say they were Tibetan fighters, remaining members of the Chushi Gangdruk, the resistance army of the Khampa warriors that rose up to fight the Chinese in the late 1950s. Others say that they were foreigners, agents from America and India that worked with those same Tibetan freedom fighters against the Chinese. I have even heard it said that they were a bunch of hippies from Kathmandu."

"Was your Dutch professor a ghost moth?"

"No. He was just someone who did what he could for us. We feel his loss as he traveled widely and collected a lot of information about what is happening to our land."

Wangdu sipped his Coke and swallowed before he continued. "I am sorry to disappoint you, Mrs. Waterman, but it is just a symbol from the old days. Our Panchen Lama cannot be found."

"So he is not actually dead then?"

"Good try, Mrs. Waterman, but I haven't let slip a secret. It is just my hope that a small boy has been allowed to grow up beyond those mountains, just as someone else here hopes that a myth might fly over them and bring him to us. It is sad to say but both are equally unlikely."

A call came in on Wangdu's phone. He answered and listened, saying something as he did so to the barman, who then switched on a television on the wall. The screen filled with a jumpy image of a bonfire within a crowd of people as a loud narrator delivered an animated voiceover. Beth struggled to comprehend what she was seeing until the screen momentarily froze to show the outline of a figure holding a sign within a tower of flame. The image speared her heart as the news feed quickly moved on to a group of people shouting, "LONG LIVE THE DALAI LAMA! LONG LIVE TIBET!" before they were dispersed by stick-wielding riot police.

"Where is this?" Beth asked.

"Kathmandu. Nepal. It just happened," Wangdu replied.

"Did you see what was drawn on that sign?"

"Yes, I did."

"Do you believe in coincidence, Wangdu?"

"No, Mrs. Waterman. I do not. For us, you must understand, everything is written."

24

PUNDIT TRICK

GADDI BAITHAK PALACE, DURBAR SQUARE, KATHMANDU, NEPAL

Sir Jack insisted Henrietta return to her apartment while he stayed to guide Green through the diplomatic aftershocks of what they had all witnessed.

"This is a huge mess. My driver will take you home. I suggest we meet for lunch tomorrow. Usual time and place," he muttered under his breath as he said goodbye. Henrietta didn't resist. She just nodded in reply, silently wondering if her own presence had in some way conditioned the horrific turn of events. The thought sickened her as Sergeant Rambhadur led her out through a bristling corridor of angry riot police to the car, which immediately joined the slow convoy of diplomatic vehicles exiting the square once she entered.

Alone in the back, Henrietta looked out on the milling, agitated crowd, but saw only the silhouette of the burning man. She shuddered, reminded of that Brocken specter in Quinn's film. The masked man had also mentioned his name. *What does Neil Quinn have to do with all this?* she asked herself. He should be back in Kathmandu by now. She needed to see him.

Finally freed from the square, the vehicle began to stretch its new legs to get her home. Even so, however fast the new car went, however dark the night got, Henrietta Richards could feel what she had just witnessed keeping pace with her.

In the past, everything took its time in Kathmandu, even the news. Multiple tides of distorted sweatshop radio, of street corner gossip, of grainy communal television and smudged newsprint were needed to carry a story into every convoluted alley and bare-brick building of that warren of a city. With each retelling, the details would be embellished a little more, the facts as fluid and clouded as the city's dirty Bagmati River.

Henrietta had made her embassy career out of tracking the flow of information through Kathmandu, trying to assemble it into truth along the way. But even there, in that ancient ramshackle city, things were different now. Events raced ahead of the scheduled media or the ambling tattletale, bouncing from cellphone to cellphone as video, texts, messages, unedited and unfiltered, no time permitted for anything that might slow the process. Despite the geography, the poverty, the matted electrical wiring that toppled down from the forked telegraph poles like black spaghetti, Kathmandu was no less obsessed with the digital than New York or Tokyo.

Henrietta opened her handbag, pushing past the prayer wheel and the skull beads to reach her cellphone. She prided herself on being "old school," only turning the device on when she needed it, determined not to be its slave, however much she welcomed the mine of information it could access. The cell came to life showing a signal.

It was a Free Tibet demonstration. They're letting it run for the moment, data-mining, she told herself. It was no secret to her, to anyone in the region, that Chinese corporations had supplied much of the city's ever-expanding communications network, including that of the Nepal police and the emergency services. It was hardly a great leap forward of imagination to also assume their secret services walked in and out of system back doors as freely as delivery boys, particularly if it had to do with Tibet.

They'll disrupt the city's power to suppress the story also, you see.

Power cuts and load shedding were now common in the overpopulated valley and, again, there were rumors they were also being manipulated to cause deliberate disruption.

You're involved. Be careful—Moscow Rules from now on!

Henrietta instantly turned her phone back off to sidestep the digital and return to the analog espionage that had underwritten her own time at the embassy: those Cold War rules of basic engagement; the whispered conversations and furtive meetings; the stolen papers and tightly folded notes; the celluloid negatives and glossy positives; the drops and pickups; even the strings of beads like those coiled in her handbag.

The coded mala really was one of the oldest tricks in the subcontinent's spy-book: a standard tool of the first "pundits," those agents of the British Raj in the nineteenth century. The name was a variation of the word *pandit*, which means *teacher* in Hindi. Selected for their education and a swarthy resemblance to Tibetans, famed explorers such as Nain Singh Rawat, Hari Ram, and the enigmatic Kinthup were sent north "beyond the ranges" disguised as wandering holy men or pilgrims, prayer beads in one hand, spinning prayer wheel or wooden staff in the other. However the rosaries of these pretend lamas did not feature the Buddhist spiritual number of one hundred and eight but the profane metric of the ever-approaching West. For every hundred paces the pundit counted off one bead. For every tenth bead they acknowledged half a mile, with every complete rotation of the hundred-bead mala looped in the left hand, five.

At day's end, with small sextants they furtively mapped the stars and dipped thin-tubed thermometers into their boiling cookpots to record the altitude; they added geographical context to the day's mala count, their distance traveled. Their findings were then hidden as micro-notes within the small cylindrical drums of their prayer wheels or secret compartments inside their walking sticks. Sometimes they were memorized as never-ending songs or rhymes that were recited like mantra. In this fashion the pundits traveled, measuring and recording those unknown lands beyond the Himalayas, some to finally return to India as experts, others to vanish, imprisoned or killed in some still uncharted place for being the spies that they were.

Yes, the one-hundred-bead mala and the accompanying prayer wheel were about as "old school" as it got. Undoubtedly why she had been given them, Henrietta thought, her handbag tightly closed on her lap as the vehicle sped on. When a motorcycle howled past the SUV to vanish into the Kathmandu night, it made her jump, disturbing her thinking about those two names the masked figure had mentioned and that symbol his sign had displayed.

For a moment it left another image of an older, slower motorcycle laden with two people and chugging its way through those same streets. It had been one of the happiest days of her life and, she reminded herself, *the start of it all.*

The driver escorted Henrietta to the front door of the old Rana building on Sukhra Path that had been her home ever since it had been converted to apartments in the '80s. Once inside, she stepped up the stairs to the third floor, moving slowly, weighed down by the burden of what she had witnessed and what her handbag might contain. Entering her apartment, she immediately switched on all the lights and dropped the deadlock behind her. The spring-loaded "snap" guillotined her bright, pristine rooms from the dirty darkness outside.

Henrietta sighed relief at the sound of the lock, and as Bodleian, her black cat, approached, tail raised in hungry greeting. But the cat stopped short, his nose twitching at the unholy smell latched to Henrietta's clothes, her hair, her skin. Revolted, the cat turned tail and strutted toward the kitchen to await a late supper by way of her apology. Despite being somewhat offended, Henrietta also smelled the vile smoke of the immolation on her clothes now that she was in her spotlessly clean apartment. She agreed that she should indeed shower, change, feed Bodleian, and have a restorative cup of tea before she did anything more; curiosity needed to be kept in check, as her long-lived cat well knew.

Those things done and the tea brewed, Henrietta returned to her living room and switched on her tall standard lamp to further illuminate her favorite reading chair. On a small side table, she readied her cup and saucer, reading spectacles, notebook and fountain pen, her cellphone, a small flashlight, and a silver candlestick with three new candles and a box of matches. Finally sitting down, she placed her handbag on both knees and said to her cat, "Well, here we go."

Henrietta gently extracted the prayer wheel, raising it into the light. Now that she could really study it, she realized that it was a magnificent piece, as ancient and special as the beads. This was no soda-can replica that could be bought for a few dollars on any Thamel street corner. The detail of the w—

There was a loud click followed by total darkness.

Power cut!

Henrietta felt for the flashlight that she had placed on the side table in anticipation and used its beam to strike a match and quickly light the three-arm candelabra just as she did every time her nighttime studies were similarly interrupted. The flames of the candles rose up to bring out even more exquisite detail in the antique prayer wheel. The cylinder was made of thick hand-beaten copper, finely crafted even if battered by use and tarnished by time. On the outside of the cylinder were raised symbols of silver and gold.

Om mani padme hum, the tireless Buddhist mantra of dedication and supplication.

With the slightest flick of her hand, the wheel began to spin on its wooden axis, the metal weight hanging to one side and lifting to circle like a fat fly on a thread. Gently Henrietta closed her hand around the spinning drum to stop its silent invocations. It was time to see what they were.

On the crown of the prayer wheel a brass acorn nut held the cylinder and its saucer-shaped lid to the axis on which it spun. Grasping the drum of the prayer wheel with her right hand, Henrietta attempted to twist the nut free with her left, but her dry fingers slipped, unable to grip, her hand cramping in arthritic protest.

Slowly getting up from her chair, she took the prayer wheel and the candelabra into the dark of her kitchen, casting a flickering light as she went, reminiscent of Florence Nightingale walking a Crimean hospital ward. There, she set the candelabra down and took a clean cotton tea-towel from a drawer as the distant sound of a police siren split the Kathmandu night, stopping her for an instant as if she was about to commit a crime. When silence returned, Henrietta arranged the cloth to get a better grip on the retaining nut and twisted again using all the strength she could muster, saying to herself slightly sardonically, "Open sesame!"

The stubborn thread held a moment more, then surrendered.

With a hesitant look beyond the candlelight out of the kitchen, Henrietta braced herself for what was about to be revealed. Slowly she turned the nut until it came away within the cotton and she could gently pry the lid from the drum with her other hand.

The lid released with a distinct pulse of pressure, energy that—however she might try and deny it to herself later—traveled up her arms, and ballooned into her head.

A single moth flew out of the drum. Small and brown, starved of light, the insect immediately began to circle the candelabra, fluttering perilously close to its three flames, suddenly spoilt for choice.

With a wave of the towel she shooed it away and looked into the copper cylinder. Surrounding the central axis tube were tightly rolled papers bound by a piece of embroidered cloth and a thin red cord. She extracted the bundle and, removing the red thread, opened the swatch of material and then the two papers held within. She smoothed all three out on her knees.

The contents shocked her, rare tears spiking her blue eyes as an irregular yet urgent beating noise filled the room. Breathless, it took a moment for Henrietta to recognize that it was the sound of her own heart.

To gather her senses, she mandated herself another cup of tea—strong and black this time—then took her flashlight into her bedroom, using the beam to cut and sweep beneath her bed to locate the small metal trunk she hid there. Returning with the black box to the kitchen, she set it on the work surface next to the candelabra, twisted the combination lock to 8-8-4-8, and removed it. The box was a necessary precaution in the event she ever had to leave her home hastily because of fire or earthquake, and its inside was crammed with her most important legal documents and backup CDs of all her climbing records.

She carefully lifted them out to reveal another layer beneath of lesser value, but equally precious to her: a series of old journals, their ragged-edged lokta paper thick with maps, photographs, and postcards. Amongst them was a battered tobacco tin, the lid featuring a fierce khaki mountain set against a black sky printed with the words, "EVEREST RUBBED FLAKE."

Henrietta took out the tin and squeezed it open to reveal a bundle of embroidered patches held by two rubber bands like a stack of old playing cards. Unhooking the bands, she began to deal the woven fabric badges onto the work surface next to the contents of the prayer wheel as if playing Solitaire.

The first line she laid out featured colorful stylized designs, stitched silhouettes of mountains combined with national flags and expedition names.

EVEREST WEST RIDGE EXPEDITION

KANGCHENJUNGA 8586 M

K2 80

NANGA PARBAT INTERNATIONAL

MAKALU NORTH 1981

Glancing at each one, she recalled the times they represented for her and for Christopher Anderson, that name from the past that had accompanied the mala beads and the prayer wheel. Next to each one she placed a journal, his diary of each climb. There was no journal for the last patch. Refusing to let herself dwell on why, she immediately began to lay out another line of badges; simple green cotton rectangles this time, lettered and edged in black that read: RANGER; LRRP; AIRBORNE; VIETNAM. Then there were others: brighter, happier, more whimsical; the type you could still buy in the city's souvenir stores. A multicolored peace sign; those famous all-seeing Buddha eyes that constantly watched over Kathmandu; a square that just said SUPER FREAK in orange and green on a blue background. Henrietta smiled, choosing to remember that one stitched to a satchel on a ride on the back of an old motorcycle.

The last patch in the tin was the one she was looking for. It too had been hand-embroidered in that Kathmandu sweatshop still located next to her old friend Pashi the barber. The badge was like new, never worn, never used. It was shaped as a moth. The body was red, the four wing segments, blue, yellow, green, and white. In each of the five segments was an individual capital letter, the stitching still tight and bold after all those years.

Henrietta put the piece of material from the prayer wheel on the top of it. That fabric was worn, dirty, and faded, the threads loose and broken but the design was identical. Undeniably it was one of the original batch given out to the small troop of climbers they had worked with to try and help Tibet all those years ago. For a moment it was as if Chris was there with her again as he sketched out the design for the first time; the shape, the colors of the prayer flag, the symbolic letters. Then they were all there once more as he distributed the patches: Piotr the Pole, the Barrett brothers, Paolo Soares, and Fuji. Henrietta had also been given one, hers destined never to grace a battered climbing jacket but to hide in that small tobacco tin of mementos for a lifetime.

The Ghost Moths.

Only her now.

It had only been her for a long time. She had written their damn obituaries, every single one, all those years ago.

Taking up the two papers the old patch had surrounded she studied the first again.

It was a copy of a drawing of a skull set within an inverted triangle, a heavily engraved skull that she realized she had once held in her own hands.

She turned her attention to the second design, a simple line drawing in black and red that showed a mountain. It looked just like a drawing that she had once made.

Christopher Anderson may well have started it all, but the two pieces of paper displayed had finished it. She shuddered at the thought.

With the candelabra, Henrietta walked to her filing cabinet with a heavy heart to open it at *M* and take out a heavy file marked MAKALU that she had only just put back following that day's Lady Huang Hsu interview. She then reached for her atlas. Mount Yudono was a new one, even for her, Henrietta Richards. From the same bookshelf she also retrieved *The Deities of Tibetan Buddhism* to better place that mask the man had been wearing. For the next hours she read, took notes, and wondered about both the past and the present until she fell asleep in her chair.

The dream was an old one, but familiar. Even the longest roads have their beginning and this, he had told her, had been the start of his, in that small town in the highlands of Colorado.

25

LAND OF BLACK SNOW

RED CLIFF, EAGLE COUNTY, COLORADO, UNITED STATES OF AMERICA
November 1958

The floorboards of the small house in Red Cliff always used to creak however lightly he trod, but that early morning, they prompted no change to his grandmother's faint snoring as he tiptoed to the frosted window. Even in the dark he could see outside that it had snowed—and, by the look of it, all night.

The young Christopher Anderson quickly shouldered his satchel, squeezed his hands into gloves, and pulled a gray wool cap over his curly blond hair. Taking down his precious Remington .22 from beneath his long dead grandfather's cane fishing rods, he glanced at the television screen set in its wood cabinet on the other side of the room. "I'll be going now," he whispered to the shadow of Clint Walker in the gray screen.

"You be careful out there, son. Back by high noon."

"Not if the Indians get me."

"There haven't been any Indians round here for seventy years, boy," came the imagined reply—but this time in his father's voice. "You read too many damn cowboy books, watch too many Westerns on that television."

Outside, the town was still, no one about. Dawn was beginning to lighten the heavy load of cloud that stuffed the sky and bring definition to the ghostly crags and skeletal aspens that lined the steep slopes below. Holding his rifle across his front as if on patrol, the boy quickly left the town behind, his only companions the metallic rattle of the too-fast-to-freeze Eagle River, the black telegraph poles that stood guard over the Union Pacific rail line like silent crows, and the Ute warriors of his imagination that were silently working their way up the valley toward him.

The boy let that fantasy drop when he reached the old metal gate that blocked the road. Always closed with a rusty chain and padlock, that morning it bore a new enameled sign bearded with icicles. Under the red skull and crossbones, black stenciled letters read:

WARNING
THIS AREA CONTAINS EXPLOSIVE ORDNANCE.
ENTRY FORBIDDEN.
RANGE OFFICER, FORT CARSON, COLORADO.
DIRECTIVE MD 2713 (1958)

Christopher knew well what had once lain beyond. During the war, it had been Camp Hale, base for the Tenth Mountain Division of the US Army. A thousand buildings—barracks, stables, mess halls, storage sheds, even a hospital—had housed fifteen thousand men who, in the highest camp in America, had learned to live and fight in the terrain that defined the regiment's existence. The coal burned by the trains that supplied them and the stoves that warmed them had produced so much soot the place had become known as "the Land of Black Snow."

They were long gone now, the snow white once more.

It was a little strange that the army should only now bother with such a sign, but Christopher climbed the gate regardless, just as he had done so many times before.

Almost immediately after, he turned left to work his way up McAllister Gulch. Rifle at the ready, he climbed slow and steady through naked cottonwoods, boots slipping and sliding for grip until he got under a roof of thick pinyon that made the going easier. When a first rabbit darted away between the tree trunks, Chris shouldered the Remington in an instant, but the brown flash twisted once and was gone.

He hiked on, getting ever higher. The chill began to bite hard so he decided to hunker down beside the trunk of an old juniper and take a break: if he stayed still enough maybe something might even appear. After a cautionary look around, he took out a cigarette he had stolen from his grandmother's pack and smoked as he watched the steep ground below his hideout. When a stick cracked, he huddled down yet more to spy on a female mule deer carefully stepping down the slope. A young calf followed. They stopped, the doe foraging, wet nostrils pushing at the snow, the calf patient. The boy studied them but knew he wouldn't shoot. He mustn't.

"You are not ready for a deer."

His grandmother didn't set many rules, but that was one of them. Besides this one had young. His mother had died young. Something disturbed them—not him—and the pair quickly turned down the hill to disappear at a run. Silence and stillness returned, filled only with the question of what had scared off the deer.

Maybe a mountain lion had followed them down intent on taking the calf?

Such heavy snow would push everything down off Resolution Mountain.

Nothing more appeared as he waited.

Not even a squirrel.

He began to shiver.

Cold. Cold. Cold.

When some sun finally pushed through trees above him, it brought little warmth, even if it made the snow below his vantage point shine.

A dark shape filled it.

Young Christopher Anderson sighted the black bulk of the huge bull elk down the narrow barrel of his rifle, concentrating so hard on it he could see the coarse hair of its coat, the white rim of its dark eye, the frothy spit at the edge of its mouth.

The Remington's sights pulsed with the rapid beating of his own heart as he lined them up on the beast, imagining a shot, clean and perfect.

A whistling sound split his imagination into two.

Sssieeuuu!

It repeated, twice more.

The boy watched dumbstruck as three arrows hit the bull elk in rapid succession.

Thunk! Thunk! Thunk!

Each impact was hard and heavy, as if the beast was made of canvas and wood, not flesh and bone. The elk coughed from their brute force then staggered and fell, its punctured chest letting out a final low groan.

In silent awe Christopher watched as three figures clad in white over-suits rose up from the snow, each holding another viciously pointed arrow to the ready in a long bow.

They were not needed.

The elk was already still.

Long knives flashed as two of the men started to work on the carcass while the third stood over them and looked all around. That figure pulled back the hood of the white cotton jacket that covered its head. The face revealed was oval, brown skinned, the eyes were slits pinpointed with black. Long glossy black hair was tied by a vivid headband as red as the elk's blood. A turquoise bead hung from one ear.

For a moment, the man seemed to stare directly at Christopher, then he turned back to help the other two lift the bull elk and go.

There was only one conclusion the twelve-year-old boy could make.

Indians had returned to Eagle County!

PART V

THE KATHMANDU EFFECT

"Kathmandu effect" is an apocryphal term utilized within spy circles to describe the proliferation of intelligence personnel within a city's diplomatic corps as a product of suspicion and paranoia rather than actual geopolitical importance.

It was said that during the Cold War there were more intelligence officers operating from the embassies of Kathmandu than in any other capital city in the world.

26

LUCKY CAT WAVING

EMBASSY OF CHINA, HATTISAR SADAK, 615, KATHMANDU, NEPAL
October 16, 2014

There was no power outage at the Chinese embassy in Kathmandu the night of October 15, and no night for that matter. Behind the compound's bare-brick and razor-wire cordon, on-site power generators had illuminated the complex so brightly in the dark city that it resembled a remote moon-base with white Toyota Land Cruisers continually coming and going like rovers.

The Kumari Jatra festival had only been under routine Chinese Ministry of State Security surveillance. Designated a Hindu event, its sudden turn to Tibetan matters had taken everyone by surprise. The immolation instantly activated a "Xizang Code 2"—the mandated response directive for any splittist activity relating to the Tibetan Autonomous Region in that zone. The presence of Senior General Haiyang of the Western Theater Command within the delegation attending the festival automatically gave him golden grade supervisory powers.

All in-city security, intelligence, and military staff had been immediately mustered at the Hattisar facility while preliminary notification of the action was sent to Beijing and Lhasa, and representatives of the Nepali law enforcement and military were summoned for "consultation." Section 17—the regional cyber management operation run from Hattisar and otherwise known as "Lucky Cat"—had the immediate tasks of assembling a multi-angle timeline video of the incident that identified all key participants, and manifesting a complete media suppression protocol.

Although the complex's air-conditioning had been designed to easily accommodate all the equipment and bodies that could fill the windowless command room, the senior general was sweating profusely as he stood in front of the immense plasma wall that displayed a hybrid satellite image of Kathmandu. "Do you understand that this is a disgrace?" he was shouting at the senior MSS officer in Kathmandu.

In response, Captain Zhang, no shrinking violet himself, was trying to explain that the Kumari festival was not related to Tibetan Buddhism and that there had been no warning of a possible demonstration from any of his team's many sources in the city.

Nothing the captain said made any difference. The senior general's demands continued. "I need to know everyone that was involved. Who they are? Who assisted them? I want pictures. I want names," he shouted.

"Our team will soon have them," Captain Zhang replied, pointing the senior general to the back of the room where, within a wall of monitors, Section 17's most senior analysts were absorbed in their work, headphones filled with the chants and screams of the crowd, the whistles and sirens of the Nepalese police; fingers racing over keyboards and blurring across touchpads to extract particular image streams. On a shelf silently overlooking their digital industry was the model of a shiny plastic cat, left arm slowly waving backward and forward. The fake feline's golden smile was fixed at the horror of the images flashing across the screens below, just as it had been when the team had successfully infiltrated the International Campaign for Tibet and the Central Tibet Administration in India from the shelter of the Hattisar facility after proving their ability against Indian defense companies in Operation Pyro the year before.

"Well tell them to get on with it!" the senior general shouted at Zhang. "I want to see it all!"

"You will, Senior General. And when you do, you will be amazed at 17's capabilities."

Across the city Sangeev Gupta arrived at Henrietta's apartment to start work at 9 a.m. as usual. The studious Indian who had assisted her for over ten years entered quietly with his own key, a recent privilege, to meet Henrietta, who sat in her living room hidden behind the wide pages of *Kantipur,* one of the biggest selling Nepali newspapers. On her side table were others: the *Annapurna Post; Gorkhapatra;* as well as her usual morning reading, the *Kathmandu Times* and the international edition of the *Daily Telegraph.* Only the latter two were always delivered to her door, so Gupta didn't need to be Sherlock Holmes to quickly deduce that Henrietta had already been down to the hole-in-the-wall newsagents that faced her apartment building. He knew also that Henrietta had been going to the Kumari Jatra with Sir Jack so could only conclude that she was trying to understand what she had witnessed just like everyone else in Kathmandu that morning. He said his habitual, "Good morning, ma'am," and then, from his satchel, added his Indian newspaper, the *Hindustan Times,* to the pile.

From behind the newsprint he heard Henrietta reply, "Good morning to you too, Sangeev. What are your country's papers saying about last night's event? There's a lot of space given to the story in these, but little by way of fact."

"It is the same. No one seems to know much beyond the horrible photographs," Gupta answered. "One editor says it is a direct result of the increasing Chinese presence in Nepal. Something that you know makes us Indians nervous."

"It makes us all nervous, Sangeev," Henrietta said. She closed the Kantipur broadsheet and reached for the Indian newspaper. Seeing her face, seemingly more lined and shadow-darkened than normal, Gupta thought Henrietta looked tired, as if she had been up all night, but without further comment—he knew better than that—he went over to his small desk area to get to work.

There, he found a stack of handwritten notes and amended pages next to the laptop that had finally replaced the faithful Compaq PC on which, for years, he had assembled her climbing records. Only after Henrietta had studied the article in the *Hindustan Times,* did she say, "Sangeev, I need to be out and about this morning and then lunch with

Sir Jack. You won't be able to call me as I'll be leaving my phone here—needs a charge after last night's power cut. On your desk you'll find my notes about the Huang Makalu meeting. If you could type them up for me but don't print or file them. I'll do that later. Can you also find out when the Snowdonia Ascents team is due back from Shishapangma and what hotel they will be staying at. I want to see the English mountain guide Neil Quinn and confirm their summits on that mountain as soon as possible. Thank you. Back anon."

A few minutes later Gupta watched Henrietta head toward the door with her trusty handbag. He glanced at his watch and then he went to the kitchen for some water. As he took the bottle of filtered water from the fridge, he noticed the silhouette of a moth flat against the white ceiling above his head. It made him think of the design on the burning man's sign. He shuddered as he tried to not see again the immolation in his mind's eye.

"But it was a suicide not a murder," Detective Jitendra Thanel of the Kathmandu Police said to Senior General Haiyang. "There is nothing to investigate."

"Take my advice, Detective," the senior general replied aggressively. "If you value your career, you will treat last night's outrage as if it had been an assassination of your prime minister. I expect to know exactly who in this stinking city of yours was involved and I have every assurance from your own minister of home affairs that this is going to happen."

Captain Zhang entered and said something into the senior general's ear, to which he replied, "At last."

Haiyang looked again at the Nepalese detective and said brusquely, "You. You will come with me."

Thanel followed the senior general into the operations room telling himself that the Chinese general could rant and rage all he wanted, but this was Kathmandu not Beijing.

The sight that met Thanel instantly contradicted his private thought.

The operations center was enormous, full of people, desks, and equipment. The room was dominated by a plasma wall filled with a satellite image that seemed to show every roof tile, every paving stone, every pigeon of Thanel's sprawling city. The scale and quality of the image was unlike anything the detective or his underfunded department could dream of.

At the senior general's signal the image quickly changed into an accelerated image of Durbar Square filling for the Kumari Jatra. People queued and clustered like worker ants. Multiple overlays of video image from ground level showed brief close-up detail from every angle before shrinking to a red indicator spot to pinpoint the source's location and vantage point. To both sides of the main screen, a continuous cascade of digital information listed the background to every video in the composite: the operator identity and known records if it was taken from a personal cellphone, or camera location and supervising organization if it was from CCTV or security within the square's many temples and historic buildings. A time bar running below the main display calibrated the display to the hundredth of a second.

The screen seemed to be feeding on all the digital data in Kathmandu with absolute freedom. As the whole room watched the immolation unfold once more, Thanel was further amazed to see that as night closed in on the proceedings, the quality of the image and the detail of the master image barely faltered, shifting only to a faintly silver-green tone from the enhanced night-vision software being applied. Also the sheer quantity of information being flagged within the display was astounding. Any person in close proximity to the act of immolation was momentarily scanned the microsecond they entered the action within tight white cross-hairs. If the facial recognition technology made a connection, that face was immediately expanded and known profile information appeared in a data box alongside the composite reconstruction.

When the reconstruction finally finished, ten data boxes of personal information grew to block the screen with a wall of Tibetan faces. Senior General Haiyang stared at them in silence then asked, "So which one of these was the man who burned himself?"

"None of them, Senior General Sir," Captain Zhang replied.

"Why do you not have that information?"

"The man's face was covered and although the material burned away, the action of the flames was such that our facial recognition could not get a positive fix against any data records we have."

"But surely you have seen the body since?" Haiyang demanded impatiently.

"No, Senior General Sir. In the confusion afterward the body appears to have disappeared."

"What do you mean it disappeared? Haven't you got it on camera?"

"Only that it was aided and moved by a number of people identified and clearly led by this man."

One of the ten data boxes expanded to show an elderly but still strong Tibetan face.

"Do you know this man?" Haiyang demanded of Thanel.

Thanel thought about lying, but the man's name and personal details were already clearly displayed.

"Yes, that is Temba Chering. He is an important man in the Tibetan and Sherpa communities of Kathmandu, a successful businessman with many operations, hotels, and restaurants, mostly in the Bhoudhanath district, the center of Tibetan culture in the city, as well as other businesses in the tourist areas." The detective did however omit the detail that Chering was seen throughout the city as either Robin Hood or Al Capone depending on which side of him you fell. Regular "donations" from Chering to help the detective support his large family on something more than his lowly police salary meant that Thanel was highly motivated to work hard on promoting the first viewpoint, as were many of his local colleagues.

"He is a good man. Gives a lot to this city and to his people . . ."

"What about these other people then?" Zhang asked as Temba Chering's data box reduced and the nine others reshuffled to fill the screen. "These men were identified as present or within close proximity of the burning man, both during the immolation and soon after. Their data says they are splittist agitators that reside in Kathmandu."

"I don't think I know any of them," Thanel obfuscated.

"Stop!" a voice commanded from behind them all.

156

A black-suited man walked around to place himself in front of the screen. He said nothing more.

"Who the hell are you?" Haiyang shouted at the man, imperiously pushing out his uniformed chest as if to emphasize his rank. The arrival's face showed no flicker of emotion beyond the tip of his tongue briefly moistening his almost nonexistent lips before he spoke again.

"Obviously I am someone that knows more about what has happened here despite all your technical bullshit, Senior General Haiyang. I am Lieutenant Yen-Tsun Lai, MSSP special division Xizang. I have been tracking the man who burned himself within our territories."

Yama passed a document to Haiyang.

"From now, this is my operation by order of the Xizang Dragon Committee with Beijing sanction. You will supply me with all the support I require."

The senior general opened his mouth to contest the matter but after he had read the document, said instead, "So who was this man that you were following?"

Yama looked at Detective Thanel. "A ghost, Senior General, in many senses of the word. That is all I need to say to you. My operation now; my need to know, not yours."

"Well, your search is finished," Captain Zhang interjected. "There is no way that man could have survived what he did to himself."

"The man was at his end, but if I know anything about Tibetans it is that to them, every end is just a beginning—however high the flames they hide behind. Run the video again."

The group, now led by Yama, studied the reconstruction again and again but each time the conclusion regarding the identified participants remained the same and no new information emerged. As a final pass was concluding, Captain Zhang was called from the room.

Zhang soon returned carrying a large black trash bag and said, "Two of my agents retrieved this from the small covered alley near to where they found an empty gasoline container. It may be unrelated, but they thought we should see it as it is Tibetan."

Zhang offered the opened plastic bag to Yama who reached in. His hand reemerged clutching a thick mass of red wool from which hung a painted wooden mask. Yama raised it up to look at it as if lifting a severed head by the scalp while he ordered one of the Lucky Cat crew to scan it. The technician stepped forward and photographed the mask's scowling multi-eyed blue face from every angle with a tablet computer. Each shot immediately displayed on the plasma screen then they all merged to become a single 3D model of the mask that began to revolve.

"What does it symbolize?" Haiyang asked Yama.

"It is a mask of Palden Lhamo, the protectress spirit of Tibet. They say she resides in a holy lake in an area that I recently visited to see . . ." He stopped speaking and continued his realization in silence. "Run a new search for that mask in the crowd."

The technician began to work quickly on his tablet screen. Once more the visual reconstruction began to reassemble the immense crowds in the Durbar Square in accelerated stop-motion until it suddenly froze. The image refocused, closed in, and then the video reversed a little to show a hunched and hooded figure almost submerged within the tight crowd stoop to put on the same mask, then rise back up to push through the people nearest and stop before another person. Although partially obscured by the crowd there was a definite meeting between them before the masked figure moved quickly away and, lowering the mask, seemed to follow it down into the crowd and disappear.

"The biometric identifiers confirm the masked figure to be the person who immolated," the technician said, his fingers tapping and swiping furiously at his small control screen. "Tell me about the other one," Yama demanded.

The Lucky Cat technician refocused on the encounter, sampling, freezing, expanding until a new image and data box filled the screen.

"Do you know that gweilo?" Haiyang immediately demanded of Thanel.

"Yes, that lady is very well known in Kathmandu. She is Henrietta Richards, a British person that has lived here for the past forty years. For a long time she worked at their embassy."

"So she is a British spy," Yama said.

Thanel had heard the rumors but, in current company, he suddenly felt protective toward the venerable Englishwoman. "No. And she retired from the embassy many years ago."

"The leopard doesn't lose its spots even when it gets old. Show me her involvement again," Yama said to the technician before looking back at Thanel and saying, "and you, keep talking. Why is she so well known?"

"She is famous in Kathmandu as a historian of our mountains and those who climb them. She also does a lot of good work for our people, particularly the Sherpa."

The encounter between Henrietta and the masked figure was rerun multiple times, blown up and slowed down from every image and angle to scrutinize every detail. As much as possible, her journey from the car that had delivered her to the square to her arrival at the Royal Palace was given the same treatment. A parallel profile was run on Sir Jack Graham, and the Gurkha, Sergeant Rambhadur when it was seen that they were accompanying her.

"You say she's retired yet she travels with the English ambassador," Yama said to Thanel, giving him a cold inquisitive stare before asking, "Is she a Buddhist?"

"No, I don't think so," Thanel said looking at the plasma wall now filled with an expanded image of Henrietta Richards holding a Tibetan prayer wheel and a set of prayer beads as she entered the Gaddi Baithak. Another appeared next to it of her clutching only her handbag as she left the car.

"So probably not her trinkets then?" Yama said, more to himself than Thanel. "Replay the encounter between them again."

27

FRIENDSHIP BRIDGE

XANGMU, NYALAM COUNTY,
TIBETAN AUTONOMOUS REGION OF THE PEOPLE'S REPUBLIC OF CHINA

At first the petty cash seemed to be doing its work. The Snowdonia Ascents team, alongside another climbing team that had been on the mountain of Cho Oyu and a tour party of wealthy Indians returning from a pilgrimage to Kailash, had been ushered to the front of the immense queue at the border booths that monitored Friendship Bridge. There, a portly official, overfed on graft and grease, stood alongside them, personally attending to the team's smooth progress back into Nepal as quickly as possible.

The processing of their stack of passports and CMA climbing permits began quickly, but stalled when a back-and-forth dialogue between the passport clerk and the fixer rapidly became heated. Resolutely shaking his head, the clerk raised a telephone and asked urgent questions. When the phone was put down, he said nothing, but restacked the team's documents and pushed the pile to one side. Soon after, two senior PLA officers arrived with four guards. One of the officers stepped inside the booth, exchanged words with the clerk, and collected the documents. The other aggressively dismissed the bribed official, who left as rapidly as his stumpy legs would carry him. That officer then ordered the soldiers to direct Quinn's team from the line and lead them to the slab-sided white office building that overlooked the bridge. The Englishman asked Gelu what he thought the problem was as they filed in.

"It seems that it is because we were on Shishapangma, Mr. Neil," the Sherpa replied. "The clerk said there was a new directive for all travelers in that region. That it was not so easy."

"What directive?"

"I don't know, Mr. Neil," Gelu said as he gave Quinn a steely look. "Maybe because of earthquake? Maybe because of those soldiers, that helicopter search you saw? Let us just be calm. No problem, Mr. Neil. I'm sure." Gelu gave Quinn another look that seemed to silently add the words, "For all our sakes, I hope."

Inside the building, they were all herded into a large waiting room and momentarily abandoned. Some of the team sat at the tables and chairs that dotted the room while others paced. All of them started grumbling.

Quinn tried to settle his clients, then turned to the window at the rear hoping that it was indeed going to be "no problem," as he looked out at Nepal on the other side of the ravine rising up in a steep wall of green foliage. It was zip-line close. Below the window a one-hundred-foot drop plummeted down onto the rocks and rapids of the torrential river that raced away beneath the high and suspiciously empty bridge.

No one is crossing, Quinn thought as a different team of border officials and soldiers entered the room making loud demands in Chinese. Gelu looked at Quinn, staring at him as he translated, "Everyone must put cameras, computers, and cellular telephones on the table." Heart lurching at the unexpected instructions, Quinn stepped back tight against the window while others in the team grumpily got up from their chairs to reach into pockets and day-packs, intent only on doing as they were told and getting out of there as fast as possible.

The first devices handed over were collected up by border guards and taken to a white-shirted Chinese technician who plugged the first into an electronic monitor. Quinn watched him almost instantly begin to scroll a button on his keyboard and pull his face close to the screen. It was clear that the man was scanning the contents. The technician quickly repeated the process on the next cellphone.

Noticing Quinn make no move toward his day-pack or his pockets, one of the soldiers gestured that he too should come forward and put what he had on the table, stabbing at the surface with a finger to demand he hurry it up. Quinn just shook his head in return, trying, nonchalantly, to indicate that he didn't have anything despite the incriminating weight of his phone multiplying in the right cargo pocket of his trousers with every passing second.

The young soldier, immediately sensing a challenge, pushed toward Quinn gesturing for the Englishman to raise his arms to be searched. Gelu quickly and deliberately inserted himself between them to offer the soldier his own old clamshell cell just as the first devices to be analyzed were returned to the table.

Big Al, the Cockney, reached for his Samsung, saying loudly, "That one's mine, mate." The soldier intent on Quinn would not be deterred.

He pushed past Gelu to get at the Englishman just as a huge roar of "What the fucking hell?" made everyone in the room jump.

"Those fucking bastards have wiped my sodding phone." The big Londoner continued to shout as he looked at the screen of his smartphone. "Everything's been deleted!"

Hearing this the Norwegian, Rasmussen, instantly leapt for the table. With both hands he grabbed his precious camera like a loose ball. Hugging it to his chest, he turned and said loudly, "My photos! No bloody way, man!" Other soldiers immediately pushed through the climbing team to take Rasmussen's camera from him. Tightly wound at best, it was the last straw for the miserable Viking who went completely berserk. He began to swear and shout, dodging and weaving, kicking and punching out wildly. Tables and chairs went flying and equipment smashed to the floor as all the soldiers tried and failed to corral the raging Norwegian. There was a distinctive popping sound from somewhere beyond the doorway and a green metal canister arced into the center of the room spewing vapor like a small rocket. The grenade clattered onto the floor to spin violently, releasing a cloud of tear gas into the enclosed area. Coughing and choking people began to scramble for the door or toward the windows.

Quinn opened the window he was standing at and forced his head out to escape the caustic fumes. Squeezing his streaming eyes to some semblance of focus, he quickly pulled his cellphone from his pocket. His fingers raced to send a message while he locked himself rigid against the window frame, his upper body sticking out over the ravine until it showed as sent.

When two masked soldiers grabbed at his jacket to pull him back inside, Quinn dropped his phone into the raging waters far below and didn't resist. Moved into another room, the soldiers emptied his pockets but found only a wallet and a small fabric toy of a once white horse. They looked at both items suspiciously but found nothing more.

28

RICKSHAW RACE

SUKHRA PATH, KATHMANDU, NEPAL

Balkumar, the newsagent, resembled an aged owl. Huge black-framed bottle-bottomed glasses dominated his wizened triangular face to look out from within the fan of newspapers and magazines that surrounded his tiny hole-in-the-wall shop. The moment Henrietta exited the front door of her building and looked across at him, the magnified eyes blinked in return and slowly lifted a copy of the *Kathmandu Times* to his left where he clipped it to his display frame with three binder clips.

She saw them immediately. Three Asians sat at a front table of the café two doors down. Each was wearing mirrored glasses. Henrietta tutted at the cliché and looked instead to the already busy roadway as one of the men saw her. He spoke to the others then got up as another began tapping into his smartphone. Somewhat theatrically, Henrietta just raised a hand to hail a bicycle rickshaw despite a number of faster taxis passing by. Stepping up onto the ripped bench seat behind the skinny rider, she took in the man's sticklike legs, totally at odds with his faded green T-shirt that showed an image of the Incredible Hulk. She told herself he was perfect as he set off with all the force of a broken-shelled snail rather than a green man-mountain, his thin body straining, the pedals clanking, one back wheel squeaking with every slow revolution. In her makeup mirror Henrietta watched as a second rickshaw bearing the Asian who had got to his feet settled in some distance behind. She tried to amuse herself with the absurdity of the chase even if she couldn't deny a concern that the Chinese must have already picked up her contact with the masked figure. She quickly focused her attention on asking a question of the rickshaw man, and when he replied affirmatively, she wrote a note on a piece of paper as the contraption clattered on, to the thought that she really did miss the old days. Things had gotten so quick, however much she might try to slow them down.

Arriving in the narrower streets of the Thamel tourist district, Henrietta was relieved to see that, despite the early hour, they were already busy. Young backpackers, white-haired boomers, delivery boys, street kids, touts, and shop owners all crowded the roads and pavements as the bright store lights burned and competing loud music thumped. When the rider turned a tight corner into another equally crowded road that momentarily separated the two rickshaws, Henrietta quickly leaned forward and told him to stop. The man did so with immediate relief as Henrietta paid with a single five-hundred rupee bill tightly folded around the small note she had written. Without waiting for any change, she stepped down quickly into the bustle of the Mandala Street market. The rickshaw man glanced at the note, smiled at the money, and wrenched up what remained of the fabric roof of his rickshaw despite the clear, powder-blue sky overhead. Ignoring another tourist seeking a ride, he slowly peddled away.

Henrietta ducked down slightly and walked directly into a melee of people as she put on a purple paisley silk headscarf she took from within her sleeve. With a glimpse backward, she saw the Asian man now standing up on the back of his rickshaw trying to locate the other rickshaw. Before she had even entered the more crowded Sagarmatha Bazaar she knew she had lost him.

Amateur.

Not looking back again, she quickly turned another corner and stepped into the Sunrise Café with a nod to the manager. She had known Kami Sherpa since he was a boy and his father had been one of the leading

Everest Sherpa alongside the place's owner, Temba Chering. "The usual, Kami," she said as he grinned at her in welcome.

Together they briskly walked past the crowded tables of the dining area and through a swing door into the equally crowded kitchen. There, Kami offered her a flask of tea as they squeezed between busy cooks and waiters to arrive at a side door that the Sherpa took out a big bunch of keys to unlock. The door swung open onto an embroidery sweatshop lined with young men and women hunched over big gray sewing machines. With a quick thank-you to the Sherpa, Henrietta walked down the center of the long room, many pairs of brown eyes looking up from the multi-colored ones they were sewing into T-shirts as they watched her pass. Over the clatter of their machines, she knocked on another door at the very end, three times.

It opened immediately.

"Miss Richards," a welcoming voice said.

Sangeev Gupta read Henrietta's handwritten memorandum of her meeting with the climber Lady Huang Hsu carefully. The report was long but the copperplate conclusion brief:

Attempt unsuccessful.

The Indian had worked with Henrietta long enough to immediately understand the significance of this rejection. There were few records left in Himalayan mountaineering that really caught the media's attention. Huang, as potentially the first woman to climb all fourteen eight-thousand-meter peaks, was laying claim to one of the biggest. This was going to be a tricky one.

Opening the laptop to log on and begin the expedition write-up, Gupta reminded himself to first find out where the Snowdonia Ascents team would be staying to get that task out of the way. It was usually the Khumbu Hotel, but as he looked for his cellphone to call and verify, he fell temptation to first open his own email. Seeing only junk, he quickly switched to the daily news and clicked on the lead story about the Durbar

Square immolation. Before his finger had even released pressure from the mouse, he sensed he had made a mistake.

The screen froze and turned black.

The black changed to scarlet.

Cats began to multiply across the screen in a golden wildfire.

"Shit!" Gupta cursed as he stabbed at the computer's power button, holding it down until its chorus of "I should be so lucky" was silenced, the screen dead.

Recovering his breath, he hoped to Shiva that the Lucky Cat virus was just being run as interference on the immolation story rather than complete infection. He had too much work to do to lose a day sorting it out. Anxious, he prepared to turn the laptop back on, readying himself to switch it to safe mode as fast as he could. He took a deep breath and lifted his finger but hesitated at the sound of a knocking on the front door. With a sigh, Gupta got up from his desk to see who it was.

Walking toward the front door he wondered if Henrietta had changed her mind about not needing her phone. He slowed, faintly panicked at the thought that she might need him to look up something on his frozen computer.

The knocking resumed, growing impatient.

"Hold on. I'm coming," he said aloud as he reached for the lock.

The second he opened it, the door slammed back into his face. The square edge of heavy wood struck his cheek, the force flinging him to the floor. Sangeev Gupta's world immediately went dark just as if someone had hit his "off" switch.

⚜

"Morning tea?" Henrietta asked as she entered the small and simple barbershop.

"Of course. I have just shut up shop as your rickshaw man's note suggested," Pashi replied while he finished turning down the grimy venetian blinds on his street-facing windows and glass door.

He returned to switch on a single fluorescent strip-light that reluctantly buzzed and clicked into life to harshly illuminate the small shop.

At its center a single chrome and black-leather barber's chair looked into a large cracked mirror over an ancient basin. To each side, the wooden shelves were scattered with narrow bladed scissors, cut-throat razors, shaving soap, and shampoos. Around the mirror were several photographs of ridiculous men's hairstyles from the 1970s. All the shop's remaining wall space was covered with postcards, stickers, pennants, and other mementos from nearly forty years of Himalayan mountaineering.

Pashi Bol, the barber, was a legend amongst the climbers who came through the city, and had been cutting their hair and massaging sense back into their heads after big climbs for longer than even Henrietta had been checking their facts. A charming gossip worthy of his trade, the little man knew as much about what was going on in the mountains and on the streets of Kathmandu as did Henrietta. They would often compare notes over cups of milky chai from Kami Sherpa's ever-ready flask, particularly at times of crisis. As usual, Henrietta poured and they each took a cup to sit on the row of waiting chairs that lined the shop's back wall, conspiratorially side by side.

"So, Pashi, what are you hearing?"

"That Lady Huang Hsu is very mad at you, Miss Richards," the little barber replied.

"Of course she is, but we all know the rules. To claim a summit you have to both set foot on it and also prove to me that you did. She did neither."

Henrietta sipped her tea as if nothing more needed be discussed on that subject but Pashi continued, "I know, but she is crazy woman, Miss Richards. All the Sherpa say it."

"They say that of me also," Henrietta replied with a smile.

"They do not. You have done much for them and they love you very much. You are their White Tara, their protector spirit in Kathmandu. It is Huang that is the mad, angry one. I know you have heard also the stories of how she treats them.

"The world record for first woman to climb all the eight-thousand-meter peaks is very important to her. It would make her a famous celebrity in Taiwan. Her country would get behind it much more than others just to be poking the finger at China if you see what I mean. You need to be careful with her, Miss Richards."

"I note what you say, Pashi. Now what about what happened last night at the Kumari Jatra?"

"With that you should be even more careful."

"Why?"

"I understand that you met the man before he burned."

Pashi's answer shocked Henrietta.

"Who told you that? Have the Chinese been asking after me already?"

"Yes, Miss Richards. I am told that they are furious about what happened and are using all their sources in the city, putting pressure on everyone, to find out who was involved. A detective I know—a good man—called and said that someone from Lhasa is now handling the matter. He said it was the one known in Tibet as 'Yama.'"

Henrietta had heard the Sherpa mention such a man in the past. "Really?"

"Yes. The detective told me that Yama was following the man," Pashi continued, "and that they have film of him meeting you in Durbar Square."

"Do they indeed. Did this Yama say who it was?"

"No, only that it was a ghost he was following. Do you know who it was?" Pashi asked directly.

"Possibly, but it makes absolutely no sense. Did anyone recognize the man after the fire?"

"No. He disappeared."

"Sorry, but what did you say?"

"In the chaos after, the burner vanished. Maybe he really was a spirit, a tulpa as some people are saying."

"Hmm," Henrietta said trying to process what she was hearing. "What did you make of the moth symbol on the banner, Pashi?"

Unusually for the most talkative man in Kathmandu, Pashi paused before he answered and, angling his head, looked back at her with a faint smile as if spotting a bluff in a poker game.

"Ghost moth sign, Miss Richards. I only ever hear about a long time ago. Not now."

"And?"

"Secret persons that help Tibet when we were both young . . ." He hesitated before adding, "To be honest I am little surprised that you ask me."

"Why would that be, Pashi?"

"Well . . . you know."

"No, Pashi, I don't know. What?"

"Your friend Christopher Anderson."

"Go on."

"Was he not a Ghost Moth?"

The truth in the answer to his question made Henrietta shiver. "What are you talking about?"

"Yes, I once heard that Christopher Anderson and some other climbers work to help the Tibetans against Chinese. They call themselves the Ghost Moths. All dead now. I always think you must know because he your very good friend, but old days, private stuff, so I not mention then or now. But please be careful, Miss Richards." Pashi Bol gave Henrietta another long yet kindly look that was etched with concern. "Sometimes the past can also be a ghost that returns to haunt us."

"Indeed it can, Pashi," Henrietta said, getting up and walking to one of the walls from which she unpinned an old faded postcard. Taking a pen from her handbag, she wrote something on the back of the postcard and then pinned it back.

"Please be sure to give that card to Mr. Neil Quinn when he comes in for his next haircut. You are always his first stop when he gets back from a climb and I need to see him. Can you also call me a taxi?"

"I will."

"And, Pashi, for his eyes only. No peeking. I am a great believer that we can't be hurt by what we don't know."

The parting comment made Pashi quickly change his mind about reading the back of the card the second she left. Instead he just looked at the pinned image of the mountain of Makalu and wondered what she was up to.

29

STUPEFIED

BHOUDHANATH PLAZA, KATHMANDU, NEPAL

The taxi stopped with a skid on the dusty tarmac, inciting a fit of honking and shouting from the cars and buses behind, while a swarm of motorcycles laden with two or even three people refused to wait for a second, screaming their engines to pull around the stationary vehicle in clouds of oily smoke. The driver ignored the abuse as if deaf to point Beth to the Tibet Guest House on the other side of the road. "It is there," he said, seemingly excusing himself with a shrug from any U-turn to its door across such a violently busy road.

Beth, tired from her early start from Dharamsala and running to catch her flight change in New Delhi, and faintly nauseous from her first experience of Kathmandu traffic, insisted the driver make the turn by flashing him a look that could kill. She got her message across even if, for the next seconds, it was *she* that thought she was going to die as the old car lurched to the opposite curb between a volley of oncoming vehicles.

Once inside the hotel's quiet sanctuary, Beth quickly checked in to her room, washed her face to settle herself, then set off again with the address given to her by Wangdu Palsang for his best contact in the city. With a faintly wry smile, Wangdu had described Temba Chering as "famous in Kathmandu," a Tibetan exile who had worked on all the great mountains and used the money earned to amass a number of businesses including the Tibet Guest House where she was now staying. When he had left Beth at Kangra Airport first thing that morning to start her hastily organized journey, he had added enigmatically, "I am sure that Temba Chering will help you find the story you seek even if you do not yet know what it is."

At the lobby, Beth showed the address where she had been told to meet Chering and was pointed back across the road where an immense stupa pointed into the sky above the shops and buildings that lined the street. She quickly ran the dusty gauntlet of the road once more to enter the focal point of the Tibetan community in Kathmandu.

Inside, surrounded by hotels, workshops, stores, cafés, shrines, and monasteries, the otherworldly structure at their center awed Beth. The huge dome at its base resembled the back of a bleached whale, the white-washed plaster stained fatty yellow and sooty gray by the valley's polluted rain. Above, a deck of peeling painted eyes looked out over the surrounding city as if staring down the cardinals of the compass. A gilt spire rose above, seemingly tethered by bowed ropes of prayer flags to stop the entire rocket-like structure from blasting into the heavens.

Instinctively Beth joined the pilgrims and tourists already merged into a slow clockwise circumambulation of the monument. The faithful devotedly held out their right arms to turn the brass prayer drums set within the base of the Bhoudhanath Stupa, the tourists mimicking them as pecking pigeons competed for empty pavement in between. As she walked, Beth searched for Temba Chering's restaurant, the Blue Poppy.

Around her, over the chatter, the mumble of mantras, and the contradictory blasts of pop and meditation music from the surrounding shops and cafés, she heard the squawk and crackle of walkie-talkies. It was coming from the narrow side streets. Beth had reported on enough demonstrations in her career to understand what it signified. She glanced in on shadowed squads of mustering paramilitary police. Armored and helmeted like black beetles, a number held fire extinguishers, others long poles. Beth quickly understood the reason for those also. The ranks of the walkers around her began to tighten, the speed of their recitations and pacing increasing until, with some relief, Beth finally saw the bright blue painted sign of the restaurant. One of the burly Tibetans at the door seemed to almost pull her inside when she said her name and asked for the owner.

She was shown to a table and told to wait. And so she did.

Every time Beth inquired about Temba Chering the reply was that he was busy but that he knew she had arrived, and she should have what she liked from the menu in the meantime.

Still unsettled from her spontaneous and hectic journey from Dharamsala to Kathmandu and suppressing the thought that she had acted irrationally on little more than a whim—even if she was trying hard to professionally justify it as a "hunch"—she ordered only green tea and drank it watching the television mounted on the far wall cycle images of the immolation between rapidly talking heads she couldn't understand.

An hour passed then another, a palpable feeling of tension growing in the restaurant as a procession of young Tibetan men came and went from the plaza. When the last to come in said something urgent to the two toughs at the door, they immediately bolted it and just as quickly dropped the blinds of the restaurant before pulling heavy brocade curtains across the window openings.

A few minutes later an older Tibetan, equally as tough looking as the men on the door—but better dressed—entered the dining room from the rear and walked directly to Beth's table. Dispensing with any introduction the man, who she instantly knew to be Temba Chering, asked urgently, "Do you have a camera, Mrs. Waterman? And not a phone, I mean, a real camera with a bloody big lens?"

"Yes. I do. In here," Beth replied, a bit taken aback by the man's gruff manner. She patted the bag looped over her shoulder that contained her Nikon.

"Good. Then please get it out and follow me."

Temba quickly led Beth up through the building onto a rooftop terrace. As they walked to the edge to look down on the square, hundreds of pigeons exploded up into the air around them like ashes from an erupting volcano. Beth watched as black streams of police armed with shields and batons began to run into the main square below.

Groups of young men deliberately blocked their way. Some were instantly snatched by the police and pulled struggling back into side streets where windowless vans, rear doors gaping, waited. Others dodged the riot policemen's grasps to run or were aided by others to create struggling clots in the panicking crowd. More people began to run from the surrounding buildings to help them.

"Come on, photograph it!" Temba ordered, prompting a momentarily stunned Beth into action as sirens blared and people screamed.

The plaza below had become a melee. Beth's lens focused on a phalanx of young Tibetans storming through it to climb onto the base of the stupa where they raised the red, blue, and gold flag of their lost land. The long flexible pole began to sway defiantly as if orchestrating the chaos below.

Beth also photographed the reply: an armored police vehicle thundering into the plaza, lights and siren blazing. Piglike, it began pushing and boring through the crowd as bricks and roof tiles rained down from the surrounding buildings. Its water cannon began to hose the demonstrators, the force of the water flinging them to the ground or pinning them against walls. The cannon's aim raised to douse the flag bearers who lost their footing, slipping and sliding down the stupa's curved mound under the deluge. The flag fell.

Beth snapped picture after picture until Temba took a call on his cellphone. He reached across to lower Beth's camera arm.

"We have to go. We haven't got long."

The Tibetan quickly led Beth down and out through the back of his restaurant. At a run he almost dragged her up an empty cobbled alley to the entrance of what appeared to Beth to be a monastery building. There, two young, tall monks standing to the sides immediately opened the door at their approach. Inside, Temba raced on, twisting and turning through a maze of dark, narrow corridors, to finally arrive at another heavyset door. There he very deliberately slowed himself, took some deep breaths, and turned to look at Beth.

"Be warned. What you are about to see will not be easy, but you can and must photograph this as well."

He tapped on the door.

The bolted wood panel silently opened onto a shadowy room lit by butter lamps. The reflection of the tapering flames shimmered on varnished painted walls decorated with mountains that rose from green valleys and blue lakes to become immense triangular snow peaks. Puffy gray clouds surrounded their towering white summits, each one carrying the image of a deity. Beneath their many eyes, in the center of the room was a single bed on which a naked man was laid out. He was being tended by a group of nuns.

Temba seemed to almost push Beth forward to the foot of the bed. There her gaze met a pair of bloodshot eyes staring from within a raw face, more skull than visage. The body below was hideously burned, but in the half-light Beth could see that what little skin remained was totally tattooed.

The Tibetan moved forward to speak quietly to the man.

A slight gesture from the man's claw of a hand caused the nuns to step aside.

The bared teeth moved.

Through the wet wheezing of ruined lungs, Beth heard him say something to Temba in reply.

"He wants you to be the witness, to show the world how his journey ended here," Temba whispered to Beth as the burned man began to cough horribly, setting off spasms of agony. A yellow fluid spewed from his mouth.

"Be quick!" Chering demanded. "I think he is going soon."

Beth took a series of photographs as the nuns worked to ease the man's suffering. When the ruined body arched once more in extreme pain, the broken hand raised again. Its two remaining fingers pointed directly to the biggest of the wall's painted mountains. "Mount Ga San," the man seemed to utter in recognition then exhaled, hand falling, spirit finally released from the suffering.

30

REALPOLITIK

SUMMIT HOTEL, KUPONDOLE HEIGHT, KATHMANDU, NEPAL

Sir Jack Graham was at their usual table on the dining terrace that overlooked the Summit Hotel's luscious gardens, the heavy leaves below thicker and greener than any salad it served. To Henrietta's disappointment he was not alone. Anthony Green was also there, talking loudly into his cellphone, a copy of the *Kathmandu Post* in front of him. Her heart sank a little at the sight. There were things she had wanted to discuss only with Jack.

Sir Jack got up and saw her to her chair, mumbling "Sorry about this" under his breath. Henrietta sat, momentarily feeling a shiver of loneliness, and with it, recognizing properly, for the first time, the cold danger of her situation. Green didn't move but when he stopped his call, he did pointedly change a setting on his phone to demonstrate that he was going to give Henrietta his full attention. "Ms. Richards, I hope you don't mind me gate-crashing your little lunch with Sir Jack, but it seems I need a lesson on what is going on here somewhat sooner than I expected."

Henrietta knew she should have answered, "Not at all," but lying was not her strong point. Instead she busied herself with her napkin as Green pressed on regardless. "Last night turned out to be a veritable diplomatic shower."

"It was something more than just that," Henrietta immediately interjected. "It was both a tragedy and a horror."

"The Chinese delegation was indeed horrified," Green continued. "I had a number of commercial meetings with them scheduled for this morning. All canceled. Extremely disappointing."

"I'm so sorry to hear that," Henrietta replied swallowing her sarcasm to add, "But it is a sad and complex situation."

"Yes, and one that we need to sort out. Obviously, I can sympathize with any peoples that have a grievance over their land and freedoms but after sixty years surely it is time for the Tibetans to accept the reality and move on?" He drummed his finger on a picture of the Dalai Lama on the front page of the newspaper. "In my book it doesn't help matters that everyone still treats this fellow like some sort of celebrity guru. It just muddies the waters."

Henrietta looked momentarily at Sir Jack as if in advance apology then spoke again. "Time might well hide history but it does not erase it. May I remind you that not much more than ten years before the Chinese marched into Tibet, Hitler was studying Britain through a pair of field glasses from the coast of France. What if he had crossed? What if his successors were still there? How would you feel about it seventy years later? Would you be speaking English or German?" Henrietta was pretty sure she could answer the last question herself as Green just replied, "But I'm not sure we're talking about the same thing in any language, Ms. Richards."

"Tibet was invaded, the land stolen, the people decimated. Sounds somewhat similar to me."

Sir Jack, beginning to fidget in his chair, jumped on the arrival of a smiling waiter to ask if they could order, more plea for calm than question.

A silence followed as they chose. That done, Sir Jack quickly spoke again before Green could reopen his mouth.

"Henrietta, why don't you tell Anthony something of your background and a bit about the recent history of this region to get us all on the same page?"

Slowly, begrudgingly, Henrietta began to talk, telling how she had also been to Oxford University then came to Kathmandu in 1969 as a junior in the Foreign Office to help the British ambassador of the time deal with the influx of hippie travelers—many of them English—who were coming unstuck in the city from drugs or illness or lack of funds. Her other task at the embassy had been as an analyst assembling the information coming out of Tibet about Mao's China, of which, at that time, relatively little was known. That task had continued and grown after her work with the hippie tide receded. As the food arrived, she continued to explain how she had become fascinated with the region, becoming an expert on its many complexities for her career, and the leading record keeper of Himalayan climbing for her own interest.

When Green asked her which mountains she had climbed—as many did—and she replied none, he questioned why she was so interested in them.

"After the indulgence and wastefulness of the hippies I was constantly having to nanny, I found the climbers more interesting," she replied. "Also, in a region with so many dimensions to everything—the religions: Hinduism, Buddhism, the Jain, the Bon; the peoples: be it tribes, castes, migrants, refugees, rich, poor; the politics: monarchy, democracy, theocracy, communism; the external influences: China, India, America, England, Pakistan, Russia, Japan, all furiously playing the field—life for a diplomat was complicated. You must understand that Kathmandu is to the Himalayan frontiers what West Berlin was to the Cold War, Dubai now is to the Middle East; a natural 'neutral zone' where many factors of suspicion intersect. Amidst all this I liked to retire at the end of the day into the simple truth of whether someone really made it to the top of a mountain. I found it therapeutic, an escape into black-and-white truth from so many shades of gray."

Green eyed Henrietta coldly. "But all your mountains have been climbed, Ms. Richards. The monarchy is gone. The Maoist guerrillas have come in from the hills to democracy. Above all, China is now the dominant power in the region—perhaps soon the whole world, whatever everyone else might try to pretend. Surely we should just be practical and accept it? I can't help thinking that what we saw last night just prolongs the agony."

"Actually it is a product of it."

"Well, it needs to stop. I'm not here to play spy versus spy but to do business for our nation. It's plain and simple. Qualities you profess to admire." Green looked at Sir Jack as if for support. "China is the future, am I not right, Sir Jack? Think of the Silk Road Economic Belt from Xinjiang to Europe, the China–Pakistan Economic Corridor, the Asian Infrastructure Investment Bank, I could go on. Each one in itself is a colossal opportunity that Team UK should seize. We must be pragmatic and not assist anything that might hinder this, particularly some bankrupt Tibetan exiles"—his eyes narrowed a little—"still intent on trouble after all these years."

"I wouldn't call it trouble," Henrietta answered.

"Well, Ms. Richards, you can call it what you want but your Tibet of *Lost Horizon* flew in 1959 alongside the Dalai Lama. The Chinese are just waiting for him to go—how old is he now? Eighty? Eighty-five? It won't be long and then they can move on. I think it's time for you to move on also, to leave the theatricals of the Free Tibet charade to the Hollywood luvvies and embrace the realpolitik. It doesn't suit someone with your intelligence."

"Well, it suits my sense of propriety," Henrietta replied. She knew Green was going to speak German sooner or later.

Beth Waterman sat across the table in Temba's office sipping a glass of water.

"I am sorry, Mrs. Waterman, that you had to see that," Chering said, "but Wangdu Palsang said you were looking for an important story after the cancellation of your article about His Holiness. Now you have two. Bhoudhanath has been our place in Kathmandu ever since the first Tibetan traders arrived here from the east over a thousand years ago. Today our hosts are pressured and bribed by the Chinese to reject that history and treat us like criminals. As for the burned man, you must be the witness he wanted you to be. He knew he was at the end of his road and wanted his last act to be a statement to the whole world. Please use your words and photographs to honor his last wish."

"Who was he?"

"Just a simple wandering monk, that's all."

"But it is not that simple. Why did he display the moth symbol on his sign?" Beth asked directly.

Temba Chering's look hardened as he replied, "Wangdu warned me that you would come looking for stories of missing lamas and mountain myths but, Mrs. Waterman, I urge you to deal with what you saw outside in the plaza and inside the monastery. A journalist of your reputation should focus on these realities. Those are your stories right there. Surely they are enough?"

One of Temba's staff came in and said something in his ear. "Detective Thanel, did you say?" he asked and instantly stood up.

"Yes," the staff member replied.

"Okay, I'm coming."

Chering took his leave of Beth. "Would you please give me a moment, as I have the police waiting for me downstairs. I think we should change where you are staying. Things are clearly going to remain difficult around here for some time. I own another place called the Khumbu Hotel in the Thamel district. It's popular with Western tourists and climbers and you'll be more at home there. I'll see that it is organized."

Temba exited quickly with the staff member leaving Beth in his office. While she sat waiting alone once again, she looked at the wall behind his desk covered with framed certificates and photographs of her host. Some were recent shots of him with dignitaries and politicians but the older ones were taken in the mountains, either in summit shots or standing with other climbers. Those pictures were getting old, the colors faded, the paper rippled. Beth got up from her chair to look at them all more closely.

Something caught her eye in one framed photo of a younger, thinner faced Temba arm in arm with a group of climbers in bulky old-fashioned down clothes. Their wild hair and heavily tanned faces, panda-eyed from ski masks, suggested they had just finished a big climb together, the elation in their eyes that it had been successful.

She pulled her face close to be sure of what she was seeing, then quickly took her own photograph of the picture. Hearing Temba return she let her camera fall on its strap even if she continued to look at the pictures as he reentered the room. "Wangdu said you were once a Sherpa, Temba?"

"The Sherpa are a tribe, Mrs. Waterman. It is not a temporary condition even if the term has become a byword for anyone who works on the highest mountains. I am actually what is known as a Bhotia, a Tibetan. I escaped to the Khumbu Valley as a youth and grew up working the same mountains I had to cross to get away. First, I was a porter on the valley trails, little more than a human yak, but then I began to carry onto the mountains assisting climbers. It was hard and dangerous, but I survived to invest the money I earned and do everything in my power to ensure that my children would not have to do as I had done. My eldest son is now a doctor, the younger, a pilot, and I remain grateful to the mountains, to Kathmandu also for permitting that. You will need to go now."

"Temba, did you ever climb Mount Ga San?"

"There is no such mountain here, Mrs. Waterman."

Chering gave Beth a long look and wondered whether Dharamsala might have underestimated the American journalist but, then again, if she had met His Holiness that was unlikely, quite the opposite in fact.

At the door of the restaurant Temba Chering spoke to one of the many policemen that was surrounding the now empty plaza. He returned to Beth to say, "I have told him you are a frightened American tourist who was having coffee at our restaurant when the riot broke out. He is going to escort you back to the Tibet Guest House. Keep your camera out of sight. A room awaits you at the Khumbu."

Back at the hotel Beth checked out and got a taxi to Thamel. Only when she was safely in the back of the cab did she get out her camera again. She scrolled the photographs to one she had taken in Temba's office. She enlarged it to show the embroidered badges affixed to the jacket of one of the climbers.

I am right, Beth thought.

Retrieving her broken phone, she searched for "Mount Ga San."

Immediately she was redirected to a "Mount Gassan."

Temba is also right.

Mount Gassan was not in the Himalayas. It was in Japan. Not a particularly high mountain, but still a famous one in its own way. Beth read as much as she could find about it before returning to the photograph on her camera and studying the Japanese flag amongst the other badges on that jacket and then the youthful, happy face above.

Green's phrase "Team UK" was stuck in Henrietta's craw as the taxi's radio rattled with news of a major riot and police roundup at Bhoudhanath Stupa. Henrietta knew damn well who was behind it, but as she lifted the key to the front door of her apartment she tried to settle with the thought that she was home—a good cup of tea beckoned—and had at least achieved the principle objective of her trip out; she better understood the playing field. Now she needed to see Neil Quinn. She was hoping that Sangeev would have left her news of his return and got a message to him. If not, the card she had marked at Pashi's should do the trick.

About to slot her door-key home, she did a double take. Her heavy apartment door was already slightly ajar. Cautiously, she gave it a push with the tip of her still outstretched key, inquiring as she did so, "Sangeev?"

The door swung back to reveal a scene of devastation.

Her beloved apartment had been ransacked. Torn books, emptied loose-leaf files, ripped papers were strewn everywhere. Plates, glasses, teacups, potpourri dishes, pictures, even her potted plants lay splintered and smashed. A smell of dry lavender and wet earth hung over the wanton destruction—in the middle of which lay Sangeev Gupta, facedown on the floor, her cat curled in the small of his back.

A horrific thought struck Henrietta. She knelt beside her assistant to find his pulse. Bodleian woke with a start and darted away, but Gupta was alive. With some difficulty Henrietta turned him over. The side of his face was swollen with deep bruising, the skin of his cheek broken and bloody. She gently shook him and Sangeev seemed to surface from a great dark depth. She helped him sit forward and waited for him to recover his senses.

"I'm sorry, Miss Richards," he eventually mumbled.

"Don't be. Just tell me what happened."

"I was on the computer when there was an attack . . . Lucky Cat."

Henrietta took a look at Bodleian who had now returned to patrol the damage, long legs delicately placing his paws between the debris as if it was a minefield.

"Oh, don't worry about him. He's fine."

"No, Miss Richards, 'Lucky Cat,' the Chinese computer virus. You know it. The virus took over my laptop when I tried to access news of last night's horrible event. I was dealing with the matter when there was a knock at the door. I was thinking perhaps you needed something but instead the door just slammed me. Then I'm gone and dreaming. Now everything is ruined."

"I'll get you some water. Stay there."

While Henrietta searched for an intact glass in the kitchen she remembered the two other Asian men at the café below. They must have remained when the other set off after her that morning. She had shaken that one off so easily she hadn't given the matter further thought other than later reconciling the surveillance with Pashi's comment that the Chinese were asking after her.

She returned to help Sangeev into a chair, administering small sips of water. "Did you notice anything about your attacker?" she asked.

"No. Nothing. I'm sorry."

"When did this happen?"

"Not so long after you left." Sangeev's eyes watered as he considered the destruction. "I am so very sorry for this mess."

His apology caused Henrietta to also look around at her life's work, shredded and scattered. She had a feeling she too should cry but it just didn't come. Instead all she heard was Green saying, "But all your mountains have been climbed, Ms. Richards." A rare fury spiked inside her, sharp and high like the peaks she studied. "Shouldn't we call the police?" Sangeev asked.

Henrietta looked to the sideboard where the apartment telephone normally sat. The phone had been ripped from the wall, the receiver smashed to pieces.

"Did you plug in my cellphone?" she asked.

"Yes."

Sangeev looked over at his small work area but there was no laptop or cellphone to be seen.

"It has been taken. Everything has been taken."

Henrietta instantly left the Indian to return to her kitchen. Stepping over more broken crockery and scattered cutlery she stiffly bent down in front of her oven. On the tiled floor before it she saw the moth from the night before, stamped to death. She quickly opened the oven and looked into its black mouth. At the back remained her equally black tin chest and, on top of it, the Makalu file. She breathed a sigh of relief when she opened the tin to also see the prayer wheel and the mala beads.

31

CHAMPAGNE TOAST

EMBASSY OF CHINA, HATTISAR SADAK, 615, KATHMANDU, NEPAL

"At our insistence the Nepali police have brought in some of the identified Tibetan activists but it seems they are saying nothing," Captain Zhang reported to Yama, who stood in the crowded room directing the operations.

"That will change when I get to speak to them," Yama replied before turning to another MSS agent. "Update me about the English lady."

"We know she was with the British ambassador and his replacement at lunch."

"What did they discuss?"

"We have the transcript taken through Green's cellphone. It seems only general matters. Nothing specific to last night's action or her possible involvement."

"What about her apartment?"

"Yes, we took a look," Zhang replied before adding, "but we were too late."

"What do you mean—'too late'?" Yama's eyes fixed on Zhang's.

"The place had already been turned over. Her assistant was unconscious on the floor. All IT and telephone equipment taken or destroyed."

"What about the prayer wheel she was given? I need to know where it is and why it was given to her."

"There was no sign of it but given the situation we left quickly."

"Who did it? The SSB?"

"The assistant is Indian so it's possible. We shall know soon as we are tracking the lady's cellphone. If it is turned on we will know immediately."

Almost as the words were said a Section 17 team member approached Captain Zhang.

"The Richards phone has been reactivated. Please come with me."

The woman led the two agents to her work area.

"Where?" Yama demanded.

"Here." Her finger pointed to a red dot on the city map displayed on the screen. A data box next to it read: *The Regency Plaza Hotel.*

"Okay. Let's go."

The trilling doorbell ripped into the hotel suite's excited conversation and laughter. Hsiao Teng, Lady Huang's manager, jumped to his feet in order to receive the champagne ordered to toast his lover's success.

The Taiwanese entrepreneur opened the door with an exaggerated flourish to let in a man in a dark suit pushing a silver trolley. Head down, the black-haired man wheeled in a bucket of ice with a penitent bottle of Dom Perignon.

At the magnum's arrival, Lady Huang looked up from the cluster of laptops arranged on the coffee table where they had been working. "Now we celebrate!" she said loudly to Hsiao in Taiwanese Hokkien. "Not only is my story that I am the first woman in the world to climb all the eight-thousand-meter peaks released to the media but that old bitch Henrietta Richards is going to be so tied up in bullshit she won't have a moment to contradict it. As a bonus, those Communist bastards on the Chinese mainland are going to have some explaining to do. Fuck them all! Let's drink to a triple success!" She stabbed a finger toward the suited man, ordering in English, "Boy, open that champagne!"

Upon her command, the man deftly swiveled the trolley around to pull the bottle's jade neck from the ice. For a moment, the magnum hung heavily as the man straightened to stare at Huang, black eyes drilling into her face, a thought coursing the mind behind.

"Get on with it!" Hsiao shouted, stepping toward the man and reaching for the champagne himself. "You don't keep a climbing superstar waiting for a second."

In less than the aforementioned second the bottle swung up in a perfect arc, a green and gold mace that curved into the side of Hsiao's unsuspecting head. Glass, bubbles, and blood exploded across the room.

Hsiao fell, instantly lifeless.

Huang Hsu screamed and leapt to her feet to dart toward the door of the suite's bedroom. Yama lunged after her, crossing the room in an instant to seize her. But Lady Huang was strong. Years of climbing the world's highest mountains had reinforced her small frame with muscles of steel. Like a wild cat, she pulled free from his grip on her robe, but then stumbled as she got free and slammed into the hotel room wall.

She spun around from the impact to meet her attacker head-on, punching, kicking, and screaming. Yama pulled the chair from a desk in the room and as if parrying the attack of a tiger used the four legs to drive her back against the wall.

Huang, momentarily pinned, smashed at the wood with her arms, but missed as one of Yama's hands pushed through to grab at her long black hair. Seizing her scalp, he pulled the chair away and then Huang after it. She fell hard onto the floor.

Yama fell on her, twisted her over, and with his knee across her chest, pinned her down and pushed her head back into the deep carpet. Lowering his mouth to her ear, he began to speak—first in Mandarin. "Do you hear me?"

Lady Huang struggled in a defiant response, drilling her heels against the floor and trying to scratch at her attacker but a suffocating pressure on her sternum from the knee and the squeeze of one of Yama's hands on her neck subdued her.

"I said, 'Do you hear me?'" Yama repeated but this time in Taiwanese. Huang fell still.

"Good. So we can begin."

Yama leaned in closer. His lips opened and his teeth closed on Huang's ear. He bit, hard, smothering her piercing scream with his other hand. Pulling his mouth away, he spat and said, "So you like things that come in threes, do you? Why don't I tell you a story of a triple success." He stopped to spit some more and clear his mouth in order to continue.

"There were once three fish in a lake. One was a very big fish. Another was very rich. The third, so pretty and vain, was, in fact, just like you.

"Despite all three being important fish in the lake, each thought those waters were not enough—too poor, too dirty, too ugly. For them, only the great ocean would do. So the three swam free. But they didn't get far.

"The big one was caught first and slowly eaten to the bone. The rich one was returned to live in a brightly lit aquarium and its golden scales were slowly picked away. Only the pretty one remained out there in that great ocean, but surrounded by sharks, it could never go far."

Yama bit on the ear again.

Huang kicked her feet against the carpet in agony.

"Doesn't taste like Tibet or Hong Kong. No this is Taiwanese fish, always a favorite for sharks or, should I say, *mainland Communist bastards* like me. So let's start with you telling me why you have the English lady's computer and telephone?"

"Fuck you!" Huang replied.

Above Yama's face locked, and he unleashed an onslaught of violence until, finally broken, Huang began to slowly talk.

It didn't save her, not at all.

Captain Zhang stood over a senior Section 17 team member who was working on the array of laptop and phones arranged on a desk in the hotel room covered in plastic sheeting. Around the suite an MSS cleanup team was at work.

"Quickly, Zhang," Yama said to the captain. "The Taiwanese said she had released a film to the media that they found on the Englishwoman's computer, a film that would screw her and us. I need to see it immediately."

Zhang spoke to the Lucky Cat, whose hands connected the laptops and the cellphones to his own unit as fast as they could move. In a matter of seconds they were all watching a video clip of a ghostly black shadow looming from dense cloud.

Yama immediately dismissed it, ordering they show the next video clip. The analyst's hands danced again on the keyboard then a new video began.

This time a Tibetan ran and fell riddled with automatic rounds. Two others were forcibly bundled into a helicopter that rose and receded into the distance. Dark shadows, visibly human bodies, rained down as it left.

"Stop!" Yama ordered. "Replay that."

He watched the video again as the analyst said, "The Taiwanese released that video about thirty minutes ago. They did it through the laptop stolen from Henrietta Richards under her name."

"Can you stop it?"

"Too late if it has already been seen by a recipient. We can however run obstruction," he replied.

"Do it now!" Yama ordered, then made a call to the Hattisar facility demanding they repeat the previous evening's wider media suppression and power-cut protocols. He turned his attention back to the room. "Was the man who burned the source of that film? I know he was there in that valley. Is that what was transferred to the English lady?"

Zhang and the analyst conferred until the captain said, "No, it seems it was sent to her by someone else, the same person who sent her the previous film of the black ghost in the clouds."

"Who?"

"A man named Quinn. He sent it to her this morning. It was in an email that contained just the film."

"Tell me more about this man."

The analyst ran a data-search, Zhang verbally summarizing the details that appeared on the screen.

"Chinese Mountaineering Association records have him as an English mountain climber that works on expeditions in the Himalayas. Neil Quinn is his full name. He has climbed Qomolangma many times and, I see, was

189

once banned from climbing in our territory for violating border formalities. Only recently reinstated."

"Why was he banned?"

"It seems that he crossed into Nepal via the summit of Qomolangma without the correct CMA authorizations."

Zhang skim-read a single page summary report.

"It seems that he was also involved in some sort of Free Tibet protest that led to the arrest of the climbing team that remained on our side of the mountain."

He stopped and put a finger to the screen in identification.

"One of those also listed as arrested was the English lady Henrietta Richards, who was visiting the Rongbuk camp at the time. They were all released without charges following intervention of the British, German, and American embassies in Beijing."

"When was that?"

"Two thousand and eleven. More recent records document him entering our territory to climb the mountain of Xixabangma Feng on the fourth of September of this year and exiting through Xangmu today. There was a minor incident at the border involving one of his clients that resulted in payment of a fine of ¥50,000 before they were permitted to leave to return to Kathmandu."

"Get this cleanup finished," Yama replied, "then run further interference through the Nepali authorities that the Englishman killed these two for releasing spy-film stolen from one of his group. I am going to speak with the old lady myself to find out what she was really given by the man who burned."

32

KHUMBU CLIMBERS
KHUMBU HOTEL, THAMEL, KATHMANDU, NEPAL

Looking out between the peeling expedition stickers that covered the side window of the hotel lobby, Beth watched a group of climbers step down from a dusty minivan as two Sherpa began unloading their rucksacks from the rear doors. Soon after, the ramshackle band entered the hotel; just as hairy, hollow-eyed, and sunburned as the climbers in the photograph Beth had taken at Temba Chering's but with none of the elation in their eyes. This bunch just looked worn out and miserable.

A tall bearded man appeared to be leading them and spoke in an English accent to another with a badly bruised face equal to her own from the attack in Dharamsala. "Look, Rasmussen, we're back," he said with obvious exasperation. "You may not have your bloody photographs but tonight you will have a comfortable hotel room rather than a Chinese prison cell so you should count yourself lucky. Take your key and go."

"Bloody bad, Neil Quinn. You know? Just bloody, bloody bad," the man grumbled as he walked away to the elevator, dragging his half empty rucksack along the floor behind him like a dead dog.

The Englishman quickly distributed the other keys, spoke briefly to the two Sherpa who had come in with them, then detoured to the small hotel bar alone.

Beth took her chance and immediately approached the Sherpa. Getting out her camera, she asked, "Can you help me?"

The older Sherpa, seeing the camera, immediately turned away from Beth to engage in a conversation with the hotel receptionist who, as they spoke, began to produce copies of the days' newspapers from beneath the reception desk, her finger pointing to the horrific photographs on the front covers. Seeing the images, the Sherpa began to quickly question the receptionist in his own language then, taking one of the newspapers, also went into the bar.

Beth pushed herself in front of the younger Sherpa. The sight of her bulky camera also seemed to set off a look of panic in his eyes. "No photo, please, miss," he said raising a bandaged arm before his face to block any attempt at a picture. Hoping to reassure him, Beth let the camera hang heavily on its strap, held up her own hands to show they were empty, and tried a different tack. "No. No. I don't want your photo. Just your help." She pointed into the bar. "Who is that man?"

"That is Mr. Neil Quinn. Our expedition leader," Nima replied.

"Does he know a lot about climbing?" Beth made a show of twisting the high-definition screen on the back of the body of her Nikon toward Nima to show the image it displayed. "Would he know who the people in this photograph are?"

Nima peered close then seemed to swallow. Giving Beth a quick sideways look he began to speak to his colleague in Sherpali as he saw him exiting the bar. The older Sherpa shook his head and they both left the hotel to join a bigger group of their countrymen standing next to the minivan and to enter into their seemingly agitated conversation.

Left alone in the lobby, Beth entered the hotel bar to approach the Englishman instead. Perched on a barstool, he was drinking a neat double whiskey and looking at the front page of the *Kathmandu Times* in silence. Even though it was partially hidden by his long hair, Beth noticed that the man's left ear was covered with medical dressing. In his left hand he was squeezing some form of grubby stress toy as he read intently. When she neared, the man let go of whatever it was and raised his glass to suddenly gulp down half of the drink. He visibly shuddered.

"Terrible images, aren't they?" Beth said gently, starting a conversation.

"Yes," Quinn replied, more to himself, lost in the newsprint.

"It happened last night at a festival," she continued.

"Yes, they just told me. The Kumari Jatra."

"The man—well, I assume it was a man—was supporting Tibet and the Dalai Lama. You can make out his sign amidst the flames."

Beth's finger stretched forward to the main photograph of the broadsheet, the tip resting just above the sign's moth symbol to draw Quinn's eyes once again to one of things in the image that had shocked him most: that same symbol he had seen on the empty kitbag in the destroyed camp.

"Bad day on Mount Everest?" Beth continued with her best smile. "Painful?" she said, pointing to his ear and pulling him from his thoughts.

The gentle question thawed Quinn a little. He looked back at Beth to notice that her own face was also scratched and bruised but said only, "Shaving cut."

Distracted again by the newspaper's horrific photograph, he added almost involuntarily, "And no, actually—not Everest this time—just a hellish journey back from another mountain But really . . . compared to . . ." He stopped, the sentence uncompleted, the Englishman lost in contemplation of such a horrible death.

"Which one was it? Mount Gassan?"

Quinn looked up at the attractive woman quizzically. "Sorry, you've lost me there. Mount what?"

"Oh, just another mountain I was reading about. Which one were you just on?"

"Shishapangma in Tibet. It's a big mountain, over eight thousand meters, but it's not Everest."

"How was it?"

"The climbing was the easy part," Quinn said, draining the rest of the whiskey in memory of its difficult aftermath.

"Can I offer you another? It looks like you might need it."

"I do. Thanks."

Beth signaled to the barkeep to refill Quinn's glass.

"Do you know much about the history of Himalayan climbing?"

"A little, it's said."

"Would you be able to tell me who the people are in this old photo-graph?"

Beth showed Quinn the screen of her camera. He looked at the group picture and instantly recognized the veteran Sherpa Temba Cher-ing with a group of mountaineers. As he looked at it she expanded the picture so that he could see each one of them in detail. The sight of one of them was just too much of a coincidence.

Quinn looked back at her a moment too long just to say, "No, sorry."

Beth saw the same look in his eyes that she had seen in those of the younger Sherpa; a mixture of recognition and shock.

"Oh well, no problem. It was worth a try," she continued as breezily as she could. "My taxi-driver told me that there is an English lady here in Kathmandu called Henrietta Richards who knows everything about the mountains and the famous climbers. He said that I should speak to her. Do you know her?"

"Vaguely," Quinn obfuscated further.

"Do you think she would help me?"

"Possibly," he muttered in reply, telling himself that if anyone needed to see Henrietta it was him. Downing the second whiskey, he got up to leave. "Look, thanks for the drink and I'm sorry I can't help you any more, Miss . . . ?"

"Waterman. My name is Beth Waterman. I'm a journalist."

Of course you are, Quinn thought, *quite a pushy one judging by the bruises and the questions,* but, telling himself to be cool, asked instead, "American?"

"Yes."

"Great. I've climbed a bit in Alaska. Rode a motorcycle around Colo-rado once. Are you here to report on what happened last night?"

"No," Beth said, looking carefully at the Englishman. "I'm not really sure why I'm here actually."

The Englishman smiled back at her.

"Well, I'm sure you'll work it out. I must go now. Good luck with your inquiries."

Gelu reappeared at the bar door just as Quinn was leaving. With an outstretched hand he beckoned Quinn urgently back into the lobby where, under his breath, he said, "Mr. Neil, big problem."

"What is it now, Gelu?"

"Your film of the helicopter is being shown on KTV news."

"What?"

"Yes, and they are saying that Henrietta Richards released it."

"Jesus."

Abandoned at the bar, Beth looked down and saw at her feet the little mascot Quinn had been squeezing in his hand as he read the newspaper. It must have fallen as he hastily pocketed it and left. She quickly picked up the small white dog or horse—or whatever it was—and went out to the lobby to give it to him, but he and the Sherpa were already gone.

At the hotel desk she tried to get the attention of one of the two receptionists, but they were glued to a computer screen. One just said, "Yes," without looking up while the other leaned in to better hear the computer's small speakers as they buzzed with rapid-fire Nepali commentary.

"Excuse me, but have either of you heard of a lady in Kathmandu called Henrietta Richards?" Beth asked loudly.

Both faces instantly looked up in unison to say simultaneously and emphatically, "Yes," before they looked at each other in surprise.

"What is it?" Beth asked.

"Miss Richards is just now in the news," one observed tapping the screen with her finger.

"What do you mean?"

"Look at this."

The receptionist turned the computer screen toward Beth to show what they were watching. As the film played again, Beth asked, "Where is this?"

They double-teamed the reply.

"They are saying in Tibet."

"Near a famous mountain called Shishapangma."

Just as Beth recalled the same name from her conversation with the Englishman, there was a loud click and the power in the hotel went out. The image on the screen vanished. Outside, the city fell into darkness to a distant chorus of barking dogs.

33

EL ALAMEIN

BRITISH EMBASSY COMPOUND, LAINCHAUR, KATHMANDU, NEPAL

Sir Jack's wife, Betsy, cleared away the supper plates as Henrietta offered thanks once more for allowing her and Bodleian to stay the night.

"Don't mention it, Henrietta," she replied sympathetically. "The least we could do after such a rotten shock. You must stay as long as you want. I really don't know what is happening in this city these days. Shall I make us some much-needed tea?"

"Yes, thank you," Henrietta replied.

"We'll take it in the study, m'dear," Sir Jack said after his wife.

Together they walked to Sir Jack's study, part of which was given over to a large diorama depicting Montgomery's Eighth Army fighting Rommel's Afrika Korps at the battle of El Alamein. As they stood over the rolling desert of model tanks and troops, each one painted exquisitely, the pear-drop odor of new paint still hanging over them, they discussed the break-in once more.

"I'm sure it was the Chinese," Henrietta said. "Just before Sangeev was attacked that Lucky Cat virus of theirs swamped our laptop."

"How is Sangeev?" Sir Jack asked.

"He'll live, but he's badly shaken up. Also mortified at everything being stolen."

"Are you sure it wasn't just that—a robbery? There's a lot more crime in the city these days and those bloody viruses turn up all the time. Why do you think it must have been the Chinese? And if it was, why you?"

Henrietta was about to answer when the landline on the study desk rang loudly.

"You'll have to excuse me, Henrietta," Sir Jack said. "As the city's power and the digital networks are down again, I need to take that. It's on the embassy's loop so it'll be important. Sorry."

Sir Jack took the call, listening more than he spoke, then returned to Henrietta. "I'm afraid that was your new friend, Green. To compound the problems of last night's immolation and today's riot at Bhoudhanath, it now seems that KTV, amongst others, are circulating a film showing Chinese soldiers murdering Tibetans in the mountains. Which is all we bloody need and undoubtedly explains why the city's power has gone out again."

"It just gets worse."

"It does indeed, Henrietta." Sir Jack paused, a grave look creasing his already craggy face as he fixed his gaze on her. "Particularly because the newscasters are saying that you released the film as a protest against the Chinese in Tibet."

"What?" Henrietta questioned. "That's complete nonsense!"

"Are you sure?"

"Yes, of course! The only film I have even received lately was Neil Quinn's video of the Brocken specter on Shishapangma. We discussed it on the way to the Jatra. Don't you remember?"

"I do. Well evidently this film is no trick of the mountain light. It is an all too real clip showing a squad of the People's Armed Police—possibly one of their new Snow Leopard Commando Units—shooting a Tibetan nomad, then brutally arresting two others before throwing both the living and the dead from a flying helicopter as it leaves."

He hesitated for a moment.

"Henrietta, the film was identified from its encryption as having been taken near to the mountain of Shishapangma . . ."

"I . . . I . . . I don't . . . kn . . ." Henrietta stopped talking. She just looked at Sir Jack and struggled, through staggered seemingly useless breaths, to say, "This is a setup, Jack . . . This film . . . The break-in . . ."

"But it repeats the question, Henrietta: Why you?"

Henrietta paused before she could speak. "Jack . . . I can only tell you what I know so far."

"Well, you are going to need to do that."

"Okay but I need some water first. I'm not feeling too good."

Quinn arrived at Henrietta Richards's apartment building to find the door onto the street open. Blacked out like the rest of the city, the only light inside came from a low wattage emergency lighting system that lined the main staircase.

Despite the post-climb fatigue still in his legs, he took the stairs two at a time. He stopped at Henrietta's door and pressed the doorbell. It didn't ring.

Urgently he knocked instead. There was still no answer. Holding his head close to the wood to listen, he heard faint movement within as a slither of light at the foot of the door revealed itself by going out.

"Henrietta, it's Neil Quinn," he said quietly. "I can understand if you don't want to see anyone, but we need to talk."

The door clicked open.

Relieved Henrietta was there, Quinn stepped into the shadows of the apartment to the crunch of broken glass beneath his feet.

He stopped, still. Even in the gloom, he began to make out that Henrietta's apartment was in complete disarray, the furniture overturned, books and papers everywhere, broken crockery and glass strewn across the floor.

"Henrietta?" he asked again, immediately concerned for her. In reply, a high-intensity beam illuminated and momentarily cauterized his eyes. Blinded, Quinn was struck by multiple unseen blows. Doubled forward and stunned, he gasped for breath as a hand grabbed the back of his neck and hurled him forward. Another light flashed, this time from the impact of his forehead being driven against the living room wall.

Stunned, Quinn fell to the floor into a deeper darkness, shadows descending swiftly on him from above.

Anthony Green strutted into the Sir Jack's study unannounced. His eyes fixed onto Henrietta, sitting, hunched, sipping at a glass of water, and speaking slowly to Sir Jack. "So you're here, Ms. Richards. At least that makes my life a little easier," he said before looking at his colleague and acknowledging his presence with the words, "Sir Jack."

Green turned back to Henrietta. "Ms. Richards, as it is your stated specialty, I am sure you will be interested to know that the Taiwanese mountaineer Lady Huang Hsu and her business manager were found dead at the Regency Plaza late this afternoon."

The man carefully watched her reaction, a shocked wordless nod of the head, before he continued. "Murdered, it seems. I have also been advised that the Nepali police are now looking for an Englishman, a mountaineer called Neil Quinn, as their prime suspect. I understand he is well known to you, Ms. Richards, part of your little climbing club it seems. The police are saying he is the same man that sent you the spy-film that was stolen by the Taiwanese and released to the world this evening."

Henrietta responded slowly, her voice weak, her breathing labored. "I don't know . . . what you are talking about. Complete . . . and utter . . . rubbish."

"So you were not in fact in dispute with Lady Huang Hsu over the veracity of her claim to be the first woman to have climbed all the world's highest peaks?"

"Well . . . yes . . . I . . . was," she admitted.

"But I thought you just said the whole thing was 'utter rubbish'?"

"Don't be pedantic, Green," Sir Jack cautioned.

"I had nothing to do with any such film," Henrietta said as firmly as she was able.

"Oh, you didn't? Well I understand that your friend Neil Quinn emailed it to you this morning from the border at Xangmu and that

Huang, having stolen it, released it to the media as payback for your nitpicking of her achievements. Was your apartment not broken into today, Ms. Richards?"

Henrietta immediately looked at Sir Jack who said to Green, "You seem to be very well informed."

"I see part of my role here, Sir Jack, as one of immediately rebuilding certain contacts that have clearly been neglected by my predecessors. The Chinese ambassador has requested my assistance in managing the diplomatic firestorm he is currently experiencing, particularly given the fact that there are two British subjects at its center. Do you know how much trade this could potentially cost us?"

Sir Jack looked at his successor with obvious disgust. "May I remind you, Green, that not everything is about money and that you are not yet the acting ambassador. I deal with such matters until you are."

"Am I not right here, right now, Sir Jack, telling you the facts just minutes after I have received them?" Green said smugly before turning his gaze back on Henrietta. "Ms. Richards, at lunch you described yourself as 'an old-fashioned slave to the truth.' So then let's keep this simple, shall we? The Chinese believe that you knew the man who immolated in Durbar Square and that, prior to his action, he transferred something to you in a Tibetan prayer wheel."

Shocked at what he was hearing, Sir Jack looked inquiringly at Henrietta, remembering the offerings—the prayer wheel and the mala beads—in her hands when he'd met her at the gates of the Royal Palace, but her gaze was elsewhere. She seemed to be being squeezed to breathlessness, her eyes fixed, her hands gripping the chair. "At first they thought it might have contained the spy-film but now, knowing the provenance of that item of espionage, they believe it must be something else intended to damage their interests."

Ignoring Henrietta's obvious distress, Green slowed to let what he was about to say next sink in. "So let's keep this simple. You are going to hand over whatever it was to me, Ms. Richards, and then you will leave this city for good. Time for you also to retire and return to England, I think. Maybe Sir Jack can give you a lift back to Blighty as I'm not necessarily sure that his diplomatic pragmatism isn't now somewhat clouded by a mutual 'olden days' romanticism."

Green gave Sir Jack a sideways look as Henrietta replied, weakly but valiantly, "I'm not going anywhere . . . This is my home from before you—"

"Not anymore, Ms. Richards. Your residency status in Kathmandu has been revoked. If you do not cooperate with me, I will leave the matter to the locals. Then you will be deported just like the hippies you used to send home all those years ago. However, you can still avoid that cruel irony by telling me what you were given and where it is."

Henrietta, suddenly conscious that her black tin box was placed alongside her hastily packed overnight bag in his guest room, turned to Sir Jack with a look of panic in her eyes.

"Jack, I—"

The heart attack struck before she could finish the sentence.

34

AN ALLIANCE

57 SUKHRA PATH, KATHMANDU, NEPAL

The Brocken specter had returned.

The black shadow within the shadows clawed its way into Quinn's consciousness, head angling as it looked down at him in silent study, digits reaching to grasp him. A thought crystallized from somewhere equally dark and unbounded that the phantom was checking it had the right prey; that he, Quinn, was indeed the first person it had seen on that freezing mountainside. The apparition spoke in inquiry, soft and low. "Can you hear me?" The words pushed into Quinn's mind like a stick being slowly driven down into mud.

"Come on. Wake up," it demanded further, more urgent this time, the command reinforced by the two hands shaking his shoulders.

Slowly coming to, the Englishman tried to answer but no words came. His mouth was sealed shut.

The voice continued to speak, the accent becoming vaguely familiar. Quinn tried to nod in reply, but his head just rolled weakly. One of the hands moved up to hold it steady while the fingers of the other dug into the hair of his beard, fingernails scratching the skin of his cheek to hook onto something. "This is probably going to sting a bit," the American voice warned. The strip of duct tape was torn away from Quinn's mouth in a single pull that ripped both bits of his beard and the word "Fuck!" from his newly freed lips.

203

"'Thank you' are actually the words you are looking for," Beth said. "I need a knife to cut these ties around your wrists and ankles."

"There's a kitchen off this room. There'll be something in there. But you?" Quinn asked after Beth as she got up to search the kitchen using the light of her cellphone. "What are you doing here?"

"The same thing as everyone else in this city it seems. Looking for Henrietta Richards."

Beth quickly returned with a long bread knife with which she sawed away at the plastic restraints on Quinn's wrists and ankles.

"But what about the people who attacked me?"

"I don't know. It was strange. I arrived here to find the building dark but wide open. From outside the apartment I heard a burst of what sounded like radio, a lot of Chinese being spoken, then suddenly they all just left. They didn't even see me."

The sound of sirens began to grow in the distance.

"And I think we should do the same. Come on, we need to get out of here!"

✤

The ambulance raced through the city, siren tearing apart the night's silence, red and blue lights ricocheting off blacked out building walls. Inside, a young doctor and two nurses worked furiously to try to stabilize Henrietta Richards after the heart attack she had suffered.

Nearing the city's Bir Hospital, the vehicle's Tamang driver suddenly had to slow for a solitary figure standing in the road waving a red lamp before a line of cars and motorcycles, hazards flashing, that completely blocked the highway. The ambulance driver—conscious of his fragile cargo—brought the vehicle to a controlled halt as best he could, but almost hit the lamp bearer who didn't move an inch.

The instant the vehicle was still, all the beams of the stationary cars switched on and, under their spotlights, masked men swarmed over the ambulance.

The vehicle's siren and flashing lights were immediately killed. The driver was pulled from his door and strong-armed to the side of the road. The nurses on board soon joined him. From there, the three of them could only watch, threatened to silence by pistols, as the cars parted and the ambulance resumed its journey with their doctor and their patient.

This time however, the ambulance stayed dark and silent as the vehicle drove straight past the entrance to the hospital without turning in. The turn it did make was farther down the road, through an archway that led onto the wide expanse of the Tundikel military parade ground.

The ambulance bumped and rolled its way over the vast expanse of turf to stop near the center of the open area where a stationary helicopter was waiting in the darkness. At a double flash of the approaching ambulance's headlights, the helicopter's engine spun into life. To an increasing crescendo of whistling and thudding, the rotors began to turn while hunched figures worked quickly below.

Within minutes, the helicopter rose up into the air above the darkened city to fly north, fast and low, toward the mountains. The doors of the empty ambulance were closed, the pirates abandoning it to recede into the Kathmandu night.

The glazed lobby of the Khumbu Hotel was a bright lantern of yellow light that illuminated the entrance courtyard now wedged with police cars and people. From the dark of the alley entrance across the street, Quinn could even see some of his own expedition members talking to the police officers—including an agitated Rasmussen at their center.

The attack at Henrietta's, combined with the thought that wherever he was the police seemed to arrive soon after, urged him to caution. He said as much to Beth.

"I think you're right," she replied. "You should wait here. I'll go in and see what is going on. Here's a little friend of yours to keep you company in the meantime." Beth passed Quinn the small fabric animal from the bar. "You dropped it in your haste to go and get yourself beaten up," she added dryly but with a hint of a smile.

Quinn looked at the small white horse, only then realizing that he was even missing it. Newly squeezing it in his hand, he moved into the narrow side street as Beth returned to the hotel to disappear into the confusion of people. Exhausted from the blow to his head, the tiresome journey back from Tibet, and the high altitude climb before, Quinn squatted down behind the stinking dumpster of a closed restaurant.

To block its stench while he waited, he pushed the cloth of the toy up against his nose. Keeping his mouth firmly shut, he inhaled through the tiny stuffed animal. The ragged toy smelled of smoke and herbs, earth and incense, and a faint woman's perfume. It made him think again of that Japanese ghost saving him, the chanting, that strange heat, those tattoos that seemingly came alive, the snakes and dragons, the warriors and the demons, and the young child who sat amidst it all just staring at him. Quinn squeezed the stuffed animal in remembrance until Beth hurried back into the alley.

"Over here," he said as loudly as he dared.

Crouching down beside him, Beth reported, "It's not good news. They are saying that a famous climber has been murdered at the Regency Plaza—a Taiwanese. The police are looking for you as the murder suspect because the Taiwanese released a spy-film they are saying you took in Tibet and sent to Henrietta Richards."

"That's complete bullshit."

"Look, I know the video came from the same mountain you just climbed, so let's cut to the chase."

"Okay, I did take the video and I did send it to Henrietta Richards, but I certainly didn't kill anyone. Something else is going on here. Something bigger."

"I agree and we need to talk—but not here. Can you get into the hotel without being seen?"

"Yes. I've been locked out of it more than a few times in the past. There is a fire escape on the building next door from which I can get up onto the roof and in. Just give me your room number and wait for me to knock. By the way—just to be clear, are you helping me or is this a story?"

"Quite a few stories, I think," she replied, "but let's start at 'helping' and take it from there."

Once they were both inside her room, Beth opened a bottle of water and poured two tumblers. Handing one to Quinn, he said, "I would have preferred something stronger."

"I'm sure you would, but I doubt it would mix too well with having just been knocked out. So, let's go, cards on the table time. I'll start if it makes it easier."

"Okay. Go ahead."

"Last week I was in India to interview the Dalai Lama for an article commissioned by *Rolling Stone,* until the piece was canceled—maybe due to advertising pressure from a Chinese financed movie, but I can't be sure.

"Anyway, paid in full but suddenly unemployed, I stayed on for a bit and learned more about the Tibetans' plight. One of the stories I kept running into was that of Gedhun Choekyi Nyima, the Dalai Lama's choice for Panchen Lama, who disappeared in 1995."

From her notebook Beth took out her postcard of the boy and passed it to Quinn. "Do you know about him?"

"Yes. But only vaguely."

"Well, you are in the minority, even for having just vague knowledge. I began to think it was a story that merited retelling as the Dalai Lama is getting old now, and the Panchen Lama is the keystone to the identification of his future replacement."

"But, Beth, that boy has been lost for twenty-odd years now. No one knows where he is," Quinn said.

"Of that I'm well aware, but some seemingly random things relating to the subject conspired to bring me here. Perhaps it's easier if I explain by showing you my photographs." Beth retrieved her laptop and called up her photos, scrolling images across the screen until she stopped at one. "This is a billboard in Dharamsala about the lost boy—similar to the postcard."

She expanded the next photo to fill the screen with the moth design that had been cut into the billboard's frame.

"I noticed that someone had carved this onto it. When I asked my guide about it, he said it was a ghost moth, an old symbol of resistance and rescue for Tibetan exiles. He tried to brush it off as nothing, but my interest in that billboard got me mugged by some sort of undercover Chinese agent pretty damn fast." She touched the now purple bruising on her temple. "When I saw the same symbol on the banner of the man that immolated, it was a fairly easy leap to conclude that it might be slightly more contemporary than my guide was admitting. So, on a hunch, I came here. My contact in Dharamsala introduced me to a Tibetan businessman called Temba Chering, who I visited at the big stupa, which you probably know."

"Yes, the Bhoudhanath, and I also know Temba Chering," Quinn said. "He was well-known to climbers back in the day. A big deal now with hotels, restaurants, shops, trekking outfits, rafting, zip-lining, you name it. He's a hard man and, the Sherpa say, a bit of a gangster. Better a friend than an enemy, that's for sure."

"Well, by meeting him I was thrown into the heart of everything going on here. From the roof of one of his restaurants in Bhoudhanath I witnessed the police rounding up some Tibetan exiles. It was brutal. Chering said they were doing it on the orders of a local commissioner who is in the pay of the Chinese. Evidently they were after Chering as well, but he said that he also has protectors in high places. He wanted me to photograph it all and then to show the pictures in America. He even gave me the details of the commissioner to reveal his identity in the media." She scrolled the photographs of the riot then stopped as if bracing herself. "While that was still going on, he then took me into one of the monasteries there. I took these pictures next."

In silence Beth showed Quinn her next sequence of photographs. They explained themselves without words, just as Chering said they would.

"The man died while I was there," she concluded.

Quinn studied the photographs in horror. Amidst the burns, the dressings, the ravaged skin, he saw scraps of those same tattoos that had come to life in the tent. In one of the final photographs a ruined hand stretched out from the man's deathbed toward the lens. In unnecessary confirmation, Quinn made out the stubbed ends of the two already missing fingers.

Beth ended her explanation by showing Quinn the same photograph of the photograph she had taken in Temba Chering's office. "And this was the one I asked you about in the bar."

"Why did you take that?"

"I'll come to that. But as I think you do know who those people are in the picture, it's your turn to do some talking. Tell me about them."

"Okay," Quinn said. "That photo dates back to sometime in the late seventies when alpine-style climbing in the Himalayas was in its heyday. After the big military-style expeditions that first summited the highest mountains, a new generation of climbers came along determined to use the least equipment possible and climb by the most difficult routes.

"The Sherpa in the picture is obviously Temba Chering. He really was one of the best at that time. Incredibly strong they said. The foreign climbers with him were also. A bunch of misfits and rebels really that took the concept of 'alpine-style' climbing to the limit on the hardest routes imaginable. While they might work with Sherpa lower down on the mountain, they tended to climb alone once they went high. In those days the Sherpa were not particularly good technical climbers."

"Who are the guys in the picture?"

"The two brothers, the Barretts, they were from the north of England. Hard as nails. They would climb anything or fight anyone at the drop of a hat, friend or foe. Complete legends. The one with the curly blond hair was an American, Christopher Anderson. He was Henrietta Richards's partner at that time and one of the boldest climbers of that era. I don't actually know the guy with the moustache—he might have been a Pole or something like that—or the one next to him but the one on the end . . ."

Quinn hesitated for a moment, still a little uncertain of the ground he was on, then he pushed through, "That's Inaka Sakata although they used to call him 'Fuji.'"

"Are any of them still alive?"

"I used to think not. They climbed hard and were all killed in the mountains sooner or later but . . ."

"What?"

"Well, the Japanese climber, Fuji, was recorded as having died on the mountain of Annapurna in 1985. However I'm pretty sure the same man saved my life last week and, judging by what you have shown me, then took his own here in Kathmandu."

Beth increased the image on the screen to show what seemed to be a small badge on Fuji's jacket in the shape of a moth, the body red, the wings blurred but showing blue, yellow, green, and white.

"Do you see it?"

Quinn nodded.

"Yet when I asked Temba about The Ghost Moths, he also brushed me off the subject just like my contact in Dharamsala. He told me to stop chasing romantic myths and focus instead on telling the world about the constant pain and suffering of the Tibetan struggle. And I get that, I do, but my instincts, like yours, are saying that there is something bigger going on here, something that also involves your famous Henrietta Richards."

Neil looked back at the light shining in Beth's eyes, the curiosity in her face, the powerful need for answers driving her, not unlike a younger version of Henrietta in her desire to get at the truth.

"Look, I certainly can't explain any of it at the moment," he said, "even if I am pretty sure that the Sherpa know more about what is going on than they are letting on. I love those guys, but their famous warmth and friendliness masks a very Asian inscrutability. And I understand why. They are Buddhists, with deep links to Tibet. They have to survive and raise their families in one of the toughest and poorest places in the world. We are just travelers who come and go, pursuing our own whims. They are not. They have to live with the daily consequences of the history, the politics, the economics of this place. Not easy."

"Well, it was indeed a Japanese man who immolated because just before he died, he mentioned a Mount Gassan," Beth continued.

"You asked me about that mountain when we met in the bar. But it's not one I've ever heard of it."

"Yes, I was fishing, just as I was showing you the photo." Beth opened her notebook and studied some notes she had taken.

"Actually, I had already looked up Mount Gassan and knew it was in Japan. Alongside Mount Haguro and Mount Yudono, it is one of the three sacred mountains of Dewa Sanzan in the Yamagata region. They are revered by the Yamabushi, a sect of ascetic mountain monks who follow the Shugendo way, a spiritual tradition that dates back to the late seventh century. The Yamabushi perceive the three mountains of Dewa as a journey of rebirth: Haguro as life in the present, Gassan as death and the past, and Yudono, as the future: a new beginning.

"Temba Chering described the man who burned as 'just a wandering monk' and perhaps he was exactly that, a Yamabushi. But this was also a man with the ability to climb anything and travel far beyond those mountains, perhaps he was even involved in looking for the rightful Panchen Lama? It's not as crazy as it seems. He showed the mark of the ghost moth. The exact same mark I saw on that sign in Dharamsala where I heard that another man, a Dutch professor who had been searching for the boy for years, had been recently killed by the Chinese."

"Well, the Chinese definitely seemed to be looking for someone or something at Shishapangma," Quinn said. "The video I took was of what happened in the aftermath. I sent it to Henrietta Richards to try and protect the record when all our media was being deleted at the border."

"Tell me about her."

Quinn explained Henrietta Richards's position in Kathmandu and the mountaineering world, saying that he had gotten to know her particularly well while resolving some problems with a French climber called Jean-Philippe Sarron. He didn't expand on it just saying, "and that really is another story."

"I'd like to hear it."

"Well, maybe some other time, but for now I am just thinking that what I did with the video was extremely stupid and I need to sort it out."

"You said that one of the guys in the photographs was Henrietta's former lover. Perhaps your timing was just bad. If those were some of the original ghost moths, if Fuji was continuing their work, then perhaps she is also in some way involved? To be sure, we'll need to find her."

"Well, I know where we can start looking tomorrow." Quinn paused, took a deep breath, then said, "There is something more, something that ties in with everything you have told me. This little detail." He held up the rag doll to Beth's face. "I think this toy belonged to a child that Fuji had with him on his last journey out of Tibet."

Beth's face lit up.

"But somewhat younger than your lost Panchen Lama I'm afraid," Quinn quickly added.

"Tell me more."

PART VI

SKY BURIAL

Till a voice, as bad as Conscience, rang
    interminable changes
On one everlasting Whisper day and
    night repeated—so:
"Something hidden. Go and find it. Go
    and look behind the Ranges—
Something lost behind the Ranges. Lost
    and waiting for you. Go!"

—Rudyard Kipling
"The Explorer"

35

NO MIDDLE WAY

EMBASSY OF CHINA, HATTISAR SADAK, 615, KATHMANDU, NEPAL
October 17, 2014

"Detective Thanel is betraying us at every turn," Zhang said to Yama as he pulled the headphones from his ears and lifted his eyes from the spiky audio waveforms on the computer screen. "He speaks often to an informant in Thamel, a barber called Pashi Bol, also to Temba Chering, the local businessman we identified as having helped the man who burned."

"Is that the reason why the Nepali police didn't bring Chering in? Also why the Englishman was not arrested at Richards's apartment last night?" Yama replied. "We left him there bound and incapacitated when we heard the old lady was at the British ambassador's instead. All those idiots had to do was go to the apartment and find him."

"Possibly. They said the apartment was empty. Quinn didn't return to his hotel room either. Perhaps the detective let him go."

An assistant approached Yama to say, "You are wanted in meeting room five, Lieutenant. Alone."

Yama entered the room to find himself before Jin Yui, the governor of the TAR, whose head and shoulders were filling a wall-mounted video screen.

"Update me on what is happening," he demanded.

"The immolator was the ghost moth. I was tracking him following the information I received from the Lhasa splittist cell and my visit to

Community Work Territory 57, Amling Zone, to interrogate the parents of that missing child Geshe Shep mentioned. We lost him at the border but then he reappeared here in Kathmandu," Yama replied.

"How could you let him video you in the mountains?" Jin Yui asked angrily. "Beijing is furious, and Party Secretary Xiaopeng is advancing himself on the back of what he is presenting as my failure."

"The ghost moth was using an old route into Nepal. It is a very difficult and forgotten way that passes an important mountain called Xixabangma Feng, well beyond the capabilities of normal travelers. It was another climber in that place who saw and filmed us after a minor earthquake complicated the situation. The ghost moth did contact the recipient of the video here in Kathmandu, but the events were not related."

"Well, what was the reason for the contact?"

"I do not yet know but I am coming to suspect it may be related to that missing child. I believe he was smuggling it over the frontier."

"Where is the child now?"

"We are looking but we don't know. There has been no trace. I suspect that was the information he gave to the Englishwoman."

"Well, I urge you to be fast and thorough in how you resolve this, Lieutenant. Whatever it takes, none of Zou's middle-way shit."

36

POSTCARD FROM THE EDGE
SURAJ ALLEY, THAMEL, KATHMANDU, NEPAL

"I am sorry, miss, but I am not cutting the ladies' hair," Pashi Bol said to the attractive tourist who had just entered his tiny shop. "I'm not after a haircut," Beth replied as the barber's scissors quickly rejoined the battle with the mop of hair on a recently returned trekker. "A friend just asked me to drop off some cards and stickers from an expedition he was on. He thought you might like them for your walls."

"And what expedition was that?" Pashi asked curiously but kept snipping.

"Snowdonia Ascents Shishapangma," Beth said slowly and deliberately. "My friend, the expedition leader, wanted to come by himself for his usual post-climb haircut, but he has been a bit tied up since he got back to Kathmandu."

Pashi instantly stopped what he was doing to look back at Beth and nod her toward the line of waiting chairs. For the next few minutes she recalled the movie *Edward Scissorhands* as the little barber raced to finish what he was doing. The second the newly shorn traveler had paid and left the shop, Pashi turned the sign on his door to Closed and drew the grubby venetian blinds on the windows to each side.

"If Mr. Neil Quinn is the expedition leader you are talking about then he is in most trouble, miss," Pashi said as he turned to Beth with a worried look in his eyes. "Many people are looking for him, saying he killed the Taiwanese climber and her friend."

"He didn't."

"I know that, miss. Mr. Neil is one of the good ones. I have a police friend who is also. The detective says he knows it is nonsense, a Chinese lie, but there are those more powerful than him that are paid a lot to be sure that they do believe it. Is Mr. Neil safe?"

"Yes, as much as he can be for the moment. But we urgently need to find Henrietta Richards. He said that you might know where she is."

"Miss, I am afraid that is another person who is also in great danger, also now missing," Pashi responded anxiously.

"Yes, we went to her apartment last night, but she was not there. Instead Neil Quinn was attacked by a Chinese man who was already inside her apartment."

"That would be the one the Tibetans call 'Yama.' He is tracking the man that burned. Yama believes he gave Henrietta Richards something important before he died."

"Do you know where she is?"

"No, miss. I do not know. It seems that she was taken ill at the house of the British ambassador last night but vanished on the way to hospital."

"Do the Chinese have her?"

"I very much hope not," Pashi said while he took one of the expedition postcards from the bundle that Beth had brought. He walked to a wall, answering a rattle of his locked front door with a shout of "Closed. Thanking you. Later!" as he stretched up to unpin another postcard from amongst the many and replace it.

He gave the card he took down to Beth.

"Henrietta Richards asked me to give Neil Quinn this if I saw him. Perhaps you could pass it on."

Beth looked at the faded postcard of the mountain of Makalu as someone tried the handle of the glass door again, this time with more force.

On the back was written, *Your next climb. We need to speak. HR.* Beneath, hastily drawn, was the ghost moth symbol.

"Still most closed!" Pashi said again raising his voice in the direction of his rattling door.

"Open up now—POLICE!" came the shouted reply.

Pashi froze. Lowering his voice, he said to Beth, "Quickly," pointing her toward another doorway at the rear of the barbershop. Sliding back its bolt, he pushed her through just as the glass of the front door shattered behind them. Masked men burst in shouting, "STOP! POLICE!" as Beth almost fell into a cavernous sweatshop.

Before her, row after row of workers, young men and women, were hunched over gray sewing machines that rattled with bright cotton threads, towers of multicolored T-shirts alongside them. Startled by Beth's entrance, lines of brown eyes looked up in unison, then widened to white panic at the shouts of "Police!" that followed her in.

An older lady walking between the aisles blew a loud blast on a piercing whistle then began to scream instructions. The workers jumped up from their stations to flee the police raid, but quickly became trapped in their narrow aisles, overturning the metal worktables, screaming and falling in their panic to get out.

Pashi turned back from Beth to try to hold his door shut, shouting "Go, miss! Go!" at her.

Beth joined the stampede toward a narrow single side door that had opened onto the street.

A logjam of escaping workers soon blocked it. Seeking an alternative, she looked back to see the door Pashi was vainly pushing against pulse twice, then slam open. The force flung the small barber to the floor, the first masked men pushing through to fall on the little barber like hungry hyenas.

Another man, unmasked, entered alone to scan the hall. Beth recognized him as the one she had seen leaving Henrietta Richards's apartment the night before, instantly understanding this was the "Yama" that Pashi had mentioned. In return, the man's black eyes narrowed to lock onto Beth's blond hair, out of place amidst the other people there.

He leapt toward her.

An alternative escape door had opened on the far side of the hall through which a young Sherpa was looking in at the commotion and talking rapidly into a cellphone.

Beth darted toward it.

Yama instantly followed, flinging people and sewing benches aside.

Trailing an arm, Beth toppled an immense pile of T-shirts that fell back onto her pursuer as she raced to the door where the Sherpa stretched to pull her through into a kitchen that was hot and crowded, steam billowing from boiling pans, oil crackling and spitting from scalding woks. He kept hold of her hand to tug her on, between cooks and waiters.

The black-suited man soon burst through the door after her. With both hands, he shoved aside a cook who was unwittingly blocking his way. The man fell against his stove with a scream. A wok overturned, the cooking oil slopping onto a burner to explode into a tower of yellow flame. The fireball instantly engulfed the cook's white jacket and hair as it ballooned up to the ceiling.

Beth's pursuer pushed that cook away to run on, snatching up a meat cleaver on the go from an already bloody chopping board heaped with dissected chicken. Swinging the deep blade wildly, he began to slash a path through the kitchen. A waiter, unable to get out of the way, caught a slicing blow to the side of the neck and became a spraying scarlet pirouette.

Beth and the Sherpa ran out into the busy café area followed by their frenzied pursuer. The café's patrons screamed and jumped up, terrified by what was happening. Tables and chairs scattered as people dived for the exit or off the open terrace. Out on the pedestrian street they all ran toward the traffic of the main road.

Yama jumped down the café steps after them.

The Sherpa tugged Beth onward and out into the traffic, dodging motorcycles and bicycles.

An orange Suzuki car suddenly swerved to a halt in front of them.

The back door opened.

"Get in," the driver screamed from within.

Beth didn't need telling twice.

The door lock was slammed down as Yama flung himself against the stationary car, one hand grabbing at a door handle.

Unable to open it he became totally enraged, attacking the vehicle with the meat cleaver, hacking at the hood and the windshield, the glass fracturing into a broken mosaic but not breaking. He struck at it again. This time the blade pierced the glass and lodged as the driver floored the accelerator.

The cleaver was torn from the Yama's hand as the vehicle sped away. Beth realized it was Temba Chering in the passenger seat as the younger driver, wearing a pilot's flight jacket, drove expertly and extremely quickly through the Kathmandu traffic.

"Do you know where Neil Quinn is?" Chering asked.

"Yes."

"Good, we need to get him to Henrietta Richards."

Beth realized her left hand still held the now-crumpled postcard that Pashi had given her. She looked at it and said, "Yes, we do."

Two MSS agents lifted a bruised and bloodied Pashi into his own barber-shop chair. Despite being stunned from repeated punches to the face, the little man understood that he was alone and in trouble. The roll of tape produced to secure his wrists to the armrests confirmed it.

Yama returned, crazed and sweating from his failed pursuit of Beth. Ordering the agents to block the broken door with their backs, he moved in front of Pashi. "I am Yama, barber-man. You will have heard of me. It is time to talk."

"I don't know anything," the barber said defiantly. Yama just turned to eye the crude tools of Pashi's trade arranged on the shelf next to the basin and, slowly and methodically, began to wash his hands. When he turned back to face Pashi he was feeling the edge of a straight razor with his thumb.

"We'll soon see about that," he said, looking around at all the post-cards and images on the walls then laying the razor's edge on the terrified man's cheek. "Why don't we start with what you know about the ghost moth?"

Pashi swallowed but said nothing.

The razor began to cut, slow and deep.

The barber squeezed his face against the pain forcing his mouth to stay closed, no sound permitted.

Yama said nothing either. He just stared as he cut, wondering how much this little man could endure. Few lasted more than a minute or two.

The silent wait was interrupted by a café chair smashing one of the barbershop's windows from the outside. The shattered glass collapsed like broken ice.

A barrage of rocks and bottles began to pound on the backs of Yama's men blocking the broken door.

The head of an ice axe broke the other shop window, then reached in and ripped away the venetian blind to better reveal what was going on inside.

The sight caused a great roar of anger from the street.

A mob began shouting, "Release him! Release him!" and "This is Nepal. Not China! Get out!" as they hurled anything they could find. Without hesitation, the Chinese began firing warning shots in return and urging Yama to leave through the sweatshop door. Seeing no alternative, he further sliced the razor across the barber's cheek and, hidden within a phalanx of armed agents, retreated. Tears of relief mingled with the blood coursing down Pashi's cheek as the first of the Thamel crowd reached him.

37

INTO THE VALLEY
TENGBOCHE MONASTERY, KHUMJUNG, NEPAL

The red-and-white H125 rescue helicopter cut between deep ravines and hopped high ridges as it raced north. Every thumping meter of distance pushed it beyond the deep greens and russets of autumn in the Kathmandu Valley and into the white world of the oncoming Himalayan winter. Immense snow-covered mountains began to wall the way, bullying the small rescue helicopter with their invisible currents and drafts.

The helicopter bucked and weaved, but thrust itself onward, guided by a pilot's hand that was light and true.

"I know this place," Quinn said to Beth through the headset as the helicopter passed a final tree-lined ridge to descend into an opening the size of a football field. "This is Tengboche Monastery. We are near to Everest here."

The helicopter whipped the snow below into a whirlwind. As the rotor slowed, Beth saw an open area surrounded by squat buildings, their backs set against the snow-laden pines and junipers that cascaded down steep drops to a river far below. Overlooking them all, on the apex of the promontory, was a monastery building, strong and proud.

The Sherpa that helped Neil and Beth from the helicopter pointed them toward it. They set off tramping through deep new snow as the helicopter took off again almost immediately, its sound retreating down the valley before they had even reached the imposing gateway encrusted with painted gods, gilt animals, and Tibetan symbols.

Beneath an ornate arch they were met by a young man dressed in pale green hospital scrubs despite the cold. The doctor introduced himself as Temba Chering's oldest son, Pema. "It was my younger brother, Pertemba, that flew you here," he explained as they entered, "as he did me last night. Henrietta Richards is also here, under our protection."

"I need to see her," Neil said urgently.

"That is not currently possible. It was a serious heart attack and she must rest. Only when she wakes can you see her, and she will tire easily when she does. She is still very ill."

"What brought it on?" Beth asked.

"Stress and shock, we think. She is not young and pushes herself too hard at the best of times," the doctor replied. "In the meantime, you two should stay warm and have some tea. We are expecting some others, including my father, who I believe you have met, Miss Waterman?" Pema looked at Beth and she nodded in return, the doctor's determined yet gentle manner reminding her more of Wangdu Palsang from Dharamsala than Temba Chering, the man's gruff, tough father.

The doctor showed them into a low-ceilinged room in which a small stove pulsed with heat. They pulled themselves close to it, and a monk soon entered to serve them cups of a milky chai, which they drank to the low rumble of chanting from the main prayer-hall. While they waited, Neil spoke quietly to Beth of the many times he had passed through Tengboche on the way to Mount Everest, explaining how it had once been a major waypoint for both travelers and refugees from Tibet who would cross the Nangpa La pass near Everest to descend into the Khumbu Valley and Nepal even if, in recent years, the route had been blocked by the Chinese.

Pema Chering eventually returned to lead them both into an area of rooms near the rear of the complex that to Beth's surprise was fitted out as a small but very modern clinic. A sign on one wall listed the international mountaineering and trekking organizations that had funded the space to serve both the local community and the many trekkers and porters that passed that way to the great mountains beyond. Inside, in a single room, they found Henrietta raised up in a new hospital bed, a bank of machines unconvincingly flashing confirmation of her continued existence.

"Neil," she said weakly, raising the fingers of her hand in recognition. "I'm sorry to drag you he—"

"No, Henrietta," Quinn said, raising his own hand to stop her. "It is I who should be sorry for sending you that bloody video."

Henrietta didn't reply, her bloodshot blue eyes tightening to focus instead on Beth. "A girlfriend?" she asked, looking back at Neil and almost shaking her head.

"No. My name is Elizabeth Waterman, Ms. Richards. I'm a journalist," Beth answered for herself.

"It's okay, Henrietta. She's helping me," Neil confirmed to Henrietta who, eyes closing, said only, "Later then," and drifted back into unconsciousness.

Pema Chering quickly began to tend to Henrietta as Neil and Beth stepped outside to the sound of the H125 returning once more. From the snow devil beneath the rotors, two more passengers appeared; Temba Chering and Sir Jack Graham, who was holding a black tin box in his gloved hands.

"Henrietta Richards, Pashi Bol—we will not let such people be openly persecuted by the Chinese in Kathmandu. They are as much the spirit of the place as any of us," Temba Chering said as he and Sir Jack warmed themselves by the stove, anger burning in his eyes. "It is time to stop them knowing more about our movements than we do ourselves, to stop them running free as if they own our city. They don't."

"I agree with the sentiment," Sir Jack said, "but you will need to be cautious and lawful in your approach, Temba."

"Those days are passed, Ambassador Sir."

Sir Jack shot a concerned look at Quinn, who—trying to redirect Temba a little from his rage—asked, "Can you tell us some more about Fuji? We know it was him who immolated."

"To us, Fuji was a protector spirit, just as is your friend Henrietta Richards in her way. The Dutch professor, Paul van der Mark, that you asked me about, Mrs. Elizabeth, he was another. They are not angels or ghosts, not even our countrymen, but just people who, under different guises, choose to help us, our religion, our lost country," Temba Chering answered.

The Tibetan continued to explain how Fuji became disillusioned with the media circus that grew up around his climbing, and depressed by the loss of his closest climbing friends. In the end, with the help of some Sherpa he trusted, he faked his death on Annapurna to walk away from it all and return to Japan. For a long, long time he was just a memory to those Sherpa that helped him, and just one more fatality statistic to be consigned to the record books to all others.

However, many years later he quietly returned to the Himalayas to continue the work he had started as one of the original members of the Ghost Moths. In Japan he had indeed trained to become a Yamabushi monk and was intent on giving all the skills he now had as both a mountaineer and an adept to protect the persecuted Buddhists he had encountered during his climbing days. He did so alone, moving relatively freely between the mountains and the wastelands of Tibet, often disguised as an impoverished pilgrim, prayer wheel in one hand, beads in the other, known only as the Ghost Moth to the people he assisted. He helped many, but always on condition of a vow of silence about his assistance.

Occasionally he sought out Sherpa he once knew and trusted in the Tibetan base camps of Everest, Cho Oyu, and Shishapangma to get supplies or to anonymously forward information on what was happening in Tibet— though he himself avoided any direct contact with his former life. He told the Sherpa that he did not want to be made into a hero a second time or coerced into the frontier games of the superpowers that did not have the honest protection of the Tibetan dharma at their hearts. The way he had chosen made him a humanitarian, not a spy, a monk not a ninja, a healer not a killer.

"Many of our people knew the original story of the Ghost Moths,"

226

Temba said. "But knowledge of the Moth that continued was a most guarded secret even amongst us. Not even Henrietta Richards was permitted to know."

Temba concluded his explanation gravely: "Over the last years, Fuji's health had begun to fail, so those supplies he sought from the Sherpa increasingly included medicine prescribed by my son Pema, who treated him when he could. In the end, Pema thought that he died as much from his illness as those flames in Durbar Square. His last trip over the frontier at Shishapangma had weakened him so much he could simply go no farther. He chose Kathmandu for his last stand; I think leaving the pieces of continuity there to be reassembled. He very deliberately chose you to be a part of that, Mr. Neil Quinn.

"The Sherpa know you as a good man. Gelu always said that you would understand, if it was possible to tell you, that the cover of your expeditions was sometimes being used to help the Ghost Moth, but it had to remain secret. When Fuji asked him which climber he thought Miss Richards trusted the most and considered to be the very best on the hardest, highest routes, Gelu said it was you, knowing all about your Everest story with Miss Richards and the Frenchman. You should have been dead when he and the other Sherpa found you on the summit that day."

"Did Fuji come to you before he immolated, Temba?" Beth asked.

"No. I was at the Kumari Jatra as a spectator but, seeing what happened and the symbol on the sign, I immediately mobilized some of my people to help get him away from Durbar Square. I soon understood who it was but, by then, as you saw, Mrs. Elizabeth, it was too late. The only person that we know he contacted before the immolation was Henrietta Richards and we only know that because the Chinese identified their meeting. Whatever else he did in Kathmandu before, we haven't yet found out. Fuji tried to hide his contact with Henrietta with masks and tricks, but I know from a police detective that Chinese surveillance capabilities in Kathmandu are now so far greater than any of us can imagine."

"Yes, he did make contact with her," Sir Jack confirmed. "I didn't see it, as I lost sight of Henrietta in the crowd when we arrived, but she reappeared with a prayer wheel and a string of mala beads that the Chinese said the ghost moth had given to her; probably the very same ones that Temba described as part of his cover when he wandered Tibet. I suspect they are in the small tin chest Henrietta had with her when she came to me yesterday after the break-in. She was most concerned about its safety when she arrived at my house, so I brought it here."

"What did his gifts contain?" Neil asked.

"Only Henrietta knows," Sir Jack answered. "She wasn't able to tell me much about what had happened before Green turned up and she became ill. Also the damn box was locked and a gentleman is loath to pry in a lady's things."

In the small hours Pema Chering stirred Quinn to tell him that Henrietta was awake.

Their second conversation was as brief as the first. She simply directed him to the locked metal tin box that Sir Jack had brought with him and was now set on a chair in the room.

"I think . . . you'll remember . . . the code. Eight . . . eight . . . four . . . eight," she said breathlessly. "Everything . . . is . . . inside."

"Okay," Quinn replied, picking up the small chest.

"You'll need to go . . . alone . . . alpine style . . . and now. Go now. You'll work it out from my notes and the pictures, new and old. It's all in the box. Pandora needs her rest now. It's not the easiest of climbs . . ." The faintest of smiles seemed to crease Henrietta's dry lips as she drifted away again, leaving Quinn to return to his room with the black tin box already suspecting—from the postcard Beth had brought from Pashi's—which mountain she was referring to.

Not the easiest of climbs at all.

There, setting the box down on the bed and tumbling the combination padlock to the height of Everest in meters, he opened it. Inside, on the top, he found a thick notebook and the Tibetan prayer wheel with the string of mala beads fashioned as tiny skulls that Sir Jack had mentioned. Quinn took them out and laid them on his bed.

Underneath was a thick file for a mountain he knew well, but had never climbed—Makalu, the fifth highest in the world at 8,463 meters. Below that was a series of much older diaries and journals, and then an old metal tobacco tin; Rothmans Everest Rubbed Flake. Curious, Quinn opened it to find a tightly rubber-banded wad of embroidered patches inside. Removing the rubber band, he flicked through them, recognizing some from their place in climbing legend as the greatest Himalayan expeditions of the '70s, but most left him really none the wiser. One of the other badges just read, SUPER FREAK, and that completely threw Quinn—*Henrietta?*— although he loved its legacy of Kathmandu's crazy hippy days.

Intent on explanations, Quinn returned to the newest looking notebook that he had first encountered. He realized it was Henrietta's current workbook, filled with notes and details of that season's expeditions. Folded within the last written pages—dated as having been written the same day as the immolation—Quinn found two hand-drawn pictures, one of a skull and the other of a mountain, and two more embroidered patches, identically fashioned as moths and bearing the letters *T.I.B.E.T.;* one seemingly very old and worn, the other almost new. They were identical to the one that Beth had identified in the photo of the climbers. It dawned on him that the older of the badges was probably the very same one.

Quinn read Henrietta's notes and let everything fall into place by studying the two pictures that accompanied them. The mountain drawing was simple, even naive, but still an accurate design of Makalu as referenced in the thick file. The drawing's black hatching precisely matched the form of the great mountain. The red lines that laced it like veins marked the same climbing route to the top that had also been hand drawn in red on a series of old black-and-white photographs in the thick file. On one of the pictures, Quinn saw the route had even been named in Henrietta's copperplate handwriting. Such route naming was still common when extreme new lines to the top of a mountain were being claimed.

Makalu: The Kapala Route.

Quinn thought about the climbing line it represented. Lower down, it seemed to be the one many climbers still took that utilized the northwest ridge—Henrietta's notes included details of the Taiwanese and Italian climbs on the mountain that had just happened—but at the top it dramatically turned off course. There it became the hardest, most technical variant imaginable up the final part of the north face: an extreme mixed climb of rock and ice at over 26,000 feet.

Her words, "Go now," cast a darker shadow still over that final desperate line. To go *now* was tantamount to undertaking a 'winter climb' of the immense rock pyramid. The autumn season had ended as Quinn had stepped off Shishapangma. Winter in the Himalayas meant increased gale-force winds, lower temperatures, violently unpredictable weather, and snow, lots of snow, combining to provide the worst and most treacherous conditions a climber could experience. To do so alpine style would mean taking the minimum equipment, and as for alone . . .

Looking at the other drawing, that of the skull, Quinn read again Henrietta's notes and understood what he had to do when he was up there—even if there were no real clues as to why.

38

THE BALLAD OF CHRISTOPHER ANDERSON

TENGBOCHE MONASTERY, KHUMJUNG, NEPAL
October 18, 2014

When Beth sought Quinn out the next morning, he made no effort to conceal the materials from Henrietta's chest spread across the low table in his room.

"What's all this?" she asked, looking curiously at the pile of journals and papers.

"My next climb, just as it said on that postcard you brought from Pashi's. Henrietta is still much too ill to talk at any length, but she gave me all this in the middle of the night. I haven't looked through everything, but I have seen what Fuji passed to her at the Kumari Jatra and the notes she made immediately after."

"So did Fuji bring out a child that last time as you suspected?" Beth questioned urgently. "Did he tell Henrietta who the boy is? Where did he hide him? Not on that mountain surely. Is the rightful Panchen Lama dead? Is the child the reincarnate?" "No, it's nothing like that," Quinn said, reluctantly stopping Beth in her excitement. "However it does relate to something essential and hidden. Look at this." Quinn passed Beth the drawing of the skull.

"What is it?" Beth asked as she looked at the picture.

"Henrietta's notes say it is a kapala, a precious Tibetan relic of engraved human bone not unlike those mala beads she was given. In the other picture, I think Fuji was drawing what he remembered of the mountain to remind Henrietta of an old climbing route. The old photographs from the file are hers. They show a possible line to climb the mountain that she worked on back in the day and called 'the Kapala Route.' On the drawing you can clearly see the same red line and markings."

"Who did the climb?"

"Her lover, Christopher Anderson—and it killed him. I suspect there are many more details that will better connect the drawings to that climb in those older diaries and journals. However, from what Temba has said of the original Ghost Moths and what I have read in Henrietta's notes, I think I know what I have to do."

Beth picked up one of the older journals and began to read.

"Like my next climb seems to have found me, I think your next story has found you," Quinn said. "In the meantime, I need to speak with Temba Chering and Sir Jack to see how all this can be organized."

Beth spent the morning piecing together the older contents of Henrietta's tin box, studying journals and maps, patches and photos of a journey through Kathmandu and the Himalayas forty years earlier. When she returned later to find Quinn assembling an assortment of climbing gear that had been hastily brought up from the trekking shops of Namche Bazaar, she asked, "So it looks like you have a plan?"

"Of a sort. I'm going to be dropped in alone by the helicopter. It needs to be as light as possible to go really high and I should still be acclimatized from my last climb, so I should be able to move relatively fast once I'm on the mountain."

"But how high? Aren't helicopters limited for altitude?"

"The H125 is new and has pretty much changed the face of high-altitude rescue over the past few years. A stripped-down prototype even touched down on the summit of Everest in 2005 and that's 29,000 feet."

"So it's just going to drop you on the top of the mountain?"

"Sadly not, but Pertemba thinks if it's just me, we can get into the Camp Two basin at 21,000 feet, which is a good head start. It seems the weather is going to hold for a bit so from there I can climb the traditional route through to a high pass on the mountain called the Makalu La and then retrace Anderson's last known steps from Henrietta's photographs. If I was going to hide something so no one could get at it, it would be on the final section of the route, a steep wall of rock above what is known as the French Couloir that leads directly up to the main summit. Very few would even consider going that way to the top."

Quinn made it sound straightforward, routine even, but Beth had read more than enough in the diaries and journals that morning to know that it wasn't.

When she asked Quinn how he was going to get off the mountain, he busied himself in making sure that the satellite phone laid on an open orange plastic flight case was properly charging.

"We've got a couple of ideas. Depends." He almost mumbled. "This old sat-phone from the gear market in Namche will allow me to communicate with Pertemba fairly anonymously just in case our Chinese friends are listening in. We also have a small rescue beacon. It looks a bit dodgy but still seems to work. I'm sure he'll get me out when the time comes." He changed the subject. "Anyway, how did you get on?"

"Good. I think I have it all pieced together now. It's a great story. Henrietta Richards and Christopher Anderson were quite the pair."

"Well, let's hear it then, and while you're at it, can you cut off all that nonsense?"

Quinn tossed Beth his penknife and pointed to an old and somewhat worn yellow down climbing suit so covered in sponsor patches it looked like a billboard.

"There's a needle and thread on the table also, for the holes."

"Really, the little lady has to do that?" Beth asked.

"No, I . . . I didn't mean it like that. I just need the help to get ready."

"I'm kidding, you jackass," Beth replied with a smile to show she was messing with him. She began to snip away at the badges as she recounted everything she had learned from the older contents of Henrietta's tin trunk. She called it, "The Ballad of Christopher Anderson."

233

The story began in the autumn of 1974 when Henrietta was still a junior at the British embassy in Kathmandu. Late one night, while she was on what was euphemistically known as "cleanup duty," dealing with those British citizens who had taken the hippie trail east and fallen foul of Kathmandu's temptations, she received a call from an exasperated police officer.

A notorious English wastrel known as "Acid Eric," was once again in the Jochne lockup just off Freak Street, totally naked and screamingly high.

Henrietta arrived to find the English lunatic sharing a cell with a host of imaginary creatures dive-bombing his head and a not imaginary American climber called Christopher Anderson, who had been arrested after punching out one of the Barrett brothers in Sam's Bar. Given that in Henrietta's book, thumping a Barrett—as well known for their hard drinking and brawling as for their tough climbs—was hardly a crime and sharing a cell with Acid Eric on a bad trip was more than punishment enough, she got the American released as well.

For Acid Eric, Kathmandu's seemingly endless patience was exhausted. He was deported on the next BOAC plane out, leaving Henrietta with his sole possession—the ex-army Norton motorcycle he had ridden there from England in the first place—to settle what she could of the cost. When Anderson later sought Henrietta out to thank her, she asked if, in return, he would help her collect the old motorbike. They did so, and together rode it back through the—in those days—traffic-free streets of Kathmandu. Enjoying themselves, the American suggested they continue to the medieval town of Bhaktapur and on to a nearby hill station called Nagarkot with a distant view of Everest. There, they ate a hastily assembled picnic and looked at the mountain on the far horizon.

Anderson talked of how he wanted to climb it and was surprised, in return, at Henrietta's already great knowledge and interest in the peak. From that day they became an item. In her diaries, Henrietta acknowledged that they were an unlikely couple: she, the straitlaced Englishwoman and he, the tightly wound American climber who had served in Vietnam. But in those days, little in Kathmandu was likely and, in her words, "the mountains had matched us well." Together they began to plan his climbs, she researching routes that challenged the idea of what was possible at that time, and he attempting them with a string of other like-minded alpinists of all nationalities.

They grew ever closer and Anderson let Henrietta in on the fact that there was something beyond climbing that had led to his presence in the ancient city. The confession came as little surprise to Henrietta who had always assumed that Anderson was partly driven to take risks in the high mountains by what he had experienced in the jungles of Southeast Asia. However, while related, it proved to be more complex than that.

Anderson was originally from Colorado. His mother had died young to leave his father alternating his broken existence between Leadville's wind-scoured molybdenum mine and equally bleak dive bars. As a result, young Christopher went to live with his maternal grandmother in a tiny mountain town nestled beneath the red cliffs with which it was eponymous. In the late '50s, while out squirrel hunting, a then twelve-year-old Anderson saw what he thought were "Indian braves" hunting on the land of what had once been Camp Hale, a remote base in the mountains where the US Army had trained its fabled Tenth Mountain Division during the Second World War.

Soon after, an army officer, who had picked up on local gossip of the encounter, came into town. Searching out Anderson and his grandmother, he told them, and subsequently everyone else still capable of listening in Red Cliffs only bar, that from then on everyone needed to stay clear of the old camp as weapon testing had been resumed. To just Anderson, he secretively explained that the "braves" he had seen were indeed a new generation of "code-talkers"—Ute this time, not Navajo—under training for a role in the ongoing Cold War. The admission was followed by the equally cold threat that if Anderson ever mentioned them again to anyone, he would be separated from his grandmother and placed into care.

Anderson's grandmother died of pneumonia just as he was finishing school, so having swapped his obsession with cowboys and Indians for hunting and climbing, he rejected his father's invite to work at the mine and dirtbagged west via the sandstone of Utah and the red rocks of Nevada to arrive at the granite walls of Yosemite. When the unofficial climbers' camp there was hosed and closed by the authorities, a number of the residents were drafted, Anderson included. His skills on a rock face and hard upbringing in the highlands of Colorado ensured that he was well suited to the army. Becoming a Ranger, he served three increasingly desperate tours in Vietnam.

During the third, Anderson was involved in a Green Beret operation over the mountainous Laotian border to exfiltrate a man known as Tommy Rowe, who had been training the indigenous Hmong people to fight the Viet Cong. Anderson helped rescue Rowe from a bitter firefight only to realize on the Huey out that he had just saved the same man that had warned him off Camp Hale all those years before.

Back in Saigon, steeped in toxic Vietnamese whiskey, Rowe told Anderson that he was with the Agency and specialized in training indigenous peoples to help America fight its wars. At Camp Hale, he revealed, they had not really been training Ute Indians, but Tibetans to fight their Communist Chinese invaders. He confessed to Christopher that of all the dirty wars he had worked in since being a teenage Marine at Iwo Jima—Korea, the Permesta rebellion in Indonesia, Vietnam itself—only the Tibetan struggle had been similarly honorable to his first fight in the Pacific. The man deeply regretted how the Tibetans had been subsequently abandoned as American interest had turned elsewhere in their ongoing battles against Asian communism.

After that third tour, Anderson, disturbed and depressed, missed his flight home and drifted to Nepal as so many were doing at that time. Climbing in the Khumbu Valley he met two Tibetans called Pema Chöje and Temba Chering, who had escaped during the Tibetan uprising and were working as Sherpa to survive. He became particularly close to Pema, who would tell him of how he had flown from his hometown "like a ghost moth" bearing a precious relic to keep it from the Chinese destruction. Inspired by Pema's story, Anderson had begun to help other refugees in the valley when he was on climbs.

Henrietta, on hearing this, had joined Anderson in his support of Tibet and, in turn, used her own contacts to disseminate the information he learned about the Cultural Revolution's persecution and destruction ravaging what was left of Tibet.

Together they recruited a small group of other climbers to help, and after Pema Chöje, they called themselves the Ghost Moths. The letters *T.I.B.E.T.* on their badges signified "Tibetan Icon & Buddhist Evacuation Team," a play on the style of Anderson's Long-Range Reconnaissance Patrol insignia from Vietnam. It was actually a sort of in-joke between the Ghost Moths, but at its heart that was exactly what they were doing, they were helping get both people and relics away from the destruction happening beyond the mountains.

For a brief period in the late 1970s the group was successful, but those same mountains were unforgiving and the attrition of the Ghost Moths was high. When Makalu took Anderson, the matter, for Henrietta, really stopped there as she became lost in her own mourning for the one person she had ever really loved. The others carried on, but when they too were taken by the mountains, it apparently finished completely. Only now had they learned that Fuji had actually survived to continue the mission in his way, but Beth said there was nothing in all Henrietta's notes to suggest that she knew.

"Was Fuji on the climb with Anderson?" Quinn asked when she'd finished. "Is that why he recognized the skull drawing?"

"No, Anderson was climbing alone when he was lost." She looked at Quinn when she realized what she had said. "I think that another of the Ghost Moths, a Pole called Piotr Glowacki, was on another mountain nearby and it was he that told everyone back in Kathmandu that Anderson had been killed—but with deliberately incorrect details of how and which route he had been climbing. Henrietta herself underwrote the Pole's report, so few queried it. Glowacki himself died on K2 a few years later. I think Fuji only knew about the route and the kapala because when he later went to climb the mountain himself, Henrietta wrote that she told him all about it and asked him to try and find Anderson's body. He made the summit on that climb, but told Henrietta that he saw no sign of Anderson."

"And what happened to the Tibetan, Pema Chöje?"

"I don't know, but I'm going to ask Temba since they worked on the mountains at the same time."

She handed Quinn back the climb suit, asking of her work, "So what do you think?"

"It's a hell of story."

"No, the suit, dummy."

Quinn looked to see it newly intact but unadorned except for Henrietta's original ghost moth badge that Beth had stitched on.

"Nice, but personally I would have preferred the 'Super Freak' patch that was in the tobacco tin," Quinn said, laughing.

"Creep," Beth replied.

"But seriously, when I set off, you'll need to go back to Kathmandu with Temba Chering and Sir Jack. If there really is a lost child that Fuji smuggled out, then that boy must be hidden somewhere in the city. He certainly won't be up Makalu, that's for sure. Do you have any clues from the diaries where he might have been left?"

"It seems the Ghost Moths sometimes housed young refugees at an orphanage called the Hello Welcome Home until onward passage to India could be arranged," Beth replied.

Quinn pointed to the prayer wheel and the mala beads. "I think you should take those with you. Perhaps the boy will recognize them. This also." He tossed Beth the small toy from Shishapangma. "It seems that nothing Fuji did was by accident. He knew his time had run out. He chose his exit I think to draw attention onto him and away from the puzzle he had left. Only that way could he be sure to protect against everything falling into Yama's hands. I think he deliberately showed part of that puzzle to Henrietta and the rest to me on Shishapangma. You are going to have to be the link that brings it all together."

"I think so too," Beth said. Looking at the small toy and then the Englishman, a thought suddenly became clear in her head about what she had to do with it.

39

SOLO

The helicopter bucked and roared in a fight to stabilize so close to the almost magnetic pull of the mountain. When its skids momentarily kissed the snow, Pertemba Chering's hasty thumbs-up signaled Quinn to drop first his rucksack and then himself from his perch in the shuddering doorway.

Quinn postholed straight down into the twisting cloud of powder. Above, the H125, instantly lightened, jumped up and away before gracefully curving back down the long glacier to the embrace of thicker air in the valley far below.

Silence and emptiness took its place overhead. Quinn rose up like a snow creature to clear his mask with the back of his glove and pull the icy buff free of his mouth. He drew in a deep, preparatory breath. The extreme cold instantly gave him a brain-freeze. Riding it out, he shook himself down, gathered up his backpack, extended his ski poles, and orientated himself to the mountain above, to the thought that while he may have been dropped halfway up it, he still had a hell of a long way to go. He immediately set to the hard labor of breaking a trail to the Camp Two site farther up the wide white basin.

The going was not so fast and not so light. The snow was thigh deep, unconsolidated. The constant struggle to wade through it punched hard despite Quinn's prior acclimatization from Shishapangma. His pack, although compact, was still heavy, everything he needed for the next days grinding on his hips and shoulders. The cold was intense. Despite it all, the Englishman knuckled down to the task, unable to deny an unexpected thrill at being alone on such a mountain with only himself to worry about, only his pace to set, only his goals to meet—the likes of Rasmussen, for once, thankfully elsewhere. The thought pushed aside the effort of constantly stumbling and falling in the deep soft snow and the lingering worry of how long the break in the weather might last to become an illogical regret that he wasn't actually going for Makalu's summit. This was his sort of challenge.

Steady.

A few tufts of old tent material and then the tip of a single pole from which blew a string of tattered prayer flags revealed the location of Camp Two. In what he judged must be the center of the area, Quinn scraped out a small platform, set up his single tent, then rested and rehydrated before determining to profit from the clear afternoon with an exploratory trip free of his heavy pack to the foot of the ice face that slipped down from the Makalu La, the high saddle in the northwest ridge, three thousand feet above. When he reached the bergschrund, Quinn was relieved to see that the gaping hole between the ice face and the snowfield below was crossable and that the wall above was mostly too steep for much snow accumulation. The pinned ropes from many previous attempts on the mountain still hung down.

Much of the fixed line was tattered and rotten but there was an almost new, blue rope that remained stitched to the side of the face. Henrietta's notes from the night of the immolation had indicated that Lady Huang Hsu's team fixed the line for their climb and would also have undoubtedly just left it in situ when they were done. Normally Quinn cursed teams that didn't take their gear down after them but, that evening, hunkered back down at Camp Two, he gave the dead a pass. When darkness fell, he sent, as agreed, a simple text message on the satellite phone.

@2

The next morning the weather had closed in to hide the mountain above. To find his way, Quinn slowly followed what remained of his previous day's tracks to the foot of the face. With a slow leap of faith, he made it over the bergschrund to find the Taiwanese blue line was still good and strongly fixed. He clipped in and, within the pale freezing haze, jugged blindly upward for what seemed like an eternity.

With every hard pull, the altitude and the cold increased but, well educated in the "science of suffering," he just pushed onward and upward in that emotionless, automatic fashion that forward progress in those high places mandated. When the face leveled out into a heavily snow-laden shelf so deep that the blue rope couldn't be pulled free, Quinn first thought he had broken the back of that day's climb to reach the high saddle that led to the upper pyramid of the mountain.

However his altimeter soon told him another story. It was just one more false summit. The level shelf was actually about halfway up, and Quinn lost a lot of time finding his way across its snow covered plateau, wading and crawling through the huge buildup to finally regain the upper portion of the ice face and the remainder of that blue rope. When he eventually crested the ridge onto a wind-blasted arctic wasteland of rock and ice, Quinn was conscious that he was walking freely into Tibet even if there was no border, no spotlit strip of no-man's land, no dogs and guns; the "death zone" of extreme altitude was guard enough.

Completely exhausted from the steep climbing, he stopped to begin a wretched night at the traditional Camp Three site, where his tiny tent was constantly lashed by a relentless north wind that funneled over the pass.

Back at the Lukla rescue center, in the warm electric light of the helicopter hangar, Pertemba Chering, working on the H125, momentarily looked at his phone when it bleeped.

@3

The next day there was just enough visibility for Quinn to take down his frozen chrysalis and continue. Pummeled by gusts and hunched against their flurries of icy snow that whipped like blown sand, he traversed the steep upper flank of the mountain to reach Camp Four, the mountain's high camp at 25,600 feet. There, as quickly as possible, he set up his tent again, spent an hour kneading his fingers and toes back to life before making a lukewarm cup of black tea and studying Henrietta's old photographs as best he could against the few glimpses of the mountain that appeared through the racing cloud.

Slowly he made out where that final great snow face curved up into sheer rock. He kept looking to identify the rising snow gully cutting left through that same rock wall to reach the snow crest of the northeast ridge. That would lead him first to a false summit—Huang's mistake—then the true summit. That steep snow gully was the French Couloir, so named for the nationality of the climbers who first used it to avoid that treacherous north wall of rock and first make it to the top nearly sixty years earlier.

Putting himself into Anderson's boots, Quinn drew an imaginary line from the approximate position of the true summit down that same wall of rock to where it intersected the couloir. That was the American's ill-fated line—vertical and extremely technical, brutal in fact. At that altitude, only an elite climber would contemplate going such a way; after a few moves even fewer would have been able to actually continue. Quinn thought it likely that hiding the kapala would have been Anderson's first objective, checking off the list before he focused on the remainder of such a difficult route to the summit.

He soon crawled into his sleeping bag, determined to start up the snow face at 2 a.m. so as to reach the couloir by sunrise. Huddled close to his small stove, preparing something more to eat and drink, it seemed that the constant drilling of the wind against the tent-fly was laughing at his plan. He ignored it and texted Pertemba.

@4^

40

BRICKSTACK

TENGBOCHE MONASTERY, KHUMJUNG, NEPAL

The H125 returned quickly from dropping Quinn into Makalu. As the gorak flew, the mountain was only twenty-five miles away.

The seats and equipment that had been removed to permit maximum lift were reinstalled, and Beth, Sir Jack, and Temba were ferried back to Lukla to pick up another ride to Kathmandu in a larger, older, Russian-made helicopter. As they left Tengboche, Beth looked out silently through the side window, trying to imagine what it would be like to be dropped so high and alone on one of those distant snow giants.

Quinn had made the task seem possible, even logical, but the sight of those immense peaks made her heart sink. The crackly sound of Sir Jack's voice filling her headset interrupted her thoughts. Turning to look at the British ambassador, he said, as if reading her mind, "Don't worry. Henrietta thinks Quinn is the best there is—even if she'd never admit it to him." That might well be so, but Beth feared for the Englishman.

She was also concerned about what to do next in Kathmandu. When Beth had raised her and Quinn's idea that Fuji might have smuggled out a last child, Temba had been particularly skeptical. "I'm sure we would know at least something about it. Fuji left Henrietta with all the clues about the kapala we needed. If there is a child, then why would he say nothing about it?"

"He only approached those he had to," she replied. "Why did he not come to you and Temba about the kapala? He knew you. You know a lot of Sherpa climbers. I also think that you knew Pema Chöje, who originally smuggled it out of Tibet."

"It's true, I did know Pema Chöje, Miss Waterman, and I still miss him. We grew up together in the same village in Tibet. It was called Amling. I was there the day he found the kapala." The old businessman's face seemed to weary a little as he told Beth about Amling, the day the soldiers came, and what followed. It was a tragic story and a deep loss hung over his every word.

"Pema and I would meet again here in the Khumbu Valley as refugees, orphans of that Chinese storm. We began carrying on expeditions to survive," he finally said. "He was a special person and the Western climbers we met recognized it, particularly Anderson. He already knew about our people's struggle and was determined to help. When Geshe Lhalu and the Khampa fighter had told Pema to fly from Amling like a ghost moth with the kapala, Anderson's group saw in that story the example of what they too could do to help.

"Pema became ill so he asked Anderson to specifically rehide the kapala—his most precious responsibility—as he knew only Anderson could truly put it out of reach until it might be needed. You must remember that we were really just porters, not expert climbers like the Ghost Moths. That was the reason Fuji went to Henrietta, because he knew only she had the facts behind Anderson's Makalu climb. He also knew from the Sherpa that Quinn had the ability to retrace Anderson's steps up the mountain."

"I'm sure you're right, Temba, but there's more to it, I think. Fuji did nothing by accident. Perhaps he left the child at the Hello Welcome Home Orphanage just as they used to back in the day? Perhaps the prayer wheel and the beads were also given to Henrietta as tools of recognition? Perhaps he deliberately showed Quinn to the child so he would link him to the kapala? Perhaps the child is a new Panchen Lama . . ."

"Miss Waterman, I understand that as a journalist questions are your trade but that orphanage has been closed for years," Temba Chering replied. "There are now at least six hundred orphanages in the Kathmandu Valley alone. It would be like looking for a needle in a haystack."

The remark reminded Beth of her conversation with the Dalai Lama. She wondered if that was coincidence or not.

Back in the city, Sir Jack returned to his embassy determined to clear the allegations against Quinn and Henrietta and to end Green's tenure in Nepal before it had even properly started. For both, he had an ace up his cuff-linked sleeve: Temba's introduction to Detective Thanel.

Beth accompanied Temba to the Blue Poppy to find the place bustling, more operations center now than restaurant, and clearly awaiting their leader's return. Temba disappeared into private meetings after telling Beth to check back into the Tibet Guest House and giving her the help of one of his assistants to identify the biggest and most centrally located orphanages in the city to, at least, test her theory. Gelu would have to go with her, he insisted, and his other conditions to the search were also firm: no cellphone usage, no computer searches, no visible blond hair, nothing that might permit Yama to track her.

The American's fluorescent highlighter soon dotted a city map with possible locations. The following morning, Gelu arrived in an aged Land Rover to crisscross the city from establishment to establishment. At each old building—many little more than stacks of red brick with battered tin roofs—Gelu would talk to the most recent arrivals, questioning them about their journey to that place while conspicuously running the mala beads through his fingers.

The assembled boys responded to his questions gladly and enthusiastically, but none reached for the beads. Instead they constantly looked at Beth in the hope that they were auditioning for foreign patronage even if they saw nothing curious in the prayer wheel strapped to the side of her day pack. None of the newest arrivals were even from Tibet, abandoned by fate much closer to no home. "That way is shut now," was the consistent answer from orphanage staff when asked about any children from beyond the mountains.

The sad plight of so many parentless children weighed on Beth alongside a growing worry as to how Quinn was faring on Makalu. When she quizzed Gelu about what it would be like to climb such a mountain at that time of year, the veteran Sherpa couldn't help but paint a bleak picture.

"Not good for the fingers or the toes. In fact . . ." The Sherpa began to say something more about a famous French climber who had tried to climb Makalu alone in winter but then, looking at Beth hanging on his every word, cut the rope by changing the subject.

Only at the end of the second day when they had returned to the Tibet Guest House from another fruitless search was the subject of Quinn even mentioned again.

"Pertemba has told his father that he is in position," Gelu reported. "Tonight we must pray to all our different gods to unite for good weather so that tomorrow he can find what he is looking for and return. Perhaps we will too."

41

BELOW

Quinn left his battered tent later than he would have liked, dismissing, with movement, the alternative of sitting out the day in the hope of better weather. There were no guarantees it would come and the physical debilitation of a stationary twenty-four hours at 25,600 feet was a certainty. It was then or never and he knew it.

He pushed himself out into the steep darkness, relentlessly forcing himself upward, once again imprisoned within that freezing bubble of high-altitude slow-motion. The beam of his lamplight showed little beyond a lattice of streaking snowflakes. The howl of the wind drowned out all other sounds, leaving only the internal metronome of his heavy breathing to count him onward and upward.

The dense cloud was lightening by the time Quinn reached the entrance of the French Couloir. The deep snow gully was acting like a flue from the high ridge above, spindrift, ice, and small rocks scouring it constantly. Quinn weathered the bombardment to move up and across the opening—so small in the photographs but seemingly never-ending in reality—to follow a slightly more sheltered line at the bottom of the rock face. The relentless grind continued.

It took the arrival of daylight to finally reveal what he was seeking—a projection in the base of the rock form where it rose into that distinctive shoulder, still mostly hidden in cloud above. Quinn began to climb up, hooking and spiking himself into the rock. Every inch of the way, he fought against the subzero cold, the wind, and the growing exposure conspiring to block his every move.

Finally making it around to a deep trough in the rock, he stopped to try to recover his battered senses and search for the slightest trace of something, anything. He squeezed his eyes to focus through the haze but there was nothing, no sign that any climber had ever been there before, just more black rock, white ice, and gray cloud. Quinn could feel that day's energy had already faded in him, sapped by the struggle to just get this far without his body freezing. The nerves in his fingers and toes had long ago receded into a blunt numbness, but now he could feel his limbs beginning to slow and stiffen at the behest of essential organs desperate for the little warmth that remained in his body. He was running out of time.

Crouched in the lee of the rock wall, Quinn laid his head back against the mountain and closed his eyes. A wave of intense fatigue released an unnatural warmth in the center of his chest. Quinn found himself wondering if the ghost of Fuji was there again, seated next to him, stripped to his tattooed skin and destroying the cold with his strange magic. But it was an older ghost, one with a German accent. "You know better than this, Mr. Quinn," it commanded. "To sleep here is to die. Move!"

Quinn jerked awake. He told himself he must do as instructed, forcing the slow command to rise into his reluctant legs just as a heavy fall of snow and grit plummeted down from above. Instinctively he turned his body into the mountain, pressing his masked face tight into the rock while the spindrift rattled on his back like an icy waterfall. Holding and waiting, his frosted eyes traveled a line scratched into the rock before him. The incision turned and looped, slowly cutting its trace into Quinn's hypoxic mind.

The symbol killed his lethargy.

Quinn immediately began to look around, pushing snow and ice from the surrounding rock with his mittened hands to find something more.

Slightly lower down he soon glimpsed a color, purple, so alien in the monochrome. It was the frayed end of a fabric sling. Using the pick of his axe, he began to hack away at the mound of snow and ice from which it projected. The tattered nylon band ran back to an old carabiner hooked onto a metal piton. Cleaning around the anchor Quinn saw something else, still mostly hidden, hanging below that same metal loop.

With a feeling of dread, he dug deeper, but revealed only a blue backpack, which he broke free from its frozen tomb. Quinn pried the stiff fabric open wondering if he was going to find the kapala but, inside, the well-preserved contents were the usual; a coil of rope, some more pitons and climbing hardware, a few personal effects, even a few bars of chocolate.

Quinn tested the strength of the old anchor from which the pack and the tattered sling hung and found it still completely solid, so he tethered himself to it just as Anderson must have done all those years before. Secure to work, he began to search elsewhere using his axe to probe the cracks in the rock, hooking and scraping them clear of snow and ice.

The first few revealed nothing, but then one began to open up the more he dug. Letting his axe fall on its lanyard, Quinn reached in, his arms pushing into the deep shelf in the rock. At the back, a round object met his hands.

Quinn swung off his rucksack, took out his own coil of rope to create space, then reached into the rock again. With a hard pull, the gabardine-covered package was released from its icy glue. After pulling it free, Quinn turned his back to the mountainside and, exhausted, slid down the ice and rock to just sit with the bundle in his lap. He eventually began, in vain, to try to undo the red cord that bound it, but the knots were too tight, his fingers too numb to make any impression on them.

He dug into his outer breast pocket for the Swiss Army knife he had stashed, surprised to find the small toy horse he thought that he had given to Beth. Confused to see it again, even a little worried, as he thought Beth was the one that needed it, he put it back and dug deeper into the pocket for the heavier knife. When he got it out however his fingers were so deadened they couldn't open even the biggest blade.

Taking up his ice axe instead, he drove the pick into the green material then tore a small opening. From the slit a single empty eye socket looked out at him just as the wind lashed the rock face once more.

I have it.

Pushing the kapala down into his own rucksack, Quinn ordered himself to get out of there while he still could. Reaching for the old carabiner and piton, he grasped and pulled himself back up onto his feet. The repeated thought that the anchor was still rock solid gave Quinn an idea. He pulled the other coil of rope from the old rucksack then rummaged around to assemble whatever else he could take from it to bolster his own equipment.

Threading the head of his rope through a new carabiner clipped onto the old piton, he then knotted Anderson's rope to it, and cast both lengths down the face. Attaching his descender to the double line, Quinn shouldered his own rucksack, trusted his life to Anderson's forty-year-old anchor, and began to rappel straight down. He lost height like an elevator, one instruction from Pertemba driving him on: "*If you can get back to the La at Camp Three, it's possible but only if the weather permits. Camp Two is best. Remember to wrap yourself in everything you have. I don't want you to freeze any more than you will have already.*"

Quinn continued to descend until the ropes got stuck on the rocks above. He fought to free them but to no avail. Reluctantly Quinn abandoned his lifelines and downclimbed until he could let the snow slope take him, sliding, rolling, and plunging back to his tiny tent at Camp Four. He arrived just as the weather worsened. Dragging himself inside, he collapsed, utterly spent. His first thought was of the satellite phone, but its battery was dead. He tried the spare, but the cold had killed that also. His next thought was a prayer that he and his small tent wouldn't blow away in the night. His last was that if it did, he wouldn't be awake to experience it anyway.

Out, cold.

42

HELLO WELCOME HOME

KATHMANDU, NEPAL
October 24, 2014

On the return journey to the Tibet Guest House brooding over another day of fruitless search, Beth couldn't help but wonder about the original Hello Welcome Home Orphanage. Despite the fact it would make her late for her daily check-in with Temba Chering at the Blue Poppy, she asked Gelu if they could, at least, drive by the place just to satisfy her curiosity about it. The Sherpa, never very talkative but always obliging, undertook a lurching U-turn through the late-afternoon traffic that incited a fanfare of disapproval from all the other vehicles on the crowded dusty road.

Not fifteen minutes later, the old Land Rover pulled up outside the entranceway of a large white house on a quiet side road. Stuccoed, ornate, and freshly painted, the small palace was a sharp contrast to the darker, seemingly only partly finished buildings that made up much of Kathmandu. A set of imposing metal gates to an inner courtyard were open, so Beth got out to take a quick look inside.

No one was visible, so she entered to find herself surrounded by what looked to now be a well-maintained private home. In the center of the courtyard she approached a small shrine erected on what resembled a carved birdbath or fountain. Much of the ancient stone platform was encrusted with red and purple pastes, to which flower petals and rice grains had stuck. The stubs of incense sticks protruded, some still smoking.

Their scents were full and sweetly heady as Beth approached the shrine, pushing her face in close to study the glazed brass box at its center. Through a hinged glass door, she saw the gilt figure of an elephant-headed, four-armed god sitting cross-legged on a lotus petal. At its feet an oil lamp burned with a smoky yellow flame. Propped to one side was a postcard of a child. Heart leaping, Beth leaned in to look closer still.

At that moment Quinn was also looking closely at something: the end of the road. All that day he had battled to descend from Camp Four but now it was over.

The worst of the night's storm had lifted by the morning. Slowly and painfully, Quinn had dragged himself from an almost fugue state to continue in visibility so poor that he got lost a number of times before he reached the Makalu La. Stumbling blindly toward the Camp Three site, he thought again about what Pertemba had said, and knew well that in those conditions it would be impossible for the pilot, however skilled, to reach him there. His own internal voice of experience warned equally that if he even stopped, he might not get started again.

Quinn had pressed on, weak and exhausted, but determined to reach those fixed blue lines that threaded their way down the ice wall to the greater possibility of safety in the Camp Two basin. With difficulty he found where they began, clipped in, and let gravity share in his burden.

The first lengths went well. With every heavy step he got a little lower, optimism growing within his exhaustion. But, when he had used the little energy he had left to wade across the snow shelf that bisected the ice wall, that optimism was instantly crushed by a dread realization.

The heavy snow that had built up on the shelf had avalanched to its lower edge. The second portion of the wall was scoured clean by the fall. The fixed line was gone. An almost vertical, virgin wall of ice remained. Too tired to turn back, Quinn determined to go on. He began to downclimb using his ice axe, crampons, and an old section of rope he scavenged from the upper ice face, but the weather began to worsen. The wind lashed at the face, threatening to strip him from his tiny points of contact with every gust. Soon he had little choice but to return to the snow shelf above to wait it out.

Once there, Quinn scraped out as much of an alcove as he could. He propped up his tent material around him to give him some shelter—and also make the most of its bright yellow color. Then he retrieved the small Namche-bought rescue beacon from his pack, and placed it inside his clothes on his bare chest to warm it as much as possible before he switched it on. When he did, Quinn was relieved to see the flashing of the unit's small red light. He did his suit up around it, masked his face, drew in his hood, cinched his pack, and tightened his harness; careful to do then anything that he might not be able to do in an hour or a day—however long it was going to take. Then he looked out on the dusky haze, fighting the closing of his eyelids from exhaustion as more snow began to fall.

Beth reached into the shrine to take out the card. It was a portrait of a young child dressed as a princess. She quickly turned it over in hope that the back of the card might feature what she was meant to find, but it was just blank. Frustrated that it bore no clue, no telltale moth hastily scribbled on it, Beth turned it around again to study the image of the young girl some more.

The exquisite face drew Beth in. Beneath an ornate red-and-gold headdress, the small child's eyes were bright, emboldened by long cow-like eyelashes and exaggerated sweeps of kohl eyeliner, and then multiplied by the addition of another vertical eye design that was painted onto a golden panel that curved across her smooth forehead. Her lips were rouged, as were the insides of her tiny nostrils, a blood-red edge to the lily-like features of that tiny, beautiful face . . .

Totally lost in the picture's detail, a stern voice from behind Beth made her jump.

"Madam, what are you doing in here? This is a private place. Not for tourists. Please put that back."

"Sorry . . . I was looking for the Hello Welcome Home Orphanage,"

Beth said, replacing the postcard quickly in order to pass her marked street map to the officious-looking woman as if it was an excuse for trespass.

The lady of the house cast a suspicious eye over it to say, "You are in the right place, but this house has not been the Hello Welcome Home Orphanage for many years. The only home it is now is a private one. You must go, please."

"Who is that?" Beth asked, trying to stall her exit by pointing back to the postcard.

"That is the Royal Kumari of Kathmandu."

"Is she Tibetan?" Beth asked, clutching at a straw.

"No, of course not. She is Nepali, a member of the Bajracharya clan. As are we, the family who now live here. Hence our shrine to her."

"Are there any boy Kumari?" Beth tried again, seeking another tack.

"No," the woman said. "The Kumari is a living goddess so that would not be possible, would it? You should go now."

Chastened by the stern woman, Beth made her exit out to the Land Rover to the sound of a faint thump in the distance. A number of pigeons that heard more to fear in the sound than Beth, instinctually flew up into the sky only to realize that they were already safe where they were. They descended just as quickly after a panicked lap of the tiled roof.

⸙

The Land Rover resumed its journey, leaving the bumpy yet quiet road of the neighborhood and plunging back into traffic on the main street that was quickly becoming more congested than normal. In the continual stop and start, Beth asked Gelu about the Kumari as he fought to make progress back to the Bhoudhanath.

"She is a Hindu god-child, Miss Beth," he explained. "Not a Buddhist thing—even if we Sherpa do see her as a protector spirit here in Kathmandu."

"Can I visit her?"

"No, Miss Beth. Outside of specific occasions and festivals like the Kumari Jatra, she lives most hidden and heavily guarded by her clan . . ."

Gelu stopped speaking.

Ahead, a towering pall of black smoke was rising above the top of the great stupa as if it were an awakening volcano.

The Tibet Guest House—when they finally reached it on foot after abandoning the Land Rover on the side of the totally blocked road—was in turmoil. The receptionist broke down and cried as she explained that the Blue Poppy had been destroyed by what people were saying was a bomb.

The stupa's inner plaza was sealed by even more angry-looking police than the day of the riot, so Beth could only wait at the hotel for further news that—when it came—was bad. Temba Chering and five other people were dead. Beth realized that if she hadn't stopped at the old orphanage she would have been there with them.

"You cannot stay here, Miss Beth," Gelu soon warned. "They are saying Yama attacked the Blue Poppy to destroy Temba Chering and those he was helping. That includes you. We must go."

Beth and Gelu raced back through the crowded streets to reach the old Land Rover and set off for Sir Jack's house, but their urgency was irrelevant to the traffic jam that held them in place as they tried to leave.

People milled between the stopped cars, trying to get to the stupa to see what had happened. In the confusion, they didn't see one of the crowd lean into the Land Rover and spray something into Gelu's face, immediately rendering him unconscious. Nor did they notice two others pull a struggling Beth Waterman from the passenger side door and strong-arm her into a dark side street where Yama was waiting.

43

LAST WORDS

TENGBOCHE MONASTERY, KHUMJUNG, NEPAL
October 25, 2014

Quinn awoke to an intense pounding inside his skull.

With difficulty he broke his mittened hands free from the snow that had fallen on him and raised them to his face. Inside, he tried to move his fingers but to no avail.

He let his hands drop back on the snow and began to wonder how long he had left.

The answer was lost in a realization: Hope is not the last thing to die. It is curiosity.

Well answer me now . . .

Not long.

You have been here all night.

Quinn tried to wriggle his toes, but the command only traveled as far as his rigid knees before bouncing back as a cold shudder that left a violent shivering in its wake. A spark was ignited somewhere near his heart, the internal fire growing quickly to arch his body in pain.

The rictus forced him to stare up at the falling snowflakes finishing their long journey to rest on his face.

Are you the ones that are going to bury me?

There it was again.

Curiosity.

Quinn tried to shield his stinging eyes from the red beams of a rising sun, vaguely understanding that it heralded the arrival of another day.

His headache began to thunder as the wind grew with the force of a whirlwind to rip what was left of his collapsed tent material away from him and lash his unprotected body with more snow and ice.

Above a black shadow appeared through the haze, a hovering specter, its noise infernal, the downdraft destroying the very mountain around him.

Quinn stared at the end of the long line that danced and slapped at the ice for some time before he understood. On the fifth flat-handed attempt he slapped its sprung hook onto his climbing harness and raised an arm to the thundering sky.

Neil Quinn exploded upward, ripped from the side of Makalu, unsure if he was being transported to heaven or hell.

$$\bowtie$$

At the designated helicopter landing area of the Makalu Base Camp, Quinn was fielded by Pertemba's crew member who had waited out the rescue there. He unclipped Quinn and helped him into the H125 when it landed. Just fifteen minutes later they were back at Tengboche.

Pertemba and Pema Chering urgently spoke of the news from Kathmandu while the latter looked over Quinn. Pertemba immediately left for Lukla, but Pema, the doctor, was insistent that he should remain. "It won't be for long, Pertemba. We'll join you as soon as we can," he said as he put Quinn on a saline drip and treated his frostbitten fingers and toes.

"You need rest, but first you must see Henrietta," he said to Quinn. "I think it is only the thought of your return that has kept her going. This IV will help so that I can least take you in to see her. We must hurry."

"Okay, but you will need to help me get some things from my pack. We'll need a scalpel also."

After he had helped Quinn into the room, Pema Chering took Henrietta's pulse, then left them alone as she woke and slowly twisted her head toward Quinn.

"And?" was all she said—all she seemed able to say, in fact.

"I got it, but only just. Pema's brother long-lined me out from the headwall above Camp Two. It seems the gods were on my side."

"In this case I would expect as much," Henrietta replied quietly. She coughed then asked faintly, "Did you find him?"

"No, Henrietta, only his rucksack." Her eyes closed on the news only to reopen as Quinn continued. "I have brought you some things."

Cupping his bandaged hands together Quinn presented Henrietta a small black journal as if it was a holy offering. "It was in the pack."

Slowly, Henrietta opened the cover. A photograph fell from the first page. She raised it close to her face and just stared at it in silence. A tear slipped down her cheek as she laid the photograph facedown on her chest next to the journal to watch Quinn place a green bundle on the edge of her bed.

Clumsily cutting the cord that bound it with the surgical knife, Quinn pushed the covering material away as if opening up a large fruit. His hands withdrew to reveal the ancient skull.

"Memento mori," Henrietta said as she gently reached for it. Her fingertips slowly began to trace the lines of its carvings, drawing Quinn's eyes into the strange letters and symbols that covered it. They stopped at the triangle carved on the forehead then, with a push, tipped the skull off the bed. The precious relic fell before Quinn—momentarily stunned by what Henrietta had done—could stop it.

The engraved cranium struck the concrete floor and, with a hollow popping sound, split into several jagged pieces.

"Damn thing. I've waited a long time to do that," Henrietta said staring at Quinn defiantly.

Quinn was dumbfounded.

"What?" was all he could say as he looked down in horror at the broken icon he had risked his life to retrieve.

"Don't look so worried, Neil," Henrietta said, the faintest of smiles creasing her lips and bringing a curl to the corner of her watery eyes. "I'm joking. Well, almost."

"I don't understand."

"The kapala is a terma, a treasure hidden to protect the future of the dharma, the Tibetan faith. It's not got laser eyes. It isn't the home of some all-powerful djinn. It's just a box, an unusual one I'll grant you that, but a box all the same. It contains texts."

Her hand loosely pointed at the floor where Quinn could see, within the split cranium, a small leather-bound package tied with red cord. He picked it up, but Henrietta motioned him to stop. "There is no point in you opening that. Only a terton will be able to read it."

"A terton?"

"A Buddhist saint empowered by his faith to understand. You could start with the Rinpoche, the abbot here, but I suspect the one you need resides somewhat farther away."

Henrietta returned to the photo from the journal. She lifted it and passed it to Quinn.

The color portrait showed an attractive young woman with thick, glossy black hair and sharp blue eyes. "I wasn't a complete bust back then was I, Neil? Talking of reading things, Neil, will you do me one last favor?"

"Of course, Henrietta."

"Will you read me Christopher's journal even if I already know how the story ends."

Quinn began to read the first handwritten entry.

"Makalu–The Kapala Route. March 16, 1981: Day 1. Leaving H for a climb is always hard . . ."

When Quinn had finished reading the journal, he left Henrietta and asked Pema to take him to the abbot. Pema showed the way, then left to let Quinn talk to the Rinpoche through a younger monk with excellent English.

Quinn showed the abbot the broken kapala and its contents while explaining what Henrietta had said. The abbot read the first folios intently then stopped to talk at length to his younger colleague. The young monk translated it all for Quinn telling him that those first pages had been written almost sixty years before by another monk called Geshe Lhalu who had studied the kapala in great detail.

Geshe Lhalu's text explained that the skull was a relic that had been passed down through many incarnations of the Dalai Lama. As was customary, one of them had made a pilgrimage to the holy lake near Geshe Lhalu's monastery seeking knowledge regarding his future reincarnation. In the waters he had seen a great vision from the lake's protectress, but understood that it was not for him but one of his successors. He transcribed the prophecy and hid it inside the kapala that was part of his retinue. He had then buried the skull near the path to the great lake to become a hidden treasure that would reveal its message when the rightful recipient passed, a future Dalai Lama also seeking to learn about his continuity in those high windswept waters.

Geshe Lhalu thought that the skull had revealed itself the day it did— on the exact day the Chinese arrived in his town of Amling—because the dharma knew that from that day forward the Dalai Lama would never be freely permitted to pass that way again. Because of this, Geshe Lhalu had organized for the kapala to be smuggled beyond the reach of the Chinese and rehidden until it was needed.

Quinn asked about the prophecy itself, but the reply was brief. The younger monk said they did not know, just like Geshe Lhalu before them. Just as Henrietta had said, it was a sacred text that only the Dalai Lama could read. It was for him and him alone.

Quinn returned to the infirmary to tell Henrietta that her suspicions were correct, but instead met a grave-faced Pema Chering. With great sadness the young doctor told him that Henrietta Richards had passed. Utterly shocked, Quinn entered the room to see her alone in the empty room. It was as if she had just fallen asleep, the journal that Quinn had brought her still in her hands.

He looked at her and then out the room's window. His eyes fell into the darkened valley below then raised up to the immense black-and-white mountains. They began to glow with the golden light of the setting sun. The sight swamped him with a feeling that the era of their discovery and exploration, her passion, his inspiration, was also over. When Quinn turned back into the room, the ghosts of those lost in those high places had already begun to arrive to pay their last respects.

Quinn left to call Sir Jack and tell him the sad news; then the ambassador imparted his own which was equally shocking.

All Quinn could do was gather up the remains of the shattered skull, the prophecy and await the helicopter in order to return to Kathmandu.

44

SNATCHED

"We should just pack it with explosives," Neil Quinn said looking into the kapala's eye sockets, the deep pits grotesquely magnified by the illuminated lens Sir Jack was using to glue the bone back together under the regimented gazes of painted soldiers and a half-assembled panzer tank.

"I don't quite think so, Neil. Even doing this seems utterly sacrilegious," Sir Jack said, mixing white and brown paint on a saucer then focusing his attention on working in tiny spots of yellow to produce a color as close to the skull's aged bone as he could. Quinn, surprised at Sir Jack's passion for military model-making and impressed by the man's evident artistry, said, "But surely Yama needs to be . . ."

"No buts, Neil," Sir Jack interjected as he began to mask imperfections in the rebuilt skull with the tiniest of brushstrokes. "It is what Chering's sons have decided. They have a plan and I think we should follow it. We are all guests in what is their house and if they wish to put it in order then I think—and I'm sure Henrietta would have agreed—they have that right."

"Okay, so be it, but we are playing for high stakes here," Neil said, worried about Beth.

"They're up to the task. Their father was a strong, resourceful man. They take after him."

"I hear you are going to be staying on for a bit," Quinn said, changing the subject.

"Indeed. A complete bore really, Betsy and I were looking forward to retirement," Sir Jack said, clearly delighted that he was staying. He turned the skull to begin masking another of the cracks. "Sadly, my rather detailed report to London about recent events has caused my replacement to be ordered back to London for the exciting opportunity to be Her Majesty's trade commissioner to Europe. Good riddance, I say!" Sir Jack raised his eyebrows at Quinn to emphasize the point then asked, "So are we all agreed on what you've got to do?"

"Yes. Do you think he'll stick to the deal?"

"Yama wants the kapala in return for your American friend and that is what he is going to get. He knows from her that we are no nearer than he is to finding any missing child that Fuji might have brought out, but that the kapala is somehow key. We set off at nine p.m. What do you think?"

Sir Jack pulled back from the old skull to let Quinn see his finished work. It looked perfect once more—even if that was not the right word.

Quinn got out of Sir Jack's new car and walked into Durbar Square alone, his back illuminated by the vehicle's headlights. His long shadow stretched ahead to divide the white river of light that pointed into the ancient place. Everything around him was vacant and still, the stacked temples silent and aloof, the normally busy thoroughfares empty, devoid of their usual tourists and vendors.

Alone and conspicuous, Quinn walked on until he reached the central area of the square. It was lit with streetlights that danced with insects, but almost the instant he reached their softer light, there was a click and the fiery filaments at their center were extinguished.

Power cut! Quinn thought as the surrounding darkness instantly flooded the square. Walking on, he braced himself for some sort of attack, holding the day pack that contained the kapala tight to his chest to prevent it from being snatched; but his progress was uninterrupted.

Just as his eyes—still raw from the Makalu climb—grew accustomed to the dark, they stung anew when, ahead and above, a single lamp illuminated to momentarily reveal the high plinth of the Maju Deval temple, then quickly extinguished.

Quinn followed the jagged smear the light left on his retinas to arrive at the stone staircase that led up to the podium of the building. Slowly and carefully he stepped up to the pillared platform beneath the stacked pagoda roofs. The moment Quinn arrived at the top, the light went back on. To the front of it appeared the black silhouette of Yama.

"The relic?" he said.

"Here."

Quinn's still bandaged hand patted the bulky contents of the day pack slung across his chest.

"Show me."

With difficulty Quinn took the kapala out and held it forward in both his hands, the single light haloing the old skull.

"Give it to me."

"Not yet. Show me Mrs. Waterman. Prove that she is okay."

Yama spoke into a small handheld radio.

"Over there."

A light went on across the square within another of the temples. Quinn saw Beth, hands bound, kneeling on the stone floor of the temple platform, a dark figure standing on either side of her.

"If you have hurt her . . ." Quinn threatened.

"You'll do what exactly, Englishman? Take another video of me? I don't think so." Yama gave another command into the radio. The lights in both temples went out.

In the darkness, the skull was snatched from Quinn's numb hands and he was shoved backward.

Quinn, all balance lost, his legs still weak from Makalu, toppled back into free air, momentarily suspended high above the long stone staircase that led up to the dais.

The microseconds of movement defied the laws of time to expand into a clear and lengthy preview of the inevitable impact.

He had always known it would end in a fall.

And fall he did.

But the impact never came.

Strong hands caught and gripped his body, strong hands that carried him down to the flagstones of the square below. There a headlamp beamed into his eyes, a shadowed yet familiar face below saying, "Mr. Neil? Mr. Neil?"

It was Gelu.

Around them, more moving lights zigzagged through the darkness like neon strands of barbed wire. Quinn got to his feet to understand that a great crowd of Sherpa and Tibetans had appeared from the shadows to fill the plaza.

He followed those nearest, toward the ghostly white form of Gaddi Baithak palace, where an open square had been formed by a silent, waiting crowd. The light of their headlamps, flashlights, and phones lit the boundaries like an electric fence.

Quinn watched as Yama was suddenly flung forward into the space.

The black-suited man ran from edge to edge, ordering, shouting, cursing but every time he was pushed back by the crowd into the open area.

He stopped and just stared at the crowd from which a group stepped forward. They seized him and wrestled him to the ground. Yama was held down as Sherpa and Tibetans went to work on him to the growing chant of, "This is our city! We are all its people! You must go!"

The shouting of the crowd began to be drowned by the sound of thunder from the air above. Bigger, brighter lights burned down from the heavens. The rush and rotation of wings beat the open area. If Henrietta could have been there, she would have told Quinn that the place where Yama was being held down was the exact same spot where the immolation had happened.

A long line hung down.

The sprung hook at the end momentarily danced on the flagstones, discharging its static, before a figure—Quinn thought it might have been Pema Chering—stood up from the scrum holding Yama down, and drew the line into it.

A hand was raised and the group dispersed at a run to the edges of the open square.

The noise above crescendoed.

The man in black was wrenched up into the night sky like a rag doll, arms and legs flung back by the force of the elevation.

As he watched, Quinn felt a set of arms reach around him. Beth clung to him as they both watched the flashing lights of the helicopter disappear to the north.

45

EIGHT BEADS

KUMARI GHAR, DURBAR SQUARE, KATHMANDU, NEPAL
October 27, 2014

"So you are sure about this?" Sir Jack asked.

"I think so," Beth replied.

"The Kumari's people are adamant that you can only meet her if she chooses."

"Yes."

"And only you, as a woman," Sir Jack reiterated.

"I understand."

"You do know the Kumari can't be the one for a whole host of reasons."

"I do, but we have to try. It's the only link I have left. We have nowhere else to turn."

The car pulled up before the palace building of the Kumari Ghar and stopped. Beth left Sir Jack and Quinn at the doorway to walk into the center of that palace's courtyard. She stopped and looked up at the ornate wooden window boxes that encrusted the two stories over her head, each opening latticed with cedar wood slats, dark shadow between.

Beth just stood there stock-still with the prayer wheel in one hand, the mala beads hanging from the other from which also protruded the soft toy that Quinn had returned to her.

Her heart counted time to the minutes passing by, but nothing happened. The only sounds were the occasional rustle of wings or cooing of the pigeons perched on the apexes of the pointed window frames. From within, there was no hint of movement, no glint of the white of an eye pushed close to see better, no whispered sound of recognition, nothing.

After he had waited what seemed a suitable time, Sir Jack called her quietly, but Beth didn't move.

"You should go in and get her out. It's not working," he said to Quinn. He did as he was asked and walked into the courtyard to stand next to Beth. "We should go," was all he said and took her hand.

"But I was so sure . . ."

They turned to leave but as they reached the entrance to the courtyard, an adult voice behind them said, "Stop."

Neil and Beth turned back to see that a small girl of about eight was now standing on the other side of the courtyard. She was holding the hand of another child, younger still, an attendant walking reverently at a slight distance to them both.

The older girl was dark haired and smoky eyed, petite. The Kumari. The smaller child was more robust with very short red hair and a strong, determined face; Beth realized that she too was a girl. The two children whispered to each other and then the older one spoke to the assistant.

"You, sir," the attendant said to Quinn. "The ghost moth said you would come for her."

The Kumari released the small child's hand. Yangchen Norgyu walked to Beth and took the small toy from her hand. She immediately gave it to Quinn as she spoke back to the Kumari. The older girl said something that the assistant translated, "She says that this is yours, that she gave it to you to keep you safe to do what the ghost moth needed you to do."

"Tell her it did," Quinn replied, trying to give the toy back to the Tibetan child, but she wouldn't take it. She spoke again to the assistant who said, "She says that you will need it still. The mountains remain."

Instead her small hand reached inside her tunic and came out clenched. Her other hand then took the mala beads from Beth. She turned the clenched fist over to reveal, in her palm, eight tiny skulls that perfectly matched those of the mala.

"The circle is now complete," Beth heard the assistant say.

46

PALDEN LHAMO

HHDL'S PRIVATE RESIDENCE, MCLEOD GANJ, DHARAMSALA, HIMACHAL PRADESH, NORTHERN INDIA
November 1, 2014

The Dalai Lama's reception room was much changed since Beth's last visit, brighter and more colorful. Yet, as she walked in with Quinn, she was overwhelmed by the feeling that she was somehow coming home.

His Holiness stood to receive them, the morning light through the windows catching the facet in the lenses of his bifocals with a glint.

"Hello again, Mrs. Elizabeth Waterman, the rock who does not roll, and welcome, Mr. Neil Quinn, the man who climbs the highest of mountains," he said jovially, breaking protocol to embrace them both warmly. "How do you like my redecorated room, Mrs. Elizabeth, to your approval? Less now like 'Exit Lounge' I am thinking. Ahaha!"

Beth smiled—that laugh as contagious as ever—then, after looking around at His Holiness's remodel, nodded. "Now sit both of you, please. You must be tired from your great efforts. Ahaha!"

Beth and Neil did as they were told while the Dalai Lama turned and spoke to his private secretary. The secretary handed him a wooden tray on which rested the kapala and the small brick of brown pages it contained. He then left the room.

"Not *Rolling Stone* magazine I am afraid, Mrs. Elizabeth, but most important reading for someone in my position," His Holiness said as he picked up the set of texts and began to lay out individual pages as if dealing cards. "A message I sent to myself from the past to explain a future I was struggling to see."

In their center he placed a page that had no words only a picture. "You found a different needle than the one I think you were looking for, Mrs. Elizabeth, and we are grateful to you both, and to your friend Sir Jack Graham for ensuring that you could deliver it to me," the Dalai Lama said as his finger rested on the faded image of a blue-skinned, red-haired goddess astride a white mule.

"The child, Yangchen Norgyu, is not the Panchen Lama, and of course, she can't be me because I am." His Holiness smiled as he let the point take. "But she is indeed a tulku, an emanation of Palden Lhamo, the protectress spirit of Tibet. The texts within my kapala said that she would come to accompany me through my final years and empower our future over those who might seek to hinder it."

The private secretary returned with Yangchen Norgyu. The child's hair was still short, but red and lustrous like burnished copper, beginning to curl like the waves of a certain lake in the high mountains. Her eyes were dark beneath curved full eyebrows and a furrowed brow. The lips pursed in an intense concentration. From her right hand hung the mala, the skullbeads clicking through her small fingers as if silently counting time. In the other hand she was holding Fuji's prayer wheel. She left the private secretary's side to sit on the right side of the Dalai Lama.

"Mrs. Elizabeth, what will you do now?" His Holiness asked.

"I think I am going to continue Henrietta Richards's work in Kathmandu. The truth is important."

"It is everything."

Yangchen whispered something to the Dalai Lama who turned to momentarily look down at the child in surprise, before saying, "If you will it."

From within his magenta robe the Dalai Lama took his Patek Philippe watch and handed it to Beth.

"You must take this."

Beth looked at the exquisite pocket watch now cradled in the palm of her hand and asked, "The masterpiece of complications?"

"Always."

"But why me?"

"She wants you to look after it for the next generation. She says that I will return and when I do, I will of course know my favorite watch just as I immediately recognized this kapala." His hand stretched forward to rest on the engraved skull. "You can return my timepiece to me then, but perhaps if I wasn't to recognize it, you would understand what that meant and take the appropriate action. We need to be sure that no counterfeit dalai lamas are being offered to the world."

The Dalai Lama turned to Neil Quinn. "And you, Mr. Quinn?"

"As Yangchen said to me, 'the mountains remain' and I will keep on climbing them and try to help your people as I do it."

Yangchen Norgyu whispered something more to the Dalai Lama and passed him Fuji's prayer wheel.

The Dalai Lama reached forward to give the prayer wheel to Neil Quinn. "It seems that you will need this for your next journey into the sky."

The child said something more to His Holiness who stared long and hard at Beth and Neil.

"Yes, I do see it now," the Dalai Lama finally said. "Two new ghost moths. So, Mrs. Elizabeth, even you must now believe in reincarnation?"

EPILOGUE
MOUNT EVEREST

Inch by inch, Quinn ascended the final thirty feet to the summit, each weary movement riven with a toxic leadenness that belied the purity of the place.

THERE!

Then . . .

Nothing.

Doubled up on his hands and knees, he just clung to that icy lip of the planet, momentarily tethered only by the sublime, exquisite understanding that there was no more up.

Slowly the pain began to recede, time and place returning with a thought.

I hope you appreciate that I did this without bottled O's.

Quinn slowly raised himself up on heavy, frozen feet to stand proud, pushing back beyond the summit and into space until a sudden gust of wind forced him to huddle back down to a realization.

That wind will help.

Shaking off his bulky mittens, a gloved hand wrenched down the iced-up zipper of his climbing suit as another pushed inside to pull something from the mesh water-bottle pocket.

The Tibetan prayer wheel was beautiful to behold up there. The wooden handle was ancient, but still strong like that of an old ice axe he had once found on those same slopes. The bare metal of the drum had been repolished with respect. The copper burned in the unfiltered light, the embossed symbols in silver and gold taut and alive, gripping it like eagle talons.

Quinn gave the wheel a turn and held it up into the sky. The cylinder rotated rapidly as if recording the three-hundred-and-sixty-degree panorama.

So do you see now?

Only when the drum had stopped turning did Quinn pull the prayer wheel back down. Clutching it close like a newborn baby, no irony intended, he picked the tape free. There was an honest intention to ball and pocket the sticky black strip, but another gust snatched it away to instinctively fly north, a writhing black eel trapped on an invisible current.

The acorn nut was carefully and slowly unscrewed. One hand pushed it into a pocket for safekeeping, the other holding the cap of the container in place.

Neil Quinn stood tall again, locking his tired legs against the wind.

Take a moment.

A poorly remembered—actually never properly known—prayer was attempted.

Ashes to ashes . . .

Quinn's inappropriate mumbling stopped as a cascade of other religions rained down onto that high summit. Uncertain as to what to say next, he chose silence, offering instead a sincere yet wordless appeal to that single everlasting spirit that logic says must oversee all faiths from such a height.

Okay. Get it done now.

The lid of the prayer wheel was released as he simultaneously pushed his arm up into the sky.

The copper cylinder unleashed an explosion of gray dust as if an artillery shell had landed on the surface of the moon. The smoky plume was instantly caught by the wind to dissolve over that fabled summit, over the other great mountains that surrounded, over that barren and abused land that stretched into the far distance.

. . . and dust to dust.

The cap was replaced and Quinn knelt to plant the wooden handle of the prayer wheel firmly into the very apex of the mountain, pushing the prayer wheel down until it was totally hidden in the snow at the top of the world.

Quinn pulled his heavy mittens on and reached for his ice axe. Standing, the rising sun caught the colors of the two badges on his climb suit. In one, the body and wings of the ghost moth momentarily burned red, yellow, blue, green, and white, emboldening within the black letters *T.I.B.E.T.* The other patch shone just as bright with the words SUPER FREAK in orange and green.

"I'll be back to visit, Henrietta," Quinn said aloud. He tapped his mittened hand against the chest pocket that contained a small white horse toy for good luck, then turned to begin the long descent.

When Neil Quinn finally pulled back into the crowded Base Camp, all the talk amongst the other foreign climbers was not of that season's first Everest summits—Quinn's, and a few others—but of a rumor that the body of a man clad only in a black cotton suit had been seen high on the mountain, frozen to death. Asked about it, Quinn said he thought it unlikely, the product, no doubt, of an oxygen-deprived mind, just another high-altitude illusion like a Brocken specter, perhaps. All the Sherpa agreed.

GLOSSARY

Annapurna The tenth highest mountain in the world at 8,091 m (26,545 ft) technically known as Annapurna 1 within a massif in Nepal that includes another thirteen peaks of over 7,000 m (23,000 ft).

Baidu Chinese web services company and search engine.

baijiu Chinese grain alcohol.

bergschrund Deep crevasse that forms when moving glacier ice separates from a steep mountainside becoming a serious obstacle for a climber moving up onto that slope.

Brocken specter The shadow of an observer cast upon clouds in the opposite direction to the sun and sometimes surrounded by halo-like rings of iridescence.

Bhoudhanath Location of the Bhouda Stupa, one of the largest in the world, originally built in the sixth century on an ancient Tibetan trade route and now home to many Tibetan religious establishments and businesses in Kathmandu.

Camp Hale US Army training facility near to the town of Red Cliff in the highlands of Colorado, constructed in 1942 for what became the Tenth Mountain Division and subsequently used during the Cold War by the CIA to train Tibetans to fight their Communist Chinese invaders.

carabiner Specialized metal shackle with a spring-loaded gate commonly used in climbing to make secure rope connections.

chuba Long-sleeved sheepskin coat traditionally worn by highland peoples in Tibet.

Central Tibetan Administration (CTA) The Tibetan government in exile located in Dharamsala.

Cho Oyu The sixth highest mountain in the world at 8,188 m (26,864 ft) located 20 km west of Mt. Everest and standing on the China-Nepal border. Considered the easiest eight-thousand-meter mountain to climb, it is a popular objective for commercial climbing expeditions.

Choson Chinese name for ancient Korea.

Chushi Gangdruk Literally the Tibetan for "Four Rivers, Six Ranges," the name of the ancient region of Kham and the name adopted in 1958 by the Tibetan guerrillas in their fight against the Chinese.

couloir French term adopted to describe a narrow gully in steep mountain terrain.

crampon Spiked metal plate that affixes to mountain boots to facilitate walking or climbing on snow, ice, and rock.

Dalai Lama The Dalai Lama is an emanation of the Bodhisattva of Compassion, Avalokiteshvara; or Chenrezig, the patron saint of Tibet; and seen as both the spiritual and secular head of the former country. The name "dalai" signifies ocean, a historic metaphor for boundless knowledge.

Dewa Savan mountains: Gassan, Haguro, and Yudona The three mountains of Dewa located in Yamagata, Japan, are sacred to the ascetic mountain belief of Shugendo as practiced by Yamabushi monks.

Dharamsala Hill town and district headquarters of Kangra district in Himachal Pradesh, India, that is the location of the Tibetan government in exile (CTA) and many displaced Tibetan institutions.

dharma The teachings of Buddha.

Durbar Square Series of historic temples, plazas, and squares in front of the old Royal Palace of the former kingdom of Kathmandu.

En no Gyoja Ascetic and mystic who founded the Shugendō sect in Japan in the seventh century and was the first of the Yamabushi monks to whom he is a saint.

fixed line The pining of lines of rope up steep or dangerous sections of mountain terrain to assist climbers.

gan bei Chinese drinking toast.

Ganesha One of the best-known and most worshipped deities of the Hindu pantheon, immediately identifiable by his elephant head.

garuda Legendary birdlike creature in Hindu, Buddhist, and Jain mythology.

Gaddi Baithak Palace in Durbar Square built in 1908 during the Rana period to a classical European architectural design.

Geshe Academic title given to a learned Tibetan monk.

gompa A Tibetan monastery or temple.

gurkha Ethnic Nepalis recruited to serve in the Nepalese, British, and Indian armies with a reputation for great loyalty and ferocity in combat.

gweilo Cantonese slang term for a Western person.

han Mainland Chinese people.

Hanuman Dhoka Another name for Durbar Square in Kathmandu, arising from the stone statue of Hanuman, the Hindu monkey god, near to the main entryway, or *dhoka*.

hmong Ethnic mountain tribes located in the highlands of Southeast Asia including Vietnam, Laos, and Southern China.

hokkien Southern Chinese dialect spoken commonly in Taiwan.

hui Northwestern Chinese people who are predominantly Muslim.

kapala Ritual implement in Tibetan Buddhism made of carved or decorated human bone.

Kailash Mt. Kailash is a 6,638 m (21,778 ft) high peak within Tibet that is sacred to the Bon, Hindu, Jain, and Buddhist religions and a place of pilgrimage. It has never been climbed.

khampa People from the Kham region in Tibet known as hunters and warriors who were instrumental in the uprising against the Chinese in the 1950s.

khata Ceremonial silk scarf that is offered as a symbol of purity and compassion.

King Gesar Legendary hero of an epic or ballad that describes the life and adventures of the great king of Ling and is an oral tradition in poetry and prose throughout Central Asia.

Kumari A young girl deemed to be a manifestation of the divine female energy and worshipped as a living goddess in the Hindu tradition until she reaches maturity.

Kumari Ghar The palace in Durbar Square where the Royal Kumari resides.

Kumari Jatra Procession of the Royal Kumari through the streets of Kathmandu that is a highlight of Yenya, an eight-day street festival in the early autumn that combines many ceremonies to pray for a good harvest and remember the dead of the past year.

La A high mountain pass in the Himalayas used as a crossing point for travelers and traders if accessible.

Leadville Town located in the highlands of Colorado, founded on mining silver but subsequently zinc, lead, and molybdenum.

Makalu The fifth highest mountain in the world at 8,485 m (27,838 ft) that stands on the China–Nepal border approximately 19 km to the southeast of Mount Everest.

mala Buddhist prayer beads used in meditation and ritual.

Maju Deval Temple Seventeenth century pagoda-roofed temple to Shiva located in Durbar Square.

Macleod Ganj Suburb of Dharamsala known as "Little Lhasa" or "Dhasa" owing to its large population of Tibetans and where the Dalai Lama has his private residence.

Ministry of State Security (MSS) The intelligence and security agency of the People's Republic of China.

momo Tibetan steamed dumpling.

Mount Everest The earth's highest mountain in the world at 8,848 m (29,029 ft) that stands on the China–Nepal border, also known as Sagarmatha in Nepal and Qomolangma in China.

Munro A peak standing higher than 914.4 m (3,000 ft) and located in Scotland.

Palden Lhamo Wrathful deity and female guardian spirit that promised the first Dalai Lama in a vision in the Lhamo La-tso mountain lake that she would protect the reincarnation lineage of the dalai lamas.

Panchen Lama The Panchen Lama is an emanation of Amithabha. The name "panchen" means "great scholar."

penitentes Spiked ice formations that develop on high altitude glaciers.

piton An eyed metal spike that is driven into rock to secure a climber's rope via a carabiner.

prayer flag Colorful flags printed with prayer text that spread goodwill and compassion through the action of the wind. The five colors represent the five elements.

prayer wheel A cylinder on an axis that contains a mantra, spinning the wheel has the same effect as saying the mantra.

puja Prayer ritual or blessing ceremony performed by the Hindu, Jain, and Buddhist religions. A puja with a constructed altar and food and drink offerings is undertaken by the Sherpa before a Himalayan climb.

Putonghua The standard Mandarin and official language of China.

rakshi Hard alcohol drink brewed from barley, millet, or rice. Common in Nepal and Tibet.

rappel The use of a doubled rope to descend a mountainside, also known as abseiling. Originally the rope was looped around the body but today the climber is connected to the rope by a metal "descender" that securely connects to the climber's harness and permits control of the rate of descent.

Red Cliff A small mountain town in Eagle County, Colorado, located in the same valley as the site of Camp Hale.

Rinpoche Title of great respect in Tibetan Buddhism given often to the abbots of Tibetan monasteries.

samsara The Buddhist cycle of death and rebirth to which life in the material world is bound.

Sashastra Seema Bal (SSB) The intelligence and security agency of India.

Shishapangma The fourteenth highest mountain in the world at 8,027 m (26,335 ft) and the highest mountain that sits entirely in Tibetan territory. Sometimes known as Gosainthan in Nepal and Xixabangma Feng in China.

Shugendo Syncretic Japanese religion that fuses practices and traditions from Buddhism, Taoism, and Shinto into an ascetic mountain way that seeks spiritual power through discipline and harmony in nature.

sirdar Indian term for a "leader," commonly applied to the head Sherpa on a climbing expedition.

sling A tied or sewn loop of webbing used to connect to an anchor, a section of rock, or a rope to secure a climber.

ta yang Chinese term for silver coinage.

Tenth Mountain Division US light infantry division founded in WW2 to undertake mountain warfare in the European theater.

terma A hidden teaching or prophecy.

Terrordactyl First generation of the lighter, more aggressively shaped ice axes that began to be used for hard ice climbing in the 1970s that was designed by Scottish climber Hamish MacInnes.

terton A revelator of hidden spiritual texts.

Thamel Commercial neighborhood in Kathmandu popular with foreign visitors.

thamzing Chinese practice of hazing political adversaries during the Cultural Revolution that involved public humiliation through repeated physical and verbal abuse.

topi Traditional brimless cap made of multicolored Dhaka cloth that is a part of the Nepalese national dress.

tsampa Tibetan barley flour, a staple in Tibet.

tulku A reincarnate child in the Tibetan Buddhist tradition.

tulpa A spirit or ghost.

tummo The practice of generating body heat through intense meditation said to be utilized by the most practiced monks in Tibet.

Ute Native American tribe that traditionally lived in the regions of Utah and Colorado.

Xizang Historic Chinese name for the land of Tibet.

Yama God of Death and Lord of Hell in both the Hindu and Buddhist traditions.

yamabushi Japanese mountain hermits that follow the Shugendo way through which they are believed to acquire supernatural powers.

yartsa gunbu Caterpillar fungus traditionally used in Himalayan folk medicine that is now a much sought after and valuable stimulant particularly in metropolitan China.

AUTHOR'S NOTE

Like its predecessor, *Summit*, *The Ghost Moths* is a novel, a fiction that combines history with a current reality at its core. For *Summit*, the history was mountaineering in the 1930s and the events that subsumed the sport—and indeed everything else—in the conflagration of World War II. The reality there was concern at growing neofascist activity in western societies that has only increased since the book was published in 2016. In *The Ghost Moths*, the historical fiction rests on the shoulders of events in the territory of Tibet since the 1950s. For those who wish to move from fiction to factual reportage I would recommend *Tibet, Tibet* by Patrick French and *The Snow Lion and the Dragon* by Melvyn C. Goldstein. Much of the true story of the Tibetan uprising from 1956 onward has died unrecorded in places such as Chagra Pembar, Nira Tsogo, Markham, and the streets of Lhasa itself. However, books such as *Buddha's Warriors* by Mikel Dunham and *Arrested Histories* by Carole McGranahan still address these matters with detail and sensitivity, matters that should be remembered.

It is a fact that between 1959 and 1964 a number of Tibetans were trained in the United States by the CIA—including a certain Anthony Poshepny, aka Tony Poe or Agent UPIN, who, some say, in his later guise as a trainer of the Hmong during the Vietnam war was partial inspiration for Colonel Kurtz in *Apocalypse Now*. Whilst the director of that film has refuted this, it is a fact that Tony Poe did survive a number of attempts in the highlands of Laos to "terminate his command with extreme prejudice" and, to his dying day, remained fiercely loyal to the tribes he worked with.

Today, in a remote valley in the highlands of Colorado, a small sign can be found. Often adorned with silk *khata* scarves and bright prayer flags, it commemorates the brave Tibetan freedom fighters that the likes of Tony Poe once trained in that remote place. The majority died fighting a largely invisible war. The books *Orphans of the Cold War* by John Kenneth Knaus and *The CIA's Secret War in Tibet* by Kenneth Conboy and James Morrison go some way to shedding light on such Cold War secrets.

The reality of *The Ghost Moths* is vested in what is often known as the "struggle for the Dalai Lama's soul," a current situation. The Dalai Lama's selection to be the reincarnated Panchen Lama, Gedhun Choekyi Nyima, has indeed been missing since 1995, and remains so. *The Search for the Panchen Lama* by Isabel Hilton describes this twenty-five-year tragedy in detail. It is still only the beginning of a high-stakes power play, a rehearsal perhaps for what is yet to come when a replacement for the Dalai Lama is necessary.

Personally I take this moment to apologize for my ignorance, and the syncretism and liberties I have taken with His Holiness within this novel, even if it comes from a desire to highlight a situation that is undoubtedly more subtle and complex than my clumsy fiction. In the end, I ask only that we don't let the pain of desire for inexpensive Chinese consumer electronics override freedom and compassion for the people of Tibet.

Before I finish it is perhaps also worth saying a little about moths. They are an ancient creature, older than the highest mountains or the seven continents, much older than mankind. But how old exactly?

In 1985, three tiny wing traces were found in the fossil rich Lias of England's Dorset coast, a layer of rock that is one hundred and ninety million years old. So *Archaeolepis mane* of the early Jurassic: the first moth.

Probably not. Only recently, a group of moth fossils similar to the ones from England were found, this time in Schandelah, northern Germany. Currently being studied by the University of Utrecht, they are already suggesting that the moth may have indeed been evolving in the earlier Triassic period.

In contrast, about two hundred thousand years ago, the first of our peoples emerged to find the two-hundred-million-year-old moth already present wherever they roamed. It's okay to think about that sentence for a minute longer if you want to. Perhaps add to it the statistic that sixty moth species have become extinct in just the past one hundred and fifty years.

To our earliest ancestors the moth was an unexplainable ancient that threaded the edge of night, their time of greatest fear and proximity to death, with unknown and silent purpose. Such powers of perception, navigation, and transformation within that shadow world could only be ascribed to the magical and the mystical. The moth: messenger, guide; spy, thief, shape-shifter, spirit, ghost.

Hepialus armoricanus Oberthür is such a moth, such a ghost, even if above all, it is simply a survivor. In the sincere hope that we might stop further extinctions of moths or peoples, I dedicate this book to the survivors.

In *Zen and the Art of Motorcycle Maintenance* Robert M. Pirsig wrote, "In the high country of the mind one has to become accustomed to the thinner air of uncertainty." The following people gave me oxygen at times when I really needed it, so thank you: Lucy Farthing, Tad Shay, David Lee, and John Huey. Eric van Leuven, one of the best linguists I have met, was also kind enough to ensure that my Dutch professor cursed correctly. Personally, I would never have made it up any mountain without guides and Sherpa. My writing is the same. To Will Roberts, my agent; Madeline Hopkins, my editor; and everyone at Blackstone, my ever-patient publisher; kudos and gratitude for making it happen. Finally, I thank my wife, Farrah, for an unconditional love and belief in me so much bigger than all the mountains of this world and the next put together.

Harry Farthing
January 31, 2020

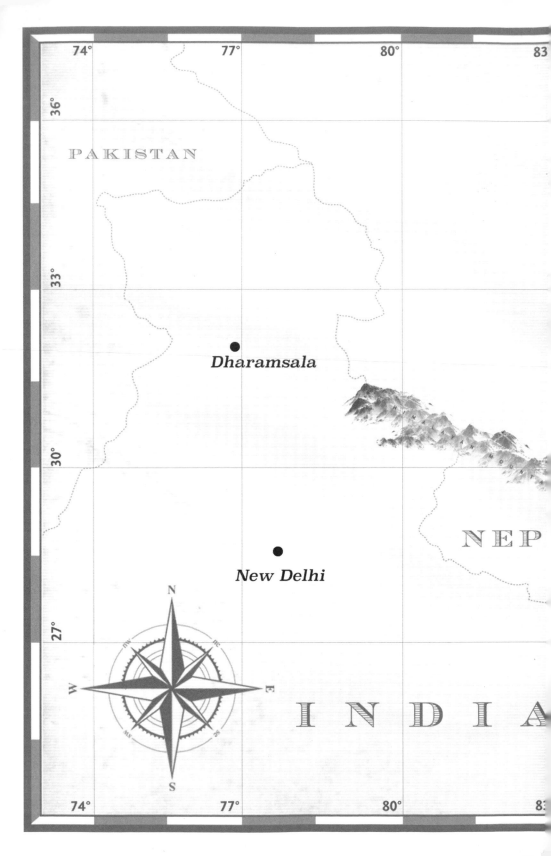